SEX IN THE CITY
PARIS

EDITED BY

MAXIM JAKUBOWSKI

Published by Accent Press Ltd – 2010

ISBN 9781907016257

Printed and bound in the UK by
CPI Bookmarque, Croydon

Cover design by
Zipline Creative

Contents

Introduction

I AM RELIABLY INFORMED that the art and practice of sex is well-known outside of major cities too, but that's another book altogether!

Our new SEX IN THE CITY series is devoted to the unique attraction that major cities worldwide provide to lovers of all things erotic. Famous places and monuments, legendary streets and avenues, unforgettable landmarks all conjugate with our memories of loves past and present, requited and unrequited, to form a map of the heart like no other. Brief encounters, long-lasting affairs and relationships, the glimpse of a face, of hidden flesh, eyes in a crowd, everything about cities can be sexy, naughty, provocative, dangerous and exciting.

Cities are not just about monuments and museums and iconic places, they are also about people at love and play in unique surroundings. With this in mind, these anthologies of erotica will imaginatively explore the secret stories of famous cities and bring them to life, by unveiling passion and love, lust and sadness, glittering flesh and sexual temptation, the art of love and a unique sense of place.

And we thought it would be a good idea to invite some of the best writers not only of erotica, but also from the mainstream and even the crime and mystery field, to offer us specially written new stories about the hidden side of some of our favourite cities, to reveal what happens behind closed doors (and sometimes even in public). And they have delivered in trumps.

The stories you are about to read cover the whole spectrum from young love to forbidden love and every sexual variation in between. Funny, harrowing, touching, sad, joyful, every human emotion is present and how could it not be when sex and the delights of love are evoked so skilfully?

Our initial batch of four volumes takes us to London, New York, Paris and Dublin, all cities with a fascinating attraction to matters of the flesh and the heart. We hope you read them all and begin to collect them, and that we shall soon be offering you further excursions to the wild shores of erotic Los Angeles, Venice, Edinburgh, New Orleans, Sydney, Tokyo, Berlin, Rio, Moscow, Barcelona and beyond. Our authors are all raring to go and have already packed their imagination so they can offer you more sexy thrills …

And it's cheaper than a plane ticket!

So, come and enjoy sex in the city.

Maxim Jakubowski

A Seduction of Vanity
by M Christian

CAFÉ LATTE BEFORE HER, steam rising into a cool morning. Her phone rang with the first few bars of a top ten hit that had slid from number two to number eight just that morning. Out of her purse, silver and slim, and up to her ear: '*Oui*?'

The voice on the other end was tight, professional, asking if she was Jacqueline – to which she replied with another *oui* – then identifying itself as a secretary working for a writer at *Le Monde*, and would she, Jacqueline, be available for an interview? Scheduled for later the next day, in the evening?

Wrapped in the latest fashion, trying to make themselves look less giggly and clumsy, two young girls four tables over chittered and chattered behind their menus, with careful, wide-eyed glances toward her.

From her purse, her sunglasses. '*Oui*,' Jacqueline said to the young man on the phone as she clicked the earpieces apart, neatly slid them over her ears, onto her nose. Details were exchanged: a date and a time. 'This number OK?'

'*Oui*,' Jacqueline said. They chatted for a bit, cool professional pleasantries, cooling latte on the table, then it was over. The phone went back into her bag.

The girls were still there, babyfat faces hunched down,

voices soft yet sharply excited, looking at each when not watching her.

Leaving her now cold, untouched coffee, Jacqueline paid and left before they could work up their courage to talk to her.

The day was hers, but there were always calls that could be made. From the bistro, she headed toward the Boulevard des Italiens. As she walked, she talked to Henri, to see if her schedule had changed. 'Glad you called,' her manager said, the clicking fingers on a computer keyboard in the background. Brusque and quick, he told her of a new appointment for a week later, some up-and-coming photographer wanting her for an outdoor shoot. Henri wasn't one to chat so the conversation was short, but before he rang off, he said 'Keep up the good work,' which made her grin.

Next call was to Bois, to check on the dress she'd ordered. Putting a creased frown on her face when she got his creature; a lithe child who managed to sneer with each word she spoke: 'I'll-tell-him-you-called.' If he wasn't the best, she never would have put up with that kind of treatment, but he was, so she did.

At a corner, the engines of traffic making progress difficult but not impossible, she checked her messages, the voice sounding far away even though the phone was pressed tightly against her ear. Henri, asking her to call – sounding even more professional, even more wound-up, and, if possible, even tighter. Delete. A rambling voice, nasal accent making it difficult to understand, finally dawning that it was that British designer – Joan Hart, was that it? – reminding her that they'd met at Lauren DeBarge's party, and on and on and on and on and on and if Jacqueline had the name and ("it would be so lovely")

4

if she had the number, of some woman who'd been at her opening. Delete. A sharp-toothed voice, leaving a simple message but far too much in the background for just the words "Call when you can." Delete, then another punch of the tiny button to make sure.

That was all. But before she called her sister back, a few other calls. Across the street, traffic quieter now that it had stopped for the light, she dialled her friend Simone. It was only after her musical voice sang to leave a message that Jacqueline remembered Simone was probably still out on her shoot, modelling for Camille – *the* Camille – and she hung up without saying anything.

Pausing to look at a purse in a window, moving on when she decided it was just a bit too gaudy for this season, which was heavy on smooth Italian designs and simple hues, she next dialled Colette. The up-and-comer who'd asked for help in learning the business had seemed pleasant enough, and a chat with someone with wide adoring eyes was just what she needed, but there too she was greeted by a sing-song voice asking her to leave a message. Again, she did not.

About to dial again – that fellow with his work coming up in *Zoom* who'd left her a message a week or so ago – it was interrupted by a ring, the not-the-top-of-the-charts tune making her sigh. Might as well, she thought, answering it.

'*Allo*?' she said, knowing full well who it was.

'*Bonjour, Jacqueline*,' said her sister, words cut and precise. 'I hope I haven't caught you at a bad time.'

'No, no,' she said, transferring the phone from one hand to the other. 'Just on the way to another posing, Audrey. Sorry I haven't called you back.'

'I know you're so … busy, Jacqueline. But since Mama was asking about you I thought I'd give you a ring.'

Knowing what the answer would be, she asked anyway, giving her sister that much: 'How's she doing?'

'She's old, Jacqueline. She doesn't have a lot of time. But you know that.'

Merde. 'I know that, Audrey. I do. It's just that things have been so busy, what with the sittings and shoots and all. In fact just the other day, Camille … maybe you've heard of her? She was just saying –'

'We're proud of you, Jacqueline. Mama reads the papers and the magazines, or I read them to her if she's too tired. She was very excited by that painting of you … the one they say is good enough to hang in the Louvre –'

'Oh, that! Escobar is such a sweetheart, a perfect gentleman. I'm so happy for him, of course. Have you seen the painting? Last I heard it's still on display in that gallery, the one near the Rue Christine. It's really nice, but then he has been described as a genius …'

'No, I haven't seen it. I have to stay here … with Mama. I hope I can see it sometime, though. I'm sure it's quite beautiful. Mama and I were just saying how you are too –'

Walking down the street, talking on her phone, danced around a rasta-curled boy also walking down the street, also talking on his phone. Walking, talking, dancing, she missed the last part of what her sister had said, replying as if she hadn't: 'I know I have to see her, Audrey, and I will. How about next week? Is that good for you?'

After a long moment: 'Anytime is OK for us. Come when you can. It would mean a lot to us. For me.'

'I promise, Audrey. I'll be there before you know it. I have another call coming in, darling,' she said quickly, even though she didn't, slipping her finger across the button to disconnect the call.

*   *   *

A few lights, a few streets, from the Boulevard she stopped again, pulling out her phone and flicking through the address book for people to call. Names and number scrolled by on the tiny screen: this model, that friend, this photographer, that painter. Almost, but then her fingers didn't complete the action that would ring <u>the</u> painter, and she went back to names and numbers flashing by.

Later, maybe later.

On the corner, a newsstand. Displayed there was a copy of *ArtNews*. An old copy, last month's copy. The copy.

Just like every other time she really couldn't recognize herself in it, at least not the Jacqueline she saw in a mirror. Reds and blues, mostly. Strong strokes. Bright colours. Eyes, a nose, lips, ears, hair. A background that looked like fire. It didn't look like something that might hang in the Louvre, but that's where some people were saying it belonged.

Not that she'd argue with them. Never.

'How much for the copy of *ArtNews*, Monsieur?'

Lifting his grey-flecked beard from where it was folded up against a sadly faded sweater, the owner looked up at her from the racing form he was reading, looking at her with bloodshot eyes. 'Eh? What did you say?'

'*ArtNews*,' she repeated, reaching down and sideways to the rack, pulling the copy free. When it came, it took a copy of *Marie Claire* with it, causing it to tumble to the ground and into a small pool of water.

'You have to buy that,' the owner grumbled, red-streaked eyes narrowing at her, daring her to argue with his pronouncement concerning his tiny kingdom.

'Of course,' she said, holding the *ArtNews* so it faced him, her hands not obscuring the painting on the cover.

7

Not recognizing her, or pretending not to, he gave her change then went back to his form. Before she turned to go, she glanced down at the other magazine, the one swelling up, pages wrinkling as it soaked up old rain. Its cover, brand new, this month's, was a photograph, not a painting. A photo of Simone.

Holding her *ArtNews* close to her chest, she left the newsstand and began to make her way slowly down the street.

Home … but she really didn't want to go home. Not yet. The sun was still in the sky, though lowering toward the rooftops; calls could be made, though none of the faintly glowing numbers – or the people attached to them – appealed to her. There were shops to browse, though none of the silks and satins, beads and belts appealed to her.

So, sun lowering, phone stuck in her purse, the shops of the Boulevard des Italiens exhausted of potential new outfits, she resigned herself that home was where she should be heading.

But she still didn't want to go there. On a corner, watching glass glide by, the lights of the city reflecting in their windows, she caught a new kind of illumination. A coffee, she decided, seeing the windows of the cafe, would be nice.

'*Bonjour, madame,*' said the hostess as Jacqueline entered, then closed the door behind her. Against the growing dust, the inside was almost too dazzling: polished brass, pale marble, frosted glass, the too-bright smile on the young woman waving her toward a table.

'*Café latte, s'il vous plaît,*' Jacqueline said, making herself comfortable: chair pulled closer to the polished table top, purse on top of it, *ArtNews* next to the purse, her face as seen by Escobar peering up at her.

How long did she look at it? Long enough to make a coffee, obviously, as a cup and saucer suddenly clicked and clacked down into the marble. 'Oh, that's beautiful,' said the hostess.

'Pardon?' Jacqueline said, looking up from the swirling dark liquid, its steam adding to the sauna spilling from the nearby bubbling brass espresso machine.

'That. Your magazine. It's a beautiful picture.'

'Thank you.'

That was it. That was all. The hostess, as sparkling and bright as the café where she worked, moved away to chat with other customers. Feeling warm and glowing, from the compliment as well as the coffee, Jacqueline stayed until she finished her cup. Then, purse over her arm, magazine in her hand, she left some coins and stepped toward the door.

Hand on the handle, pushing it open she realized something, a shiver like the night outside. Madame. The hostess had called her madame ...

Then her phone sang that less-than-popular tune again. Pulling it quickly out of her purse she glanced down at the screen, the text message there from Annette, another model, another sort-of friend. PARTY? it said.

II

So, home it was. But having a place to go to after the taxi ride to the Rue du Faubourg-Saint-Honoré, the street of beauty, and then to just around the corner, into the street of her flat, she made the journey with a tight smile on her face.

From the cab, returning the driver's grin and handing him a generous tip, she went to the foyer door. Bernardo, the doorman, as always showing his old man teeth as he shuffled to the door, turned the gleaming steel handle to let her in. 'Bonjour,' he said, dipping his head as she swept past him and in toward the lift.

Then up to the clean lines of the hall, the clean lines of her door, the clean lines of her apartment, the door shutting behind her with a soft hush of expensive precision.

It was a beautiful place: a glowing wooden slab of a coffee table, polished swirls and perfect knots; floor to ceiling prism class windows, the clear blue of thick protection, the view beyond a faery kingdom of late twilight Paris; Terzani lamps hovering high above, glimmering crystal throwing brilliant perfection all around; against one wall a Campaniello sofa, creamy leather as soft as a blown kiss; on the other a Matteucci-designed sideboard, tranquillity in luxurious teak.

It was a place to show, to stroll through in silk. The few pictures that hung were of her. Subtle, only the most transparent of ghostly arrogance in black and white photographs.

Heels clicking on the Italian flagstones that led from the entry to the bedroom, she carefully laid her purse down on the bedside table, cautious that it did not fall back against the stiff cream diamond shade of the Estiluz lamp, turning its perfect placement into clumsy misalignment.

Wood and steel, crystal and stone, bright and flawless. It was a beautiful flat and she was proud of it. With a few practiced pushes of buttons on the lacquer-black stereo system, a mix of the most popular songs of that week surged from hidden speakers, bass and treble putting dance into her movements as she slipped off her dress, a satin descent adding a drum fan to the thundering music.

Then the shower. She was proud of the apartment, the

way it had all come together from her suggestions and an expert decorator's skill, but she loved the bathroom. Bra and panties neatly lowered into the hamper, she stepped into the elegant obsidian-tiled stall and, with a few turns of a well-tooled Rohl faucet, the water roared down onto her, drowning out the teeth-on-edge chilling lines and eternal coldness of the apartment with warm splashing.

On her body. Out there it was theirs, in here it was hers.

Water jetted a steaming massage on her face, down her neck, between her breasts, onto her belly, on one thigh then the other as she shifted and moved under the shower. The building had an old outside, but the plumbing was brand new: she had plenty of hot water.

Hand roaming, she brought a mild soap to her face – something benign that wouldn't argue with her usual, more serious regimen. It came off when she put her face under the spray, lather rolling down her belly and then spiralling down the drain. From the same tiny shelf came another bottle, a dollop that cost as much as a good dinner out. It was health in a pearlescent plastic bottle, a specially formulated glow of sensuality. All so she'd look like a goddess for the cameras, or the brush of a master painter.

It also felt damned good. The wraps and plucks and peels and astringents and masks and cucumbers and the rest were OK sometimes, painful others, but that little bit of slipping and sliding felt wonderful.

Fingers spread, she applied it everywhere: her belly and around and around the perfect dimple of her navel, the gentle rises of her ribs to her thighs, along the tight muscles of her slim neck, the bumps of her spine to the sculpted rises of each rear cheek, shoulder to shoulder then down to the upsweep of her breasts.

11

Clean lines carefully maintained and perfected, everything in its place: an ideal form. The apartment as well as her.

But in the shower they were just breasts that felt good to touch; an ass that was thrilling to caress, and between her thighs ... that was the best place of all to touch or caress.

In the shower, she could. Once, after the apartment had been finished, she'd tried, sprawling out on the vast black, silk-sheeted bed but couldn't. It was only in frustration that she'd taken a shower to relax that she realized, away from the cold lines and precise corners, for the first time she was actually comfortable.

Hot water. Lather, rinse, repeat. Under the pounding spray, Jacqueline put everything aside – except her hands and her body.

Cupped, then squeezed, then kneaded, then thumb and forefinger to nipple, then pull, then pinch, then squeezed hard, the right then the left then together, putting her face into the stream of water, opening her mouth to let the jet pound her tongue – her breasts.

Caressed, then slapped, then spanked, then gripped hard, then walked apart, then hand down between the right and the left, touching the back of her lips and running a finger from where they were swelling up fat and plump past the wrinkle of her anus and then up to where they blended into her back – the cheeks of her ass.

Slicked, then relished, then stroked, then spread wide, then finger seeking the tiny hard point among slippery hot folds, a dance, a tinkle, a stroke, a rub, a circling, then to make it last longer, away from it to explore the much hotter, much wetter depths of herself.

From one to another then back again, one hand on a breast, another between her legs, to one hand on a breast and another fondling herself from behind, to both hands on her breasts pulling and rubbing her nipples, to both hands exploring the molten heat and throbbing clit of her quim, to both hands rubbing and squeezing the muscles of her ass.

Which fantasy? They bubbled and roared in her head: bent over the railing of a yacht bobbing on a too-blue Aegean Sea? On a beach in St Tropez at midnight, priceless skirt hitched up around her hips, alone except for the rock star kneeling between her legs? Masturbating in the changing room of a boutique while a famous photographer snapped shot after shot of her performance? Naked, maybe, on the runway, the applause of the crowd like a million hands on her tight and fine body?

Knees buckling, breath wheezing, eyes closing, hands out to catch an-almost-collapsing fall, she moaned in thundering release, an orgasm that brought stars to her eyes and quivers and quakes to her legs.

Sitting in the bottom of the black well of the shower, she panted for a few minutes, letting the body rush fade to a general bliss. Then, strength returning to her legs she got up, soaped and lathered again, and stepped out of the shower. Taking dozens of controlling, calming breaths, she looked in the mirror, frowning at her wet disarray.

Hair, facial, makeup – so much to do if she was going to be presentable for the party.

Without a smile on her face, she set to work.

The cab knew the way, so the trip was quick and efficient; merging elegantly with the city traffic, gliding up to and then away from lights, never getting too close or too far from the cars in front of them, and not a single tap of the horn.

Getting out of the taxi as carefully as he'd driven –

stepping gracefully out and away, stylishly turning back, carefully opening her little purse – she passed him a neat fold of bills: the fare and a handsome tip for his eyes surreptitiously watching her in the rear view mirror and for never once calling her madame.

Annette lived away from things, on a barely lit street in a nearly forgotten corner of the city, that only a few years ago would have been dead to everything but the rumbling and quaking of late night trucks hauling this or that to or fro. The avenue was still mostly dark, but with a mischievous hope of life: music faintly played and scurried, bouncing between the heavily shuttered warehouses, as stretched shadows danced on their plastered walls.

Walking up to the party, the tune got louder, identifiable as a techno beat, and the shadows shrank to a handful of men and women who'd spilled out of Annette's brightly lit doorway, smoking and chatting and drinking and laughing.

'Darling!' came a chiming laugh as Jacqueline walked up. The royalty's here, Jacqueline thought as arms wrapped around her and a pair of lips landed in a flighty kiss on her cheek. Kings as well as queens. 'Now all the pretty people are here!'

Letting Daniel lead her inside, she laughed and smiled and kissed and hugged her way through the pressing crowd that was either leaving early or arriving fashionably late.

'So glad you made it.' Annette was elegant and simple, a nymph wrapped in Audrey Hepburn purple, with a blast of Monroe lipstick. 'It wouldn't have been a good party without you.'

'I was just telling her the very same thing,' the dresser said, uncoiling himself from around her arm. 'Now you

14

two chat or something fashionable while I go mingle – and get me some of those wonderful canapés before some fat cow eats them all.'

Air kisses and he was gone, sliding between a photographer and a junior set designer from the opera. 'So how have you been, Jackie? Bet things have been crazy since that posing.'

'Oh, you know how it is,' Jacqueline said, who hated to be called anything but her full name. Annette, she knew, didn't know *how it was* as she was new to the profession. 'Phone ringing all the time, one job after another.'

'I can imagine,' the other woman said, waving past Jacqueline's shoulder at someone moving through the crowd. 'But being busy has got to be better than not having anything going on, right? Wanted rather than not and all that.'

'I guess. But to be honest things have been so crazy lately, not having something would be a nice little vacation.'

'Well, I hope you get a break. Don't want you to be working too hard.'

'In fact, just today I got a call from Henri – he always seems to be calling me for one thing or another – with a new assignment. A new photographer. Jorge, I think his name was.'

'Oh, I know, Jorge! Such a sweet man, and very talented. I saw him ... two weeks ago, I think? Did a lovely set with him. In fact he said he wanted me to come back and see him, and maybe not just to pose again, if you know what I mean.'

Jacqueline did, but didn't say. 'That's very nice, Annie,' she did say, knowing the other woman also didn't like to have her name trimmed down. 'I'm so glad for you. I hope Jorge and I will have just as nice a time when I see him.'

'Oh, I'm sure you will, Jackie. I'm sure you will. He even told me he was looking to work with someone … more unique.'

Face flush, face hot. She knew what she meant, but still didn't say. But she did say: 'Well, they say being unique is far better than being common, Annie.'

Then, before the other woman could say something, Jacqueline pretended to see someone behind her. 'Oh, look,' she forcefully gushed and chirped. 'Isn't that Depaulo? I must say hello to him. See you later, Annie.'

Stepping around her and away into the crowd, she turned to look behind her, catching Annette's eye and, with a royal wave of her hand, Jacqueline said. 'Thank you for inviting me, by the way. It looks to be quite a lovely party,' before a curtain of men with drinks and women laughing like musical instruments came between them.

Toasted fresh shrimp set in a bed of tapenade, on a tiny wedge of dark rye; some kind of rich pate on a light cracker; carefully manicured cones of fragrant cheese, summer pears dusted with cinnamon and sugar.

She'd drifted somehow, or was moved by the unconscious Brownian motion of the party, from the front room to the hall and eventually back to the kitchen. Kisses and hugs had preceded her retreat – or exile, but she didn't think about that – through the low-ceilinged space. Compliments were fluttered and gossip was acidly whispered to her as she shuffled from one area of the apartment to the other, bubbles of amusement between the two. Escobar's name came up often, as did the possibility of his portrait of her hanging in the Louvre, but all the flattery couldn't melt the frozen smile on her face.

Inexplicably tired, she rocked back and forth in her heels, stretching one foot and then the other, trying not to let the spikes of either catch in the tiles that floored Annette's kitchen. Unlike Jacqueline's clean and cold lines, the other woman's apartment was tight and cluttered. Wrought iron shelves up against thick plaster walls, curls and coils of sometimes fake brass and veined blue glass, and sometimes real vines; plates painted with scenes of pastoral simplicity. It looked more like the rooms of a dowager artist than a runway walker.

The food looked tempting but even though she ached to do something, anything, other than just stand there, she resisted. It was one thing to be someone who'd drifted from the living room to the kitchen, an added shame to be the one there stuffing her face.

'Pardon! God, I'm sorry – I didn't mean to stare.'

Not having noticed him come in, she started, catching her heel-teetering before it turned into an embarrassing stumble. 'N-no, it's alright,' she said, shooting her smile toward what she thought was a warmer and more sincere one.

'Nothing looking appetizing?' he replied, stepping all the way into the tight kitchen.

'Oh, no. It all looks fantastic. I'm just not all that hungry.'

'At least let me get you a glass of wine.'

Did she really want some? Older than she was by what looked to be five, maybe even seven, years, he moved well, like he knew at all times where his elbows and knees were. Salt and pepper beard, salt and pepper hair, but with a face that said the spices were premature. A ready and bright smile, blue eyes that flashed with light humour. He was dressed down, in just a pair of jeans and a similarly

17

blue denim shirt, which could have meant a lot of things, but what she took to suggest the kind of comfortable that came with success. 'That'd be nice.'

'An impertinent little vintage,' he said, choosing an unopened bottle from the white linen catering table and filling two glasses. 'Cheers!'

The chime of their toast was loud in the tiny kitchen.

'*Merci*,' she said, trying to figure out exactly where he fitted in, casting him in quickly flickering roles of agent, director, photographer, journalist, painter, designer, hairdresser … but rejecting her casting as he was too nice, too polite, too sloppy, not sloppy enough, too smart, too charming. 'Very nice,' she said, after having a sip.

'You know, I actually had to fight to urge to say, "not as nice as you". Beauty,' he said with a sigh, 'always makes me a fool.'

Laughing, she swirled the contents of her glass. 'But you did say it!'

'*Merde*. So I did. A fool. A complete and total one at that. See what I mean?'

'I've met worse.'

'I could say "I bet", but that would imply that you're surrounded by legions of fools. But what I would have meant, if I had said that, is that you're so handsome that you must reduce other men to being that way. Fools, I mean.'

Banter, not nerves. Had it been the latter, she probably would have put the cold smile back on, maybe even pretended that she had to be somewhere else. But it wasn't – at least not completely – so she didn't. Instead, she said: 'We're all allowed to be fools sometimes. Even the best of us.'

'That I find very hard to believe,' he said with staged solemnity. 'I'm afraid you've reduced to me other clichés.

I know I've seen you somewhere. You have to be part of the business.'

'Very possibly,' she said. 'I am.'

'I knew it! But you are far too beautiful for that, unless you're legendary and I am simply too much of a fool to be aware of it. A fact we have already established.'

Banter, not smarm. Had it been the latter she absolutely would have put the frozen grin back on, definitely pretended she had to be somewhere else, fast. But it wasn't – it didn't feel that way at all – so she didn't. Instead, she said: 'I'd hardly call you a fool.'

'Normally I wouldn't either. But tonight, mademoiselle, I am a complete and utter one.' Sipping his own glass, he seemed to take a deep breath at the same time. 'Believe it or not, this isn't easy.'

Raising a perfectly executed eyebrow – one that Rodriguez had called, pausing in the middle of a barrage of machine-gun rapid strobe shooting, "the best in the business" – she said, 'And why is that?'

Slowly, almost solemnly: 'You're unearthly. Almost too beautiful. The first time I saw you I really didn't know what to think. If I were a painter, I know I wouldn't be good enough to paint you. Same if I was a photographer: I'd never be able to do you justice.'

The banter had been fun, a circling little game. This was … different, but she still didn't feel the need to retreat. If not painter or photographer, then maybe an agent, director, journalist, designer, hairdresser? 'You are too kind. I'm really just a woman.'

'I would never call you *just* anything. But then by now you must be getting tired of these asinine compliments.'

Flushed, she laughed to cover it, swallowed a bit more wine to cover it even more. 'I wouldn't call them that. You're very sweet.'

Salt and pepper rose at the corners, his grin wide and animated. 'It's my pleasure,' breaking off from looking into her eyes, he glanced to the left, out of the room. 'Things seem to be dying down a bit. All and all I think it was a success, but you usually can't know about such things until the morning after.'

'Well, I had a good time. If that helps.'

'It's the only thing that matters,' he said, taking a bow. 'I should make a quick check, I guess. Shake some hands, kiss some cheeks. It's been a true pleasure. Honestly.'

Extending his hand, she saw elegant fingers, clean nails. No rings. 'Luc,' he said. 'Luc Bressian.'

His grip was light but present. Lips to the back of her hand, dry, firm, and elegantly and respectfully quick. 'It's been a pleasure,' she echoed, meaning it. Feeling the need to say something else, she added: 'Jacqueline Montelle,' even though she suspected he already knew it.

Hands parting, he looked up at her, catching but this time holding her sight. 'Jacqueline Montelle,' he said, saying her name with careful weight. 'I will hate myself more for not asking this than for saying so, but would you like to have a drink with me?'

Choices … visualized and dismissed again and again with cinematic speed: home, staying at the party, dinner alone. Puzzled, then: what was he if not painter or photographer or agent, director, journalist, designer, or hairdresser?

Whichever, he glowed and smiled being around her, which did the same to her. '*Oui*,' she said, putting out her arm so that he could lead her out.

III

The wine bar at the end of the still-dark street was

swollen with similar refugees from Annette's party, to get in and get glasses would have meant sliding shoulders across shoulders and mumbling too many 'pardons,' so by unspoken mutual consent they moved toward the distant traffic flashes of a major Parisian artery.

As they walked, he occasionally made a quick witty remark about the party, to which she responded with a short pulse of laughter. His arm, still linked in hers, was warm and strong.

Even though they hadn't had that drink, and she'd only had two small glasses at Annette's, Jacqueline floated, drifted, bobbed along at his side. Had it been that long since she'd been wobbly on the arm of a man? It hadn't. Not really. Nameless gropes and sometimes more at other thundering and pulsing parties, hands on her body, between her legs, cupping her breasts as techno vibrated her bones. A long afternoon only a month or so ago, sliding between the sheets at a moderate Roman hotel with Bertoli, a smooth-chested and muscled pretty boy. But that had been nothing but a sticky and slick release; the stress of them both parading for the editors of a new Italian fashion magazine, let go in cocktails in the bar then growling and scratching in his room.

Afterward, they had returned to the gliding steps and haughty demeanour of their professions, weighing the value of each other's company on what could be gained, or harmed, by their association. Bertoli hadn't called afterward, but she hadn't called him either.

Traffic, the roar of cheap cars and the purr of expensive ones, and she looked up from where she'd been looking into herself to see they were at the Avenue. A few metres toward the rushing traffic was another café, this one with only a few couples bent over tables. More than enough room for one more evening pairing.

'How about here?' Luc said, with a nod toward the door.

'It looks nice. Let's,' she said, with a smile toward him.

At a table, a bottle and two glasses soon brought, they chatted with short, grinning bursts about nothing – or nothing she remembered. Looking at him, at his honest black and white hair and beard, at his sincere laughter, she tried to place him yet again, to figure out what he was.

But despite her confusion about his role, she still didn't ask.

'This is quite amazing,' he said, eyes twinkling at her over the rim of his glass.

'Actually I think it's more than a bit average,' she said, thinking he meant the vintage.

Shock and disappointment were there on his face, a lowering of peppered eyebrows, a turning down of the corners of his mouth.

Before he could say anything, a laugh came up and out of her with loud sincerity that made the few other late night sippers and chatters turn toward them. 'The wine, I mean. Not you.'

'*Merci*,' he said, relief evident on his face. 'Had me worried there for a second.'

It continued from there: chatter, chuckles, smiles, then a surreptitious touching of his hand on hers, hers not moving away; she pouring for him, he pouring for her.

If not painter or photographer or an agent, director, journalist, designer, hairdresser then what? It was important to her, but, that night, his opinion of her as the most beautiful woman in the world was all that mattered.

He lived nearby, or at least within a reasonable walk. When they left the little café, she thought about Danielle.

22

A vertical line of a girl, streamlined and frightfully purposeful, she'd told her one day as they sat in the bar during a hiatus in a long Danish swimsuit shoot that it was all a game: the industry, her appearance, people, the world, everything. It was a something you either lost or won. Her way of winning one battle was to make a man beg for her, to put herself on top of every facet – from flirt to kiss to strip to fuck. To make him wait and wait and wait until he'd practically explode, then after he'd had a taste, make him do it all over again.

Luc's arm was around her waist, a nervous daring that made her want to laugh loudly again. Playfully, she took his hand away, waving a warning finger at his panicked face. 'Not too forward,' she stage-whispered.

It *was* a game. Gone from it after she lost by marrying some third-rate director of commercials; Danielle was right, even if she was a poor player. Maybe not a painter or a photographer, but perhaps an agent, director, journalist, designer, or hairdresser. Luc was dangling at the end of her hook; and although she wasn't going to make him beg, she was enjoying her own version of Danielle's competition.

But by the time their walk ended at a heavy oak door in another dark and half-forgotten curl of a Paris street, she had to admit to herself that he was scoring considerably as well. Eyes shimmering with both desire and awe, his touches were equally warm, then heated.

At the door, they kissed for the first time. Not planned, not strategized, no rook to king, no grand slam, just an occurrence: his key in his lock, a turn to look at her, she moving in, he moving in, then lips to lips.

Danielle would have been disappointed. Jacqueline wasn't.

The game was completely abandoned beyond the very

modern and very heavy metal door: a narrow flight of stairs climbing steeply upward, diamond-plate steps and a brass railing completing the industrial ascent.

On the first few steps, they moved in unison but apart. As the stairs narrowed, it pushed them together – an architectural matchmaker.

Whose hands first? Hard to say. Maybe at the same time, but definitely different places: her fingers sliding between the buttons of his shirt, tips touching the curls and swirls of his coarse chest hair; his dropping down to the flat of her back and then the rise of her ass. In response to her, he grinned and leaned forward for another kiss. In response to him, she pulled herself closer for another kiss.

It was hot, it was wet, it was strong, and it travelled from her lips and tongue down her body, ringing her already aching nipples and down between her legs where it released a weight and warmth of readiness.

As the kiss continued – hotter, wetter, stronger – she felt Luc's own response pressed up against her, persistent, long, and very hard.

Before she was even aware, she'd slipped her hand from between those buttons and had dropped it down to, instead, a zipper. A grip told her that her initial reaction hadn't been exaggerated: indeed very long and very, very hard.

He moaned into her mouth, breaking the seal between them to give a quick series of pants. His hands went from caresses to fervent squeezing of her ass, which made her even more daring in her fondling of him.

Somehow during all this, the door to the street had been closed, which she realized was good because she was burning far too much to have cared if they had an audience or not.

For some reason, what was happening struck her as funny, and she went from hissing between her teeth in her own melody of excitement to giggling into his shoulder.

'Shouldn't … we get upstairs?' she whispered into blue denim.

'*Oui, oui,*' he said, his own stammer deep and rough.

Turning away was very difficult; their hands had become powerful magnets not wanting to break from their touchings, holding, strokings, and kneadings.

Leading the way, she took the steps slowly in her dizziness. Holding the railing tightly – instantly wishing it was his own muscular pole she was gripping – the attraction between them grew too strong again, especially for him, as she almost immediately felt his hands cup and then grip her ass. Stopping, each foot on a different step, she hissed and pushed herself back into him.

Fine silk sliding. She felt like she was going to pass out. Thankfully did not.

Knowing what he would be seeing as he slid her dress up made her even hotter, even wetter. She hadn't selected the lacy thong with the intention of it being seen, had made no plans to show it to anyone, which made it all the more exciting. The thrill of their mutual surprise; she for being revealed, he for seeing.

A kiss, one on each cheek. A ritual. Holding back for two simple gestures of affection. Then his hands, one also on each cheek, and a gentle parting – and as he did she felt herself further, and almost completely, liquefy. She might have been showing him the silken thread of her panties, but she also knew she was also showing her very plump, very wet lips.

Knew, as well, because he touched them. Again, slowly, cautiously, almost respectfully: one single finger beginning at the top, then down and going down, then in the barest amount. The contact, that barest touch, was a bolt of lightning. It made her gasp, hiss, and moan from there, her clit, to there, her lips.

Spreading her legs, giving him permission, demanding his attention, she also pushed back toward him.

Agreeing with quick fingers, he began. At first she thought he was going to drive her completely insane: he rubbed her swollen lips, played with the muscular ring that introduced her vagina, tickled where quim became anus, and then circled, but here quite touched that pulsing button.

Just when she was about to scream in frustration, to stop her heavy panting to yell at the top of her lungs, he stopped his teasing. Tap, tap, tap, rub, rub, rub, he went, playing her and in playing her drawing out steady deep-body moans instead of any kind of demand.

It came – her coming – unexpectedly. Normally, even with the most sophisticated of partners, she had to descend into a fantasy, picture instead of boyish models, anonymous fucks on pulsing dance floors, or sweaty managers in dressing rooms, someone else and somewhere else. Places of refinement and sophistication, fine silks on her back, jewels around her neck, and men rippling with muscles or immaculate hair, but this time, in a stairway off a cheap street in a cheap part of the city, she screamed louder than she ever had before.

Knees failing, she collapsed onto the stairs – at least partially. She would have collapsed all the way down onto the steel steps, but Luc put his hands under her, supporting her until she could see, breathe, and carefully pull herself up onto her feet.

Then he took her hand and led her all the way to the top.

Not really looking, not really seeing, she didn't

perceive the apartment as anything but quick images, tiny details that slipped past her glistening perspiration, fluttering heart, weak legs, panting breaths: huge, very modern kitchen – all polished brass and chrome, streaked marble, and blue tinted glass – full of well-used pots and pans, and plastic bins full of greens and even some browns; huge dining table roughly hewn out of what looked like one huge slab of mahogany, surrounded by mismatched chairs. Low bookcases containing a jumbled chaos of bright covers, then the bed, a great pad of an unmade futon.

Then, the bed. On it in a tumble of hands and lips and clothes. She licked his fingers, tasting herself. She nibbled his lips, tasting herself there as well, though not as strong.

A pause, he sprawled, shirt unbuttoned, head between his own huge pillows. Eyes glittering in the low light, looking entranced, hypnotized.

Hypnotized, by her. She knew that, understood that. It was more exciting to her than any cold tryst with plucked and waxed models, any ham-handed gropes or bathroom blowjobs in clubs, any career moves on her knees in dressing rooms – far better than any gleaming fantasy of yachts and gold and jewels and applause.

Jacqueline was the woman he'd heard about, read about, seen in magazines, walking the runway on television, and hanging on gallery walls as immortalized by a true and spectacular genius. She was the woman in the portrait by Escobar.

Here and now, just for him, she was the legendary Jacqueline.

While sitting on rumpled sheets, she strolled into his most intimate of dreams, of fantasies, by reaching down and taking hold of the hem of her fine dress and carefully, almost cruelly pulling it steadily up and up and up and

27

then off, to fall loosely to the floor.

No bra. Hard nipples. Shimmering sweat between them. His expression said it all: awe, delight, amazement and most of all, total and complete desire.

Rising slowly up from where he'd been sprawled, he gazed at her with every climbing inch, clearly drinking in her renowned beauty, absorbing every detail of her body, ending up nose to nose, looking deeply into her eyes.

Locked together, she saw herself reflected in his gaze. Saw herself the way he saw her.

Perfect.

Flawless.

Ideal.

Beauty.

Then his clothes were gone, joining her in nothing but skin and sweat. From a corner table, a quick moment of reality, a tiny plastic wrapper tossed to the floor, a condom rolled down the length of his cock.

While he lay on his back, bobbing with desire, she climbed up, on top of him, positioning herself carefully so that he was just *there*, at the entrance of herself.

Down. In. Together. His dream, his fantasy, made real.

And hers – in being his – as well.

IV

During the night, two more times. Twilight hands, twilight bodies, not enough illumination from the street outside to see much beyond the smooth rise of a hip, the halo of uncombed hair, a hand outlined against the soft gloom, the gleam and glimmer of eyes in delight, or teeth in passionate smiles.

Then sleep, heavy and deep. Warm, wrapped right in thick blankets and satin sheets, it was dreamless and still.

No tossing. No turning.

Sunlight woke her, intense brightness coming through those same windows: a hard day heading straight into her rapidly blinking eyes. Rubbing them, she sat up, a sudden sharp concern with it that she was alone in the bed.

Eyes clearing finally, she saw him at the far end of the room. Naked, on the phone, he paced back and forth in and out of the kitchen.

Watching him, she grinned, trying to decide how to draw him back to bed. She never felt more beautiful. More perfect. Agent, director, journalist, designer, hairdresser – whatever he was, she liked being his ideal, his dream come true.

'I'm happy you liked them. I did think they came out especially well,' he was saying into his tiny silver phone. Seeing her see him, he grinned back and blew her a kiss, his eyes as wide as his broad gesture.

'Sorry I didn't hang around to check in with the cleanup,' he continued, stopping to listen to a response. 'Excellent. I knew Marie would take care of it. She's wonderful.' More that only he could hear, then: 'Jacqueline? Why, yes, we had a wonderful time. Thanks for asking.' Still more, still only what he could hear. Finally: 'Well, I'm very pleased that you're pleased. If you're having another event, please keep Pomme in mind for all your catering needs.'

'Good morning, beautiful,' he said, stretching as he walked back toward the bed. Closing the phone, he set it down neatly on the dining room table as he passed it. 'That was nice. Annette said the party went wonderfully. I'm glad because normally I hang around to make sure, but Marie is very capable and … well, with you on my arm I really couldn't think about anything else.'

At the edge of the bed, he sat, arm reaching out to

29

stroke one of her bare legs. 'She asked about you, by the way. Hope you don't mind if I said we had a nice night. No details mind you, I do try to be a gentleman in such matters. No gossip, I! You know, if you ever want to quit waitressing, I would be more than willing to take you on, as it were. I always need servers, and, well, my food would taste like the ambrosia of the Gods by just being near such a beautiful and amazing woman ... I'm sorry, did I say something wrong?'

Her feet hurt, but she kept walking. She didn't know where was going until she turned one corner and recognized the neighbourhood.

The day was busy, lots of people about: doing this, doing that, on the way from some things, going to other things. Jacqueline knew she must not have looked ... her best, with the same dress she'd worn the night before, scuffed heels, smeared make-up, hair frayed and wild, but even though she still cared, she was too lost, too alone amid all the bustle and rush to do anything about it.

A caterer.

A police car rushed by, its wailing cutting through any other sound that day. It made her stop on the corner, and with the stop came a few other sensations with the ache in her ears from the *gendarme's* siren. Her eyes burned and smarted, swimming in close-to-crying tears; her feet hurt, a pulsing throb from her toes to her ankles and then all the way up her legs; her chest ached, muscles fisting in her rib cage.

She'd gone home with the caterer.

Breathing in, breathing out, biting her lip, she fought the battle of her tears. One battle won, her nose pulled a surprise end-run strategy and began to run freely. Tissue, she needed a tissue. Her purse, there was probably one in there. Swinging it around, she popped the clasp and began to dig.

She'd fucked *the caterer.*

Cell phone, sunglasses case, makeup, wallet, keys, miscellaneous slips of paper … tissue, wadded, wrinkled, torn … good enough. Stepping away from the edge of the curb, back close to but not touching the wall of a dry-cleaning establishment, she dabbed, then gingerly blew in what she hoped, prayed, was a dignified, ladylike manner.

Annette knew.

The damp tissue went into a nearby trash bin. Taking a deep breath she tried to release some of the tension, to shake it away, to push it out. Fingers through her hair, she tried to tame it, snapping knots carelessly, not caring in her rush for tsk-tsks from hairdressers in the future.

The neighbourhood *was* familiar. She was real close. Why not? She might as well stop by. Yes, that was a good idea. Yes … a good idea.

Across the street, down the avenue. In the near distance, just a few hundred metres or so, the pure white of the façade. Was she presentable? Suspecting she wasn't, she decided to go ahead anyway.

A waitress.

L'Art, that was the name of it – the name of the gallery – the memory bubbling as she walked up to the door. A small place, known for the pomposity of its name and one recent discovery. Four months. Was that how long it had been since she'd been there last?

Flashing cameras, lenses turned toward her; tart champagne in fine crystal; black beads of fine caviar on fine porcelain; journalists asking questions; beautiful women. Faces dark with jealousy; Escobar looking uncomfortable; his wife looking even more uncomfort-able.

Four months? It felt like only a few days. Jacqueline wished it really had been four days since the party, the unveiling of that new work, a month later the cover of *ArtNews* with the same beautiful work gracing its cover.

The painting. Her portrait by Escobar.

Seeing it again would be good. No, it would be wonderful. It would make her feel better. Not like a woman who'd fuck a caterer. Who people thought was a waitress. It would make her feel beautiful; make her special.

Adjusting her dress, trying to sweep off a few of the more noticeable wrinkles, she held off opening the door and going in – like a present where the anticipation was almost as precious as the contents.

But then she stopped smoothing her silk. L'Art was small, just one large pale-walled space. To one side was a desk, a slab of heavy blue glass; on the other, a narrow ascent of stairs to probably an office.

It was still early, the gallery clearly just having opened. It was empty aside from the owner, a man whose name she couldn't remember. Large and slow, yet dressed in a finely tailored suit, he busied himself with papers and documents, wide back to her and the front window.

One wall was that glass, the other two were for art. On one of them – she looked once, then again and again – were the explosive colours, brilliant sweeps, refined compositions of Escobar.

But none of them were her. None of them were the painting he'd done of her. It was gone.

A waitress. He thought he'd spent the night making love to a waitress – a plain, ordinary, waitress.

Not Jacqueline.

During her second shower that evening, the phone rang. An expired, tired, past-its-prime tune. Even though it came as hot water was smashing down on her, steam clouding the room, she still quickly twisted off the flow and jumped out of the bathroom to grab it.

Flipping it open: '*Allo?*' she said, droplets from her wet hair tapping onto the tops of her bare feet.

'Jacqueline?' came the voice on the other side, flat Francoise with American accent. 'It's Sheri of *Le Monde*. My editor said you were available for an interview …?'

'*Oui, oui*!' she gushed, automatically wishing she were dressed in something fine as opposed to her damp skin. Crooking the phone between ear and shoulder, she rushed back into the still-steaming bathroom, quickly pulled her towel from the bar, began to wrap it around herself. 'Of course, I remember. How are you?' she said, a spontaneous stall as she pulled and tugged the towel into place.

'Um … I'm fine. Is this a good time? This won't take very long. We're planning on featuring Escobar in an upcoming issue and it would be great if we could get some comments from you as one of his models.'

Sitting on the edge of her bed, not caring for the moment that she was getting the Miazaki spread wet: 'I'm so flattered! Thank you for thinking of me.'

'Well, I'm trying to give the piece some depth. I just got finished talking with his wife, Constance.'

'A wonderful woman. Of course, I've only met her once or twice. But she's always struck me as being very … dignified, I guess you could say. I always got the impression she hasn't been very comfortable with her husband's – well, his life as it's become. Maybe even a bit jealous of him and me. I was just saying to Simone – you know Simone, right? I was just saying how this life, the life of art and artists, I mean, can be wonderful but how it can also sometimes bring out the absolute worst in people.'

'The worst? Yes, I could easily see that. I guess I should ask what Escobar was like to work with?'

'Escobar? Oh, he was wonderful, darling. Absolutely fantastic. A genius, of course, and like all those kinds of people, completely focused on his work. Not that he was rude or anything. Not at all. Treated me like a princess – if not better, if you know what I mean. Always made sure I was comfortable, brought me drinks, rubbed my neck when it got sore. Posing takes some time, you know – that kind of thing.'

'Um, yes. So you'd say he appeared to be conscientious?'

'Oh, more than that. Much more than that. But then artists, especially great artists, are like that. Very sensual people. Guess it must have something to the way they look at the world, eh? Always trying to make love to everything with their art ...'

'So you and he were actually ... intimate? Can I ask that?'

'Well, you can ask it, certainly! But a lady would never tell, and I may be a lot of things but I always try to be discreet.'

'Oh, I think I understand.' Not great, just good, but Jacqueline could still hear through her French that she did understand what was being implied. 'It also sort of agrees with what I've heard.'

'Now, now,' she *tsked* into the phone. 'Mustn't gossip.'

The journalist's laugh was rough and loud. Very

American. 'So, Jacqueline, what was it like to have the privilege of being immortalized by a master?'

'It … it was good, but while I know the painting's been considered a masterpiece and all that – I've even heard talk of hanging it in the Louvre, if I remember correctly – it's just something to hang on a wall. Being with Escobar, a man like that … to have that kind of experience … well, it can change … a waitress, say, into a princess.'

'But what was it for you?'

'It was magnificent. Truly magnificent.'

About the Story

A SEDUCTION OF VANITY is a chapter from *Brushes*, a novel I recently wrote. The book is about all the people around Escobar, a famous artist: his wife, his manager, the forger, his brother and many others, told through interconnected chapters.

There is just something about Paris – its history, flavour, atmosphere, a mix of the very old with cutting-edge contemporary – that lends itself perfectly for all kinds of stories, including erotica. That *something* for me is so strong I – even though I don't speak a word of French (I have a hard enough time with English) – have often dreamed about living in that very special city. While that may never happen, the allure of Paris is still there: a magnificent snail's-shell of culture, food, eroticism, romance, and laughter. A true city of dreams … all kinds of dreams.

Belleville Blue
by Carrie Williams

MONA HADN'T SPOKEN TO or even seen any of her neighbours in weeks. She'd been holed up in her garret, hooked up to the internet or knee-deep in box files, researching her *Encyclopaedica Erotica*. As the work absorbed her more and more, so the human contact diminished, until all she was left with were her occasional trips to the grocer's and her brief calls to her editor, updating him on her progress.

Nights, after working to the point where she couldn't think straight, she'd sit in her window with the shutters thrown open, listening to the Paris night. This area, Oberkampf spilling out of the 11th into the 20th, was one of the city's hippest, and from every direction she could hear people calling to one another, music spilling from bars and clubs, animated chatter wafting up from the restaurant and café terraces. The place pulsated with life, while hers seemed to have become something stagnant and stale.

One morning, walking home from the local market with her string bag full of fruit, vegetables and little packets of meat bound up in greaseproof paper, she stopped, on a whim, outside the town hall of her *arrondissement* and studied the notices on the board. It was only then that she realised that it was the eve of the day people like her, lonely people, dreaded more than any other: Bastille Day, the city's – indeed, the nation's – biggest party. A day for celebrating with loved ones. A day for fireworks and fun. But what if there was no one to have fun with?

Just as she was turning away, a second notice snagged her attention: a ball at the local fire station, that evening. She smiled to herself. She'd heard about these *bals pompiers* some time ago. Fire stations across the capital held them every year, on the eve of Bastille Day. She studied the notice in more detail: there were to be 'country fair style games', a bar, traditional music, and a *petite surprise*. This time she almost laughed out loud. The French had some funny ideas about what constituted a good night out.

At home, she put away her shopping and made herself a cup of coffee, which she placed on her desk, by her mouse mat. Logging onto the 'net, she typed in the website address of the Louvre and, after a few minutes spent keying in various search words, leaned forward in her chair to get a better view of the erotic artworks and artefacts that flashed up before her – men and women, or women and women, carved into figurines, on Attic vases, on rings, or in paintings by Delacroix, Ingres and others. From time to time she would lean forward to make notes on a little lined pad beside her, highlighting ones that she particularly wanted to see in the flesh the next time she visited the museum.

Her favourite, and one she had already visited in person several times over, was Ingres' *Le bain turc,* or *Turkish Bath*. She loved it both for its composition – a harem scene full of arabesques – and for its history. Ingres, aged eight-two at the time of the painting, had enjoyed the irony of creating an erotic work in old age, telling friends that he 'retained all the fire of a man of thirty years' and even going so far as to detail his age, AETATIS LXXXII, on the canvas itself.

Mona also loved the audacity of the painter in depicting one of the nude female bathers openly caressing the breast of another, and the fact that the bather in the right foreground, arms raised above her head, was based on a sketch that the painter had made of his wife, Madeleine Chapelle, almost half a century before. Another wife, Empress Eugenie, so disliked the work that she made her husband, Napoléon III, return it to the painter just days after receiving it. Before making its way to the Louvre, it had found a more welcome home with Khalil Bey, a former diplomat and art lover with a renowned collection of erotica that had also included Courbet's *L'Origine du monde*, a close-up oil painting of the lower half of a woman's body, legs spread, and his *Les Dormeuses* or *The Sleepers*, an overt depiction of naked lesbian lovers entwined, almost certainly post-coitally, on a bed.

The afternoon passed quickly, productively, and when Mona next glanced up, dusk had fallen outside her window. She stood up to look around, pulled her cardigan more closely around her. She didn't mind the days, but the nights were hard.

She cooked herself a simple supper, but even the robust Toulouse sausage, oven-warmed bread and red wine failed to warm her. She sat in her armchair wrapped in a much-loved pashmina, re-reading a favourite work by Anaïs Nin, *Spy in the House of Love*. Lulled by the slow burn of the prose and the luxuriousness of the sensual experiences described, she soon fell into a rêverie from which only the sound of the bells chiming in the church beside her apartment block roused her. She counted down the hour: eight o'clock. Just eight. How was she to get through the rest of the night?

She held out until nine, when the words began to blur before her eyes. Then, folding the blanket and placing it on her work chair, she went upstairs and ran herself a bath, adding a few drops of aromatic oils – her own mix of jasmine, ylang ylang and mandarin. Then she stripped off and sunk into it as far as her chin, holding her hair up in a ponytail with one hand. With her other she played with her right nipple, almost unconsciously.

She stared down below the clear water, at the flat expanse of her stomach terminating in the gentle incline of her mound of Venus and the fluff of golden-brown hair, rather unkempt since she had been living here, since she had been alone. She let her ponytail tumble down and the freed hand glide over her body, move across the plump cushion of her mons, thread its way through the silken fronds and play around her lips. She closed her eyes, gave herself up to the delicious melting feeling. As it grew stronger, she hooked her thumb round and pressed it against her clit, massaged it from side to side. A jag of pleasure like an electric shock had her arch up, sloshing water over the side of the bath as she climaxed.

Afterwards, she dressed warmly before locking the apartment and heading out into the night.

She was surprised by the number of people heading into the fire station – the promise of traditional musical entertainment seemed to have brought the locals out in droves. She stood still in the road for a moment, looking at the building. She didn't even know why she was here, besides the fact that she couldn't be alone anymore. But who was she going to talk to? She knew no one. And no one knew her.

She breathed in deeply and pushed open the door. Inside, people were drinking and chatting in low voices. A few of them turned their eyes to her as she handed over a few euros to the woman collecting the entrance fees, and she nodded self-consciously in their direction as she made her way to the trestle table in front of them and bought a glass of red wine. She turned back to face the room, looking around every so often for a friendly face encouraging her to start a conversation. But the momentarily inquisitive adults had all turned back to their little groups, shouldering her out.

After twenty minutes or so, she was just thinking of creeping away and making her way home when a mike was set up on a makeshift little stage at the front of the room. Some men she hadn't noticed until that point materialised from one corner of the room and took to the stage, one carrying a trumpet, another an acoustic guitar, and a third a piano accordion.

Mona watched as they assembled themselves, tuned up their instruments, psyched themselves up. The accordionist, in particular, drew her attention: tall and slightly built, he had almost white-blond hair and chestnut-brown eyes – a combination that had always intrigued her. She didn't remove her gaze from him as he took the large, boxy instrument between his hands, ran his long slender fingers up and down the piano keyboard.

After a few minutes, the band struck up a waltz, and she was pushed back as a tide of people surged forward and the space in front of the stage was transformed into a dance floor by swaying couples. She felt another pang of loneliness as she counted out the coins for a second glass of wine, which she emptied rapidly. Over the dancers' heads she could see the accordionist gently rocking on his parted legs as he compressed and released the bellows

41

with one arm. One hand operated the button keyboard on the left of the bellows, the digits of the other caressed the piano keys. His mastery of the cumbersome-looking contraption was complete.

In her mind, as the wine infiltrated her bloodstream and her focus on the blond accordion player grew more intent, the sound of the other instruments almost wholly died away. She was fascinated by how the swirling sound of the accordion simultaneously evoked in her a sense of sprightly cheeriness and a kind of wistfulness, perhaps even melancholy. Utterly and unmistakeably French, it put her in mind of black berets and clouds of cigarette smoke – some of the clichés she thought she abhorred. She found herself swaying a little in time to the music, then tapping her feet, shimmying her shoulders a tad. No one could see her anyway, hidden away as she was at the back of the room.

As the evening advanced, the pace heightened, with the band working their way through an impressive repertoire of polkas, mazurkas, foxtrots, *paso dobles* and javas. The latter, in which the swaggering dancers wrapped their arms around their partners and clasped their buttocks, thrilled her with its loucheness. It put her in mind of the old *bal-musettes* she had read about. Almost against her will, she found herself moving forwards towards the dance floor, surrendering her body to the cadence. The couples, lost to each other, scarcely noticed as she slipped between them, eased herself into the centre. As another tune began, she threw her head back, closed her eyes, and let herself be carried away by the tempo.

She wasn't sure how long she'd been dancing when she opened her eyes to see the accordionist's fixed firmly on her, the corners of his mouth twisted up in a wry smile. He nodded at her when she saw him, winked. She smiled back, moved a little closer to the stage now that the crowd had thinned out a little. With her hips and shoulders she writhed like a serpent, enjoying the way her breasts swayed wantonly in her flimsy bra, the feel of the blond's eyes on her as the band launched into a rousing finale.

The music stopped and the musicians stepped forward to take a bow. The rough wine coursing in her veins, combined with the intoxication of the dance, made her step forward to steady herself against the stage. She closed her eyes again. She was showing herself up in front of all these strangers, she reprimanded herself. She looked towards the door, wondered if she could make it that far without falling over.

As she straightened herself up, she felt a firm hand on her shoulder.

'*Ca va?*' she heard a voice say, and she looked up to see the accordion player lowering himself to sit on the edge of the stage beside her.

'*Oui, oui,*' she said rapidly.

'Ah, you're English?'

She nodded.

'Are you on holiday?'

'No, I just moved here, not long ago. I live just off Oberkampf, towards the Canal Saint-Martin.'

'I don't know it. I'm not from here. We travel around. We're vagabonds.' He smiled, held out a hand. 'My name is Louis,' he said, as she felt his warm palm against hers. 'What's yours?'

'Mona.'

'*C'est joli*. Listen, Mona, I need to pack up my accordion but I'd love to have a drink. How say we take a couple of glasses outside with us?' He looked around him. 'It's getting a bit stale and sweaty in here.'

'Sure,' she said, losing herself in the soft brown eyes

that regarded her, dark as pools of spilt ink. She followed him across the now-deserted space of the dance floor.

'What did you think of the entertainment?' he said, as she reached for two glasses. He headed towards the door, which she stood against to hold open as he manoeuvred his bulky instrument outside.

'I loved it,' she replied, a little embarrassed as she remembered how she had lost herself on the dance floor, how she had opened her eyes to find him staring right at her. Sensing her discomfiture, he added, 'It's nice to see someone with a bit of rhythm.'

She laughed.

'Seriously,' he said. 'So what brought you to Paris?'

She frowned, looked past him. There had been nights, other nights, when, crazed and cracked by solitude, she had walked and walked, following the streets until she had to ask a stranger for directions back to Belleville.

'I'm a writer,' she said at last. 'And Paris is a city of writers. *For* writers.'

He nodded thoughtfully, lit up a cigarette, offering her one. Fire danced in his eyes as he struck a match and brought it to the tip. He took a deep drag, blew smoke out around him.

'Shall we go for a walk?' he said. 'I don't know this part of Paris at all. Which is silly, since this is the territory of Piaf, my heroine.'

Mona gestured back down the Rue de Ménilmontant, and he nodded, placing the undrunk glasses of wine on the pavement before following her.

They walked in silence for a while, and then, feeling the need to break the silence, Mona said, 'So why the accordion?'

'The squeezebox, or 'trembling box' – *boîte à*

frissons – as the slang word has it?' he said, then paused reflectively. 'Well, why not?' he continued after a moment, flashing her a smile that made her feel weak.

'Why not indeed? But it's quite a rare instrument. Why did you choose it over, say, a guitar?'

'Oh, I play the guitar too. And a few other instruments besides. But I'm a romantic, and there is something so old-fashioned about the accordion. I've been in love with the idea of it ever since I first heard the Piaf song *L'Accordeoniste.*'

'About an accordion player?'

He nodded, eyes fixed on the road ahead. 'About a doomed love affair between a *bal-musette* accordionist and a prostitute. Cheery stuff. And what about you?'

'What about me?'

'What kind of thing do you write?'

She squirmed a little. Depending on who she was talking to, she was more or less evasive about her job as an historian of the erotic. Not that she was ashamed of it. But she had found that it gave people certain ideas about her, that it made them think, all too often, that she was some kind of nymphomaniac. Sadly, the converse was true. She would have loved to be a sexual tigress, but she had grown to accept that she just didn't have it in her.

He had noticed her hesitation and was just about to open his mouth to coax her when she saw the Café Charbon up on their right and was happy to have the opportunity to deflect any further questioning, at least for the moment.

'A drink?' she said. 'This is the best bar in the neighbourhood, so they say.'

He looked at the façade, then down it past the street. 'How about a dance?' he said, gesturing with his chin towards a different venue.

She looked. It was the Nouveau Casino, a famous club and live music venue. She'd never been.

She must have pulled a face, for he said, 'We don't have to.' Then he linked his arms through hers. 'But it might be quite fun if we do.'

She didn't want any more to drink, she felt dehydrated from the cheap red wine at the *bal*. But on the dance floor with Louis, resting her head against his shoulder and feeling his pelvis grinding into her, feeling the coil of his dick straining at his trousers, seeking, of its own accord, what nested between her own legs, she felt light-headed, drunk with desire and longing. Around them people swayed in time to the electro tunes, sometimes moving other body parts too – arms, hands, fingers, shoulders, head or hips. Some of them whooped and bounced, showing off to the rest of their crowd. Others, falling into tune with the music, with the intensification of the beats and melody that the DJ was engineering at his turntables, looked to be falling into some kind of trance state.

She didn't know if she were imagining it, but the DJ seemed to be trying to work the room up to some sort of climactic highpoint, lifting the dancers, perhaps without them realising, to some higher plane of consciousness. It was a question, she sensed, of letting go, of submitting, and she had never been very good at that. But what had happened as Louis had played his accordion back there in the fire station had shown her that she was capable of it, that she could allow herself to lose control. It was all a matter of trust.

She lifted her head, looked Louis fiercely in the eyes, then let her head loll back away from him, closed her own eyes. The strobes sent multicoloured waves of light racing over the insides of her lids. The music pounded away inside her brain, up through her body, like some kind of powerful narcotic. Her cunt ached, ached for this man whose delicate but sure hands were the only thing between her and the floor. It was all she could do not to reach down and start rubbing at her palpitating clit.

She must have been about to pass out, or to look as if she might, for before long Louis scooped her up in his arms and carried her out of the club. The July night was cooling now. He set her down on her feet, gently.

'Told you it would be fun,' she heard him say, 'in a weird kind of way. Not that I'm a big fan of modern music. Give me Piaf any day. Or John Coltrane. Or Gershwin.'

Not eliciting any response from her, he began to hum, and then to sing:

Fascinating rhythm
You got me on a go
Fascinating rhythm
I'm all a-quiver
What a mess you're makin'
The neighbours want to know
Why I'm always shakin'
Just like a flivver.'

As they began to walk back up towards the fire station, he stopped singing, turned his head to her. 'You've gone awfully quiet,' he said. When she didn't reply, he took her hand and they continued in silence.

As they approached the fire station, raucous cries could be heard through the windows open onto the night. Louis turned to smile at Mona.

'*La surprise,*' he said, and mischief flickered in his eyes like wild fire. He made for the door, beckoning her to follow him.

When they stepped inside, the room was even more

packed than before, and the temperature had risen perceptibly. But the dance floor was still, all bodies turned towards the stage, backs to the door from which Louis and Mona had entered.

Mona raised her eyes to the stage and let out a low moan. On it, five or six firemen were gyrating to the music emanating from the loudspeakers on either side of it. Slowly, tantalisingly, they were stripping off their tight navy uniforms. Mona swallowed, almost painfully, as she watched taut limbs being unveiled, as bronzed biceps and well-define six-packs were revealed, and honed buttocks signalled their firm presence through crisp white boxer shorts.

The men danced on, obviously enjoying the eyes on them, revelling in the power of their manliness, savouring the thrill of performing this act normally forbidden to them, alien to their daily lives and vocation. Running their powerful hands over skin that looked, in its sheen, to have been lightly oiled but may just have been slick with perspiration, they let their eyes roam the audience, occasionally winking at someone who caught their eye, giving them a cheeky grin and a come-hither look.

As the pace quickened, Mona became aware that she was moving in time to the music, swaying her hips then her torso and shoulders, almost aping the firemen's moves. Half-closing her eyes, she imagined for a moment she was up there with them, stepping up to one of them, running her hand down over his bare, smooth chest, insinuating a finger into the top of his boxers, starting to inch them down, by infinitesimal little tugs, until she could feel the soft hair of his groin lap at her fingertips.

She must have staggered again, almost fallen, for suddenly she was in Louis's arms for the second time, and his face was in hers, half anxious, half lustful, shining with a film of sweat. He too, she sensed, was not unmoved by the sight of the muscular bodies on the stage.

'Time to go home,' breathed Louis, and she nodded.

He carried her back down the Ménilmontant hill, paying no heed to the passers-by who stared at them. Then, where she pointed, he turned right off Oberkampf onto Rue Saint Maur. After a few moments, he prompted gently, 'Where do you live?'

'Opposite the church,' she uttered with effort, weakly waving a hand towards her apartment block.

He moved towards it. She felt in her pocket, produced the key and handed it to him.

As if bringing his bride over the threshold, he carried her in and began to ascend the staircase, looking down at her.

Mona smiled at him. She felt like a child in his arms. She felt safe.

In her studio, walking over to her big old *lit bateau*, Louis threw her down. The rough action woke Mona from her dream-like state and she jumped up, encircled his slim wrists with her hands.

'Come here,' she half-snarled, pulling him towards her, twisting him round as she did so, so that he fell backwards onto the bed and it was her on top. The somnolent effects of the alcohol and the repetitive music had worn off now, and she felt incredibly clearheaded, lucid. She knew what she wanted, for the first time in a long while. Perhaps for the first time in her life.

Leaning over him, hair pouring down onto him like water, she ripped his shirt off, too impatient to fiddle with the buttons. Then she pulled the T-shirt beneath it up over his head, at the same time bringing her face down and fastening her front teeth on first one nipple, then the other.

As he moaned and wriggled beneath her, she chewed at them in turn, varying the intensity. With her hands she reached down to where her cunt was drizzling his groin with her nectar, took hold of the hard baton of his penis. With her thumb she massaged the head, paying special attention to the ridge of the corona. Then she grasped the shaft firmly in her fist and set in motion a series of regular strokes, listening to his joyful gasps at the up- and down-beats. When his breaths and groans seemed to be rising to a crescendo, she kneeled up above him, presented him with her cunt.

He cupped the succulent mound with one hand, levered himself down and through her legs until his face was directly underneath her. His tongue peeked out from between his lips, tauntingly. She lowered herself, mashed herself against his jaw, his mouth. He opened wide, took a big mouthful of her pussy, his tongue at the centre stabbing at her clit. She juddered, rising towards her climax. When it seemed inevitable, she lifted her haunches and backed up, lowering herself onto his cock. Taking him into the far reaches of herself, she held on as he galloped beneath her, squeezing and releasing him with her walls until both of them were being battered by their orgasms.

She collapsed down on top of him, and as she began to let herself succumb to sleep, clutching her still-throbbing pussy, she was certain that, although the Nouveau Casino was a good few minutes' walk from her house, she could feel the music from the club pulsing up through her floor.

In the morning she found him frying eggs in the kitchenette, as coffee brewed in the pot, richly scenting the room. Music was playing on the radio – some vapid pop hit – and he was wiggling his fine arse around in time to the beat, clad only in his striped boxer shorts.

She sat down, smiled uncertainly. Memories of the firemen in their underwear flitted through her mind, like the uncertain traces of a dying dream. She was astonished by what she had done the night before, by what the music and the firemen's striptease had loosed in her, as if she were a dam stopped up for too long. How much had she needed this release?

'So how long have you been writing erotica?' he said casually, jerking his head towards a pile of papers that she had left on the corner of the kitchen table.

She didn't return his gaze, rubbed at an invisible stain on the tabletop. 'Oh, a couple of years. I'm – I'm just writing an encyclopaedia.'

'I can't say I'm surprised,' he replied.

'What do you mean?'

'Well, a woman with appetites like yours. The way you … the way you went for me last night. Like something possessed.' He looked towards her, trying gauge her reaction, hoping he hadn't overstepped the mark.

She smiled inwardly. *If only you knew*, she thought.

'What about fiction?' he went on, flipping the eggs in the pan.

She shrugged. 'I've tried, but …' Her words tailed off.

'But what?'

'I don't know. It's the characters. They never really come alive. Which means the sex doesn't either.'

'Perhaps you need a muse?'

'Maybe,' she said, thinking again of how the music from Louis's accordion, the previous evening, had stirred in her some animal longing that she hadn't even known existed. She stood up, letting her kimono fall open.

He rose too, eyes riveted to the strip of ivory skin that had been revealed. 'I've been thinking of leaving the band

51

for a while. I'm sick of the wandering life,'' he said. His voice had a sudden edge to it – desire, certainly, but desire tinged with fear, or awe.

Her kimono fell to the floor. Pushing him down onto the chair, she yanked his boxers down.

'Inspire me,' she growled, but she didn't hear his reply. Her head was filled with the wildest, murkiest and most euphoric cacophony, one that she knew no words could ever translate.

About the Story

LIKE ALL BIG CITIES, Paris can be an unwelcoming and lonely place, for those new in town, without friends or family. Similarly to the heroine of my tale, having moved to Paris for a year to research my thesis on the women Surrealists, I found myself a little lost. Or at least for a while.

For Paris is also the place where much of my erotic education took place. For all those clichés about the city being the capital of *lurrvv* and romance, Paris is indeed ripe with sex and longing, which sizzle in the most unexpected places. The corridors of the Sorbonne, the library of the Centre Pompidou, the winding paths of the Parc des Buttes Chaumont... All these and other everyday spots proved just as conducive to passion as the Eiffel Tower, the Louvre, the Sacré Coeur.

Among the various characters I met who helped me on my way to finding myself, as a woman, were a mathematician, a model, a jazz singer, a policeman, and even a cinema usherette, who makes an appearance in a story I wrote under the pseudonym Candy Wong. In 'Second Skin' (*Wicked Words Sex in Uniform*), a picture-house off the Champs-Elysées becomes the setting for a tale of seduction suffused by subterfuge.

I've set much of my fiction, under my own name and others, in Paris. But the Belleville neighbourhood has always been particularly dear to me, as the place where I first lived and where I began my journey of sexual wakening. In this part of Paris, on Rue Oberkampf, Rue de Ménilmontant and surrounding streets, among the couscous houses, the junk shops and the Oriental boutiques,

I got to know an authentic Paris peopled by true Parisians. In old-time cabarets and smoky dives, I became a part of Belleville.

My most memorable night in Paris was indeed the eve of Bastille Day, when I did watch *pompiers* stripping at the local fire-station, and where I was persuaded to dance the foxtrot with a handsome stranger. Like Mona's, mine was a night of abandonment, a night when louche music and the sight of gorgeous men dancing in their underwear loosed something within me, changing me forever.

My fourth novel, a work in progress, is set partly in Paris and partly in London, both cities that I consider 'home'. This time my setting is Pigalle, the red-light district, where one of my characters works as an exotic dancer.

The Window-Dresser
by Alcamia Payne

MONSIEUR FICELLE FOLLOWS ME around the apartment staring at the seam running up the rear of my nylons. He's wondering if underneath the fashionable short skirt and ruffled blouse I wear underwear, or if I'm the answer to all his fantasies, and I'm simply smooth and tantalisingly bare.

Unlatching the shutters I throw them wide open, letting in the cacophony of street sounds.

'You see,' Ficelle comments. 'It has the most fabulous view of the Pont and the Seine. It's exceptional *n'est-ce pas*?'

'Yes, it'll do nicely. I'll take it. I told Monsieur Démage, if I liked it, I'd need tenancy immediately.' Reaching up a hand I finger the pearl necklace encircling my throat.

'*Bien entendu*. Of course, Madame Pucette. As you can see it comes decently furnished.'

The apartment, a study in faded bourgeois opulence, is absolutely perfect for my little game of charades. It has a salon whose shuttered French windows open onto a wide balcony with views up the leafy boulevard and across the river. Extensively renovated in the nineteen-twenties, I can feel the decadent ghosts as I move through the tall high-ceiled rooms.

There's a woman who lives across the landing and her name is Madame Culotte. I can tell she is distinctly suspicious of me as I've developed a sixth sense regarding the neighbours I rub shoulders with. When I moved in she stood in the doorway to the neighbouring apartment with her small dog in her arms, and her dark eyes glittered in fierce appraisal. She was thinking to herself. This woman is a whore, she wears seamed stockings and her skirts are far too short. I think I shall have to make her my next project. I shall observe the putain and discover if she's undertaking whorish activities. Then I shall telephone that nice man Monsieur Démage, and tell him he gave the tenancy to a whore and he must expel her instantly. This is one of the more affluent arrondissements in Paris and we only have residents of the highest calibre. Dignitaries and actors have lived here and I was once the neighbour of a Russian diplomat. We simply can't lower the tone of the apartments.

When I go out later, it is as if she is waiting for me. I flash Madame Culotte my most brilliant smile as I reach out to stroke her dog. 'I once had a poodle exactly like this. They make such devoted companions don't they?' Bending down, I kiss Madame Culotte's cheeks in the familiar French greeting. Perhaps on reflection, I'm being a little presumptuous. 'My name's Madame Pucette, like the flea. Baby flea that's what my father used to call me. I hope we can be good neighbours.' Beaming at her, I attempt to draw a reluctant smile out of her stony façade but Madame Culotte remains inscrutable.

'Fleas are undesirable little irritations.' She mutters, sotto voce. 'I always think one should get rid of them as quickly as possible.'

But despite her supposition, she cannot fail to like me,

I think. I shall make that an important project – to change Madame's opinion of me. Her black eyes flash the warning that she'll be impervious to me.

Leaning forward in expectancy, Madame Culotte is waiting for an explanation, but I'm not about to give her one. I've met them before of course, the eavesdroppers; it's the same wherever I go. There's always a curious person wanting to know my business, ready to upset the well rehearsed execution of the plot. Women notice my opulent ring and they immediately wonder if I'm a widow or if there's a Monsieur Pucette, and if so where he is. Well I'm not about to tell them; they can go to hell. Part of the excitement is the evasion and subterfuge and it fills me with a wet, perverse thrill.

'It's a big apartment for a woman.' She says. 'These places were built for families; always they were full of people and laughter. Naturally your husband and children will be joining you later on?'

'No, madam. I'll be far too busy to think about the emptiness. I'm always busy, always on the go.'

'Ah you're a business woman.' She strokes the dog's head and her with lips tightening in a grimace she nods, as if saying to herself. There you are. I was right. I'm never wrong with this instinct I have for people and whorish women in particular. She's a slut and that's her profession. She's not a common street whore. No, she has far too much class for that. She's a high-class society whore who entertains men. I don't know which is worse. In a way you can forgive the Parisienne gutter girls because they have to earn a crust and no employer will give a job to a vulgar little mademoiselle with her skirt up around her neck and her cunt showing. But high-class putains, they're the worst. They do it because they're bored and they enjoy it.

Only yesterday I saw Madame encounter just such a gutter girl sprawled in the doorway to the entrance of the Place Pigalle metro. The girl was totally out of it; everyone could see that and as Madame Culotte disdainfully stepped over her, she'd clutched fiercely at Madame's ankle and whimpered. 'Do you have a few euros to spare?'

Later on, I sit down on the faded sofa and I roll down my stockings. I smooth my hands against my bare skin and my flesh tingles. A whore indeed? Never in a million years could I consider myself a harlot. No, I'm simply the girl in the window. I'm the window dresser, *la femme à la fenêtre*, and that's quite a respectable profession in my opinion.

Opening a bottle of Burgundy, I sip the warming liquid, and I continue easing the stockings off my toes and wonder what it would feel like for Paolo to suck them.

My first ever lover sucked my toes. He took each one in his mouth, and as he ran his tongue around them I finger fucked my cunt. My husband, Paolo is not very demonstrative in the arena of sex though. It isn't his fault, it's just the kind of man he is. Men like Paolo were brought up governed by strict rules concerning sexuality and when I married him I knew his conservative Catholic parents had ruined him. 'I want you, Evasin.' He'd said. 'I know all about you and I know you consider yourself a little damaged, but that doesn't matter. I love your sense of self and your sex strength and that's what attracts me to you. What's a little fetish, a little smudge on your sex landscape? *De rien*.' Paolo presented me with a glittering opal in a silver setting. 'An opal is perfect for you. It's fire and beauty, yet it's also fragile and changeable.' Kissing me chastely, Paolo pushed the ring onto my finger. 'Now say it and make me the happiest man in the world. Repeat after me. Paolo I'll be your wife.'

'Darling, you say you accept my little, how can I put it … idiosyncrasy. But you don't know how deeply this addiction affects me.' I persisted.

'The sex fetish is nothing. It fulfils you and makes you glow. It's harmless,' he said, kissing my fingertips.

Stretching out on the sofa with my arms above my head I convince myself I'm not the demon whore Madame thinks I am, I could never be a slut and I could never permit any other man than Paolo to fuck me.

I do indulge, however, in a very daring addiction which flouts all the rules of etiquette, and addictions are not that easy to stop once they take hold of you. To be honest I don't even know if I want to stop it. Naturally I could try to, but I have tried before and I can't break the cycle. Actually, it's mentally painful to try to do so, and if I deny myself my addictive pleasures, Paolo sees the light and colour in my personality begin to dwindle and he can't stand it. Then, he begs me to rekindle the old Evasin and once again he presses me to pursue my addiction.

Paolo adores every facet of the damaged Evasin: my vivacity, my humour and individuality, but in order to retain it, he knows he must allow me to indulge myself every so often. In little sips, when I cannot withstand denial any longer. Always, darling Paolo senses when the time is coming for the necessary fix and he'll turn to me late at night and, pressing his body against me and stroking my hair, he'll say, 'Evasin, it's becoming painful for you, holding it all in. Tomorrow you must buy a ticket. Actually I'll order it for you over the internet. Now where would you like to go? Would you want it to be far away from here? How about a little trip to America this time?'

'Oh no! Not America.' Running my fingers through my hair, in the nervous way I have, I smile dreamily. 'I think I'd like it to be Paris again. Paris always has the atmosphere. And the apartments there are better suited to window dressing than those in America. There's no better place for me in the world than Paris.'

This is true. Doubtless there are apartments in America ideally suited to my purpose, but there's a certain magic about the old Parisian apartments and in particular the *maison particulière*, with its tall stylised windows and airy balconies, which draws out the creative eroticism of the window dresser.

I keep telling myself this addiction is harmless and since it's harmless no one seems to care about it. Paolo accepts it. On our wedding night he made it clear to me. 'I'm all right with it, perfectly all right. However I make one condition. You must never discuss the details of it and you must never totally fuck the bastards and let them into that hot little love tunnel. Make me that promise now darling.'

'That's easy, Paolo. I love you and I'm devoted to you. I'll never talk about it.' I said, as I tenderly massaged his dick, lubricating his tip with tiny movements of my fingers. 'Never. You can trust me, you know I have integrity. I will never "cunt fuck" them.'

'And you definitely won't fall in love with a man will you?'

'Oh, it doesn't work like that, my sweet. I'd never truly fallen in love until I met you and now you've stolen my heart. No, it's all very divorced from reality really. I can't describe it, but it's like acting one of my little parts in a show or going out shopping. For instance, I look in the shop window from time to time and occasionally I touch the goods. Or I walk out onto the stage and I execute my little performance and then I step down, take the applause, change out of costume and into my day clothes, and life goes on as usual. It's like you, Paolo. I'm sure on certain occasions you admire a beautiful woman. You go up behind her and you follow her for a few blocks and you think she's beautiful and I shall flirt when she turns around. And soon feeling your eyes on her, she does turn around. So the two of you play out this little scene of make believe, for a while. But because you love me you don't approach her to sleep with her. You might pinch her butt or even fleetingly brush her breast but that's all right. All right, because there's no actual intercourse. Nothing beyond the window dressing.'

There's no telephone in the apartment and I don't require one. Monsieur Démage said he would happily have one connected, but I don't want any distractions. I'm hungry for my own peculiar thrills and when I'm this ravenous I don't want anything at all to interfere in the process. If someone now walked into the apartment he would not know who I am since my persona is so carefully disguised. I wear natural hair wigs and I cleverly apply my make-up so I am not Signora Sobrani, married to the industrialist Paolo Sobrani, but Madame Pucette, the cheeky little flea. Furthermore, there are only a few carefully selected items of clothing in my closet since I have no use for them. I leave no paper trails as to my identity.

For several days before I arrived here, I lay waiting for the stirring to mature because there's no hurrying it. It's powerful and it comes upon me first of all as a ripple and then with increasing strength until the waves wash over me, wash me away. The ripples started a few weeks ago when I became restless. Then the obsession began to edge me once more towards the precipice. It was a familiar scene as Paolo watched me pack a small suitcase. I kissed him on the cheek, feeling the familiar swell of love for my husband. 'I won't be long darling. It'll be the usual. Just a little vacation for me to find myself and before you know it, I'll be back. On my return, I'll be new and glowing and not this dark little thing with no light. I'll be a better woman. Things will be calmer and we can settle back into our little groove. That's how it works isn't it?'

'Sweetheart.' Hugging me, I felt the pounding of his heart through his expensive shirt. 'You know I'll miss you like hell. But I'll welcome the return of your light.'

Madame is standing in the window again. When I look up at the apartment from the boulevard, she's watching me. Actually she's observing me through a pair of opera glasses. Smiling I raise my hand and she turns away. Did she think I wouldn't see her? Does she want me to know she has her beady eye on me? I expect Madame has a little black book on the bureau by her piano into which she is writing her observations.

I will have to be careful. She could be tricky. She doesn't seem to have much at all to do, except observe me and instruct the odd child in music. If she's not looking out of the window, she's standing on the landing, and she has only to hear a footfall on the staircase or the creak of that naughty apartment door which I shall have to make a point of oiling – and there she is – with the same calculating look on her face. Little does Madame know that she is making the execution of the game so much more appealing by presenting an almost insurmountable difficulty.

I'm not a beautiful woman but I exude what Paolo calls that certain *something*. I have a particular chemistry. I exude it. I'm the original femme fatale. Wherever I go men stare at me and they don't understand why they are staring. I am the indefinable essence of sex. They see a woman who is somewhat petite, with short bobbed hair, but my outstanding attributes are my huge, luminous eyes. Paolo tells me it's my eyes he first noticed across a crowded room. He said I had power with those eyes and wherever I moved they followed him and entered him in strange and exciting ways. Yes that's what he said. My eyes had the uncanny ability to enter and capture him and stir things in him. I analyse myself in shop windows and mirrors and I see the eyes staring back. They are incredibly expressive, large sumptuous almond-shaped lakes of deepest green, which can portray the most startling range of emotions. Men are hypnotised by them and I learnt, early on in my acting career, that my eyes were the major tool of my audience seduction. I practised for so long getting the look just right that I now have a catalogue of suggestive expressions with which to hook movie directors and, more importantly, my prey. I don't like to stalk the window shopper. I like for him to scent me, like a dog scents the bitch.

I adjust my seamed stockings, apply a spray of scent, and then leave the apartment and stroll down to the Quai, and beneath the echoing bridges I apply myself to the advertisement of my presence with the coquettish angle of my head, the rise of my skirt and the discreet loosening of a button or two. Then for a while I sit in the jardin des Tuileries.

The air is hot and dry and bites at the back of my throat. There's no heat like that of Paris in August. Swirls of dust tickle my legs and hot drops of rain dew my hair. The atmosphere is prickling with a storm so I head back across the river, buying a crepe on the way because I'm ravenous. I tear into it with my strong teeth.

Pausing for a moment on the Pont, the familiar shiver clambers up my spine. Leaning over the stone parapet, I see my face reflected in the inky water, together with the paler reflection of the window shopper as he observes me. It's another aspect of my sixth sense that I know he desires me. He's staring at the swell of my breasts and my taut nipples. Sexually intent, he thinks he'd like to approach me.

Yes! This one will do, this one will satisfy the addiction. I feel a tremor of satisfaction and the contraction and flexing of my sex. This is the kind of sexual attraction which compels me to run my fingers under the elastic of my sexy knickers and bring myself to orgasm then and there.

I engage him, throwing out a length of invisible string which will lasso him. Then strolling away, with occasional backward glances, I reel him in to me, over the wide bridge and across the road, before I dart into the doorway and vanish up the stairwell to my apartment. Running to the balcony I fling open the shutters and look down at him. Yes there he is.

This is the curtain raiser to my whole performance and intended to whet his appetite. I smile seductively, widen my eyes, take a step backwards behind the shutters and shrugging out of my silk dress, I reveal my exquisite French bra and panties.

I'm so irresistibly aroused, my heart's beating like a schoolgirl's. I'd forgotten how good it is to be in the grip of the addiction, and now the delight pulses through me like a narcotic. I push the couch as close to the window as I can and sit astride it; my thighs wide, wriggling my butt as I imagine how it would feel for him to touch my secret bud with his fingertips. I intend to thrill him and colour his monotone life, by eventually showing him my breasts, then my cunt. Today though I simply draw his gaze with my finger, pinching my nipples into firm raspberry nubs, placing my hands on my thighs so my breasts jut forward provocatively. Next, I part my lips with my fingers and trail them down my throat, circling my breasts, before moving them lower over my rounded abdomen, to the moist swelling below. Watch me. Window shop me.

This is my addiction. I am the window dresser who sits in her apartment window and flagrantly displays herself. Sometimes I wonder how I've got away with it for so long, but I suppose I'm just clever at what I do. Like any performer I have adjusted to the circumstances. I try to make sure no one else is looking up at the window when I reveal myself, and I have a robe close by just in case I should be caught red-handed. Furthermore, my senses are finely tuned to those who may take pains to discover my identity and expose Signora Sobrani.

I can't get him out of my head and the next day I'm raging with feverish sexual urges. I walk about the apartment so aroused, even the brush of my clothes brings me close to climax. I imagine his generous mouth on my neck, my shoulders, raining kisses on my back. I press my lubed glass dildo against my anus, and I feel the resistance as I contract my sphincter muscles around it. I have only to visualise his cock and the dildo slides in easily. I rock back and forth on the artificial cock, concentrating on my own pleasure as I touch my bare breasts and stare down the road.

He walks across the bridge at the same time each day and I enjoy making up stories about him. I don't imagine he works in the city; I think he must be a dancer, as he walks with a loose, loping stride and his limbs are free and dextrous. Today I slide off my bra and I lift and cup my breasts saucily, before I make my next move, slithering onto the arm of the couch, and spreading my thighs in my French knickers to their fullest extremity.

He leans against a lamppost and, sliding my hand beneath the silk and squeezing my cunt like a ripe peach, I rub my finger around my dark hole, before pressing the trembling bud of my clit. My orgasm shudders and my thighs jerk in tight spasms.

I cannot tell whether my performance surprises or offends him because he simply looks at me thoughtfully before pushing his hands in his pockets and crossing the road.

I bite hard on my bottom lip. I'm indignant. Yet the fact that he is not easily seduced is also a thrill. Always, they fall too easily and that's no game at all. Everyone knows that anything worth having is worth fighting for. Well I'll have to polish my performance.

Friday, when at last I expose my cunt, he smiles at me. I ought to give him a name. I will call him Tom. 'Tom,' I say out loud, touching my fingers to my lips and moving them suggestively inside my mouth. Once more I trail my hand over my body, jerking down the French knickers before pulling open my sex lips and moving my finger up and down the slit. I climax spontaneously, but this time Tom does not walk away and he never breaks eye contact. Gliding to my feet and posing by the window, I smile and I pull the shutters closed.

On Saturday Tom's face is drawn into a tight mask of desire; his face pale from lack of sleep. The hunger has turned to lust and it's time to finish dressing the window. I play with the shutters for awhile. Half closing them, I dart behind them, so he catches tantalising glimpses of bare skin, before I push them wide open again. I use the shutters as a skilful stage prop, in the same way a Las Vegas dancer uses her fans in her seductive dance.

Tom sits on the bench opposite my window and as usual I take up my position on the couch with my legs spread wide, raising myself up out of my hips, showing him my glass dildo, and the place where it will go. I move the dildo against my hole, then roll it around my nipples.

Whenever I masturbate, I usually insert my dildo and press my thighs together to increase the delicious pressure whilst I rub hard on my clit. But today, I need to do it with my legs spread wide and Tom's eyes on me.

I orgasm violently and quickly, my mouth open in an *O* of pleasure and a small spurt of my juice marks the couch. I walk to the window, and press my hands to the glass. I blow on it until it mists and with the tip of my finger I write my name: Evasin. I dance for him, undulating my curvaceous body in tune with the jazz from my CD player, pirouetting with my arms above my head. If he comes tomorrow, I will use a larger dildo and I'll slide it all the way inside my hot tunnel as he watches. I'm so self-absorbed, so high on the shot of pleasure, I don't see her. But there she is, standing right by the lamp post. Madame Culotte. For a moment I'm frozen, before snatching my robe from the back of the sofa, I quickly cover myself.

Madame Culotte fires her fist at the door with impatient staccato shots. 'Come out Madame Pucette, I know you're in there.'

When I open it, I'm confronted by her face drawn into a mask of rage and there are two spots of high colour on her cheeks.

'You whore.' She says raising her fist. 'Don't pretend you weren't doing that filthy thing because I saw you. I've never experienced such behaviour. How could you,

67

you dirty putain? Do you want to give me a heart attack?'

'No,I don't want to give you a heart attack, Madame, but just what exactly did you see?'

'You know damn well what I saw, you licentious bitch. I shall call Monsieur Démage and the police. There must be laws about women who walk up and down naked in front of their windows flaunting and touching themselves in full view of the whole world. It's indecent exposure.'

'They wouldn't believe you, you know. Besides, you're mistaken in what you saw. Look. Why not come in for a cup of coffee and I'll explain how I like to walk around the flat naked. It's not that unusual, Madame. Thousands of people do it.'

'You must be joking. Me, enter the whore's boudoir. And you needn't try and make out I'm a senile old woman. I know what I saw.'

'Madame Culotte, Suzanne.' I say in placatory fashion. 'I really didn't mean to upset you in any way. I think you have me very wrong. After all if I was a whore wouldn't strange men be arriving and departing at all times of the day and night? Anyway it would be so disingenuous of me to even think of prostituting myself with you watching me so closely.'

Madame leans closer, so close in fact, I can smell her pastille-scented breath. 'Listen to me, you minx.' She shakes her finger in my face emphasising each point. 'You think you're a clever little thing. All whores are clever. But believe me there are whores and whores. Your whoredom is of a different flavour to the usual, that's all. I know what you're up to. You play a dangerous game. You dangle yourself like a lure. You enjoy tantalising men. Well one day the fish will bite and he'll gobble you up and there'll be no more Madame Pucette.'

I laugh. 'You can think what you like. You seem to

know an awful lot about my supposed profession.'

'I'm not as stupid as you think. I know nothing about you, and you know nothing about me. I could have run the most notorious brothel in all of Paris and how could you prove I didn't? Hey.' Her knifelike finger jabs my breast.

'Ouch!' I exclaim. 'That hurt. There's no reason to get physical.'

'You little bitch whore, you think you're so clever and so smart with your words and excuses.'

The next day Tom does not appear. I sit at the kitchen table in sad contemplation, crumbling a croissant into pieces. I've lost my appetite. I haven't eaten since yesterday morning because I've been delirious with lust. When the addiction is upon me I become possessed by a fever, and all I need to live on is the thrill of seduction. It's like falling in love again and again yet without the hazards of emotional entanglement and the threat of a broken heart. I'm safe within Paolo's love.

How could Tom not come? I've never failed, I'm a one hundred per cent success story. When I first created the game I made a ruling that I could never fail. I picked my victims with a formidable intuition. If that failed, the window dressing failed. Well, for the first time my sixth sense must have tricked me. Evidently, Tom's not so sexually adventurous after all and I've offended him by pushing the boundaries too far. The trouble is, Tom is now in my head and I am mesmerised by his lips and presence. It seems impossible that this time I could have failed in the game, right when he seemed so enamoured of me and I could see the approach of the dénouement.

I wander aimlessly around the apartment; occasionally I press my hand to the window. It's raining heavily. There are ominous rumbles of thunder. People scurry over the bridge, huddled deeply into their raincoats. Across the landing I can hear the soothing strains of Chopin as Madame Culotte gives one of her music lessons. She's really quite a talented pianist. 'Where are you Tom?' I glance at the ormolu clock on the mantelpiece. It's now time, and he's never late.

Sighing, I wander through to the kitchen and place the coffee pot on the hob. I am just spooning coffee into the filter when I hear it, a distinct tap at my door and feel the breeze as the door I left off the latch in anticipation is pushed wider. It's not Madame Culotte as I can hear her anxious raised voice quite clearly, as she chastises her student.

I hold my breath, dare I believe it? Dare I believe it's Tom? Closing my eyes I lean against the countertop, suspended in a fever of sexual anticipation. I should have known, I should have had more belief in my convictions. I am a talented window dresser and I never fail. They always come.

Satisfaction swells inside me, pops like a bubble, and is followed by a rush of arousal so intense it burns. In preparation for Tom I have been the most exacting *étalagiste*. I have bathed in rose oil before massaging my skin with lotions. Shaved my sex to ultimate smoothness and lightly sprayed myself with my favourite erotic scent.

'I thought you didn't enjoy me any more?' I whisper.

He comes to me and, wrapping his arms around me from behind, he squeezes my breasts and rubs my nipples with rhythmical motions of his fingers.

'How could I not enjoy such a breathtaking performance, Evasin?'

I turn to him and assault his lips with my own as I push him against the wall reaching for his pants' zipper. Then I drop to my knees and, taking his penis in my hand, I slide

70

my lips up and down the slick length of him until he is groaning with lust. My performance never fails to excite them.

Taking his hand I lead him into the salon where I push him onto the sofa and, gripping his turgid staff, I move my hand rhythmically up and down his pole. He swells and stiffens, the penis becoming taut and red and bursting with juice. I raise myself above him and, pushing my cunt to his mouth, I let him taste me. His tongue darts out, moves in and around, up and down, as he devours me. 'You taste so good,' he says huskily as he licks and sucks. 'Jesus, so good.'

'Taste me more.' I press against him, urging his tongue on my clit.

'Oh that's it.' My hand sinks into his hair as I pull him hard onto my sex. Yet this is the limit. I never allow a man to do more than taste my delicacies, because my inner sanctum belongs to Paolo. I part my flaccid red lips and he gives a sigh and plunges his greedy mouth back down on me, the lips and tongue working in a frenzy to give me the orgasm I so desire. When it comes it tears through me like a rip tide. I'm victorious once more.

'Evasin.' He groans. 'Let me make love to you properly, let me put my dick inside you?'

'No, my darling.'

'Why not? Aren't you even tempted?' He sighs.

'It'll be just as erotic like this, *chéri*. Just lie back and enjoy.'

His body arches in spasm as I press down with my thirsty lips to meet him. I have complete self-mastery over the game. I am the window dresser.

Satiated by the provocative whore of tongue and finger, he sleeps.

Moving stealthily, I slide out from under the

bedcovers, evading his hand which reaches for me. I slip silently and expertly into my dress and pull on my shoes. I am curious because there's something different about Tom, something intense in the way his eyes bore deeply into mine as if he hopes he can be the key to unlock me. For an instant I think of Madame. What was it she said? One day a fish may gobble me up? Aha, never Madame.

My hands search through his clothes pockets. I expect to find police ID. Once I was so very nearly caught. But he's clean. Leaning over him I wet my finger in my cunt and then I press it to his cheek in a butterfly kiss. Madame Culotte you're a fucker. I guess you ought to be pleased with yourself as you're making me paranoid. It won't stop me, you know. It's not that easy to stop an addiction.

I feel so high I am flying. It's like taking a really heavy-duty shot of a stimulant. With the hardened addict it hurts a little, and maybe it frightens you shitless for an instant, but you always do it again.

I slide the small case from inside the wardrobe door and I feel the familiar sense of satisfaction. Once again I am complete, I am repaired; at least until the next time. Within me there is a warm pool and it is spilling its contents and spreading through me, filling me with a renewed passion for the loving Paolo. I have taken my medicine, but soon I will appear in the next shabby vacant apartment. Perhaps in Paris. It could be Milan. Actually I quite fancy Venice at about the time of the Masquerade ball.

I leave no note of farewell. Well, what could I say? Darling Tom, you were the antibiotic that failed to cure the incurable virus?

When he wakes up I'll be gone and he'll preserve me as a simple fantasy, and that is best and for the best. The rented flat will soon be home to someone else, but he will always wonder. Who was that woman called Evasin, who enticed him from the window? And Madame Culotte will say, 'Thank goodness. Now I can put away these opera glasses and forget about that filthy putain.'

About the Story

I KNEW MY FRIEND'S apartment situated in an atmospheric maison particulière would one day provide the perfect setting for a story. In this case it was part of my inspiration for 'The Window Dresser'.

'The Window Dresser' is a tableau drama. It is not a sexual procession of physical liaisons, but a simple little observation about monogamy, love and addiction.

For this story, I wanted to focus more on ambiance and gradual seduction, using a strong heroine.

Why Paris? Well Pucette is a charming whore sophisticate, and, to my mind, she could not execute her little game in any city other than Paris. The layout of the typical bourgeois apartment is the perfect sexual prop for this talented and sensual actress. Indeed the apartment is her theatre, the window her stage. The Parisian populace her audience and Tom her leading man.

Certainly every city has its charm and its unique genus of woman. Pucette could only be Parisienne though since she possesses the unique and intriguing idiosyncrasies of the Paris femme. Outwardly chic and sophisticated, but beneath the classic polish beats the heart of a stylish Paris whore. Only a Parisienne can be both respectable and a putain.

Many other observations led to the 'Window Dresser'. A man leaning against a lamp post smoking a cigarette, as he watched a girl and undressed her with his eyes. A woman on the arm of her husband, crossing the road outside the Galéries Lafayette. They were evidently in love but she had naughty eyes which intercepted men, giving suggestive glances of which the husband was aware but indulgent. Did the couple share a secret sexual accord, permitting erotic leniency?

A Madame Culotte exists I am sure, in every apartment block in Paris. She's probably the concierge, but may be a lonely Madame with nothing to do but recall her vivid sexual youth.

For me, Paris is simply Paris and always enchanting. Uniquely inspirational to poets and writers, painters and musicians; it is the city par excellence of artfully concealed human dramas. It is a distinctive blend of eclectic personalities and salacious undertones which Parisians are so good at creating. It is a city elegant, scintillating and possessed of panache, yet at its heartwood darkly erotic and dirty.

Unexpected Emotion
by Debra Gray De Noux & O'Neil De Noux

SHE CAME OUT OF the rain and stopped just inside the doorway of the small café. LaStanza watched her wipe the water from her arms, lean forward and squeeze the water from her long dark hair. A sudden coolness filled the café, damp with the smell of rain. She closed the door with her right foot.

She was a looker, wearing a tight charcoal-grey dress, mid-thigh in length. LaStanza's eyes traced the sleek lines of her body as she wrung out her hair. When she stopped, she looked right at him with bright green eyes. He narrowed his own eyes, also green, but much paler. He also ran his left index finger and thumb down over his moustache, which he did automatically when nervous, or excited.

The café smelled of coffee again and sugar and faintly of milk. The lone waiter, a portly man with balding grey hair and a clichéd white apron around his midriff, moved to the girl with a white towel in his hand. She smiled at him and said something in French. LaStanza understood only one word of the conversation, '*Merci.*' Her lips, painted a deep crimson, stood in direct contrast with her ivory skin.

The rain continued slamming against the picture window at the front of the café. Dabbing herself with the towel, the girl stepped over to a table next to the window. Her high heels, the identical colour grey to her dress, clapped on the tile floor as she moved. LaStanza watched her sit in profile to him and run the towel down each leg. She wore black stockings, which seemed to accentuate her long legs. Placing the towel on her table, she crossed her legs.

A deep moan of thunder rumbled through the café – through all of Paris. She ordered coffee from the waiter and turned her gaze to the picture window, to look out at the dark sky over the Rue St André. A wicked slice of lightning flashed across the rooftops of the Latin Quarter. LaStanza saw it, through the glass above the girl's head.

He watched her, trying not to be obvious watching her. He loved watching women. He especially liked the fine lines of this girl's face in profile. She was young, probably in her early-twenties. He was thinking how he'd like to know her, how he'd like to touch her.

LaStanza felt that hollow, lonesome feeling a man gets when he sees a woman he'll never know, that hollow yearning for someone who's beyond reach. He remembered feeling that same way about his wife, when he first met her. Silly, he told himself, he was acting like a schoolboy. Hell, he was almost thirty-four now.

She was waiting for someone, he told himself. Just like he was. She watched the window; waiting for someone, he told himself. Then she'll be gone.

The waiter brought her a steamy cup of coffee, nodded and left. On his way past he asked LaStanza, 'More coffee, monsieur?'

LaStanza nodded. As the waiter stepped away, the girl looked at LaStanza again. Her face remained expressionless, like fine porcelain and her eyes were so bright.

LaStanza was the only other customer in Café Degas that stormy afternoon. He loosened his red tie and unbuttoned the top button of his white dress shirt. In his dark blue suit, he figured he looked like a typical American tourist. If there was one thing he learned in seven days in Paris, the French could spot a foreigner miles away.

The waiter returned with a fresh cup of café-au-lait and removed his old cup. LaStanza stirred in two spoons of sugar.

He had been day-dreaming when she came in about a movie he and his wife had seen two nights earlier, an unlikely story of a man and a woman on a sea that was a blue dream. It was a boy meets girl story – boy loses girl – boy gets girl story. It was a French movie, of course, without the typical puritanical American restrictions. Which meant there was plenty of nudity, full frontal, female and male. The sex scenes were hot, NC-17 if shown at a U.S. theatre.

The lead woman was immediately drawn to the man, but fell to the temptation of a younger man and wound up making love to both separately as the three sailed across the Caribbean. Neither man knew the woman was screwing both. There was a lot of titsucking and simulated cocksucking and fucking that looked pretty real, may have been.

The best scene was shot behind a waterfall where the woman is first seduced by the young man, then as he slips away, the other man comes and finds her lying on the rocks and climbs atop her and she's panting again with the cooling water flowing around them in mists. Good cinematography with a gorgeous background and a beautiful naked woman kept LaStanza's attention.

He took a sip of café-au-lait, rested an elbow on the

table, cupped his chin in the palm of his hand, and began to feel very drowsy. He went back to his day-dream of the lovers on the blue sea, feeling a stuffiness a few moments into his day-dream, a sudden heat. He didn't hear her, but felt her just before she said, 'You are American, are you not?'

He felt the coolness of the rain on her dress as she stood next to him now.

Blinking, he sat up and said, 'Yes. I'm American.'

'I like Americans.' She flashed a shy smile at him. Her voice was smooth, like velvet, coated with a French accent that added a sensual tone to her words. She shifted her weight from her right leg to her left.

'May I sit with you?'

'Sure.' *Absolutely*, he thought.

He noticed she had her cup and saucer in hand. She placed it on the table in front of the chair to his left. She moved around to his side of the chair, before sitting. He could hear the faint, sexy sound of nylon brushing nylon as she crossed her legs. She put a small purse, which matched the colour of her dress, on the table.

'My name is Juliette.' She extended her hand to shake.

It was cool and still damp.

'LaStanza,' he said. 'Dino LaStanza.'

'That is a nice name.' She took her hand back. 'Italian, is it not?'

'Sicilian.'

'My last name is Le Bourget. Like the old airport.'

He nodded, although he hadn't he faintest idea what that meant. She brushed her hair back with her hands and smiled at him. Her eyes looked even brighter up close.

'What part of America are you from?'

'New Orleans.'

'Nouvelle Orléans?' Her eyebrows raised. 'You speak

79

French?'

LaStanza shrugged. 'Naw. I can say merci, oui. No. That's about it.'

Juliette smiled broadly, then took a sip of coffee and put her cup down in the saucer. He noticed she did not return her cup to the centre of the saucer. Rather, she placed it to one side, sort of askew.

She stared into his eyes, those dark eyes suddenly sad, widening as she looked at him for long moments. They moved slightly as if searching for something within his eyes. Her chest rose and she took in a deep breath.

'I work for a bookseller,' she said. 'Here in the Latin Quarter. What do you do, Monsieur LaStanza?'

'I'm a policeman.'

She blinked twice and sat back, a slight smile to her lips. 'Do you drive a motorcycle?'

It was his turn to smile. 'I'm a detective.'

Juliette leaned forward, put her elbows on the table, cupping her chin in the upturned palms of her hands.

'Are you from Paris?'

'No,' her voice was lower now. 'I am from Provence. In the south. A town called Arles.'

He had no idea where that was. She could probably tell from his eyes, because she added, 'It is near Marseille. Van Gogh, the artist, painted there.'

He reached for his coffee again. They both took sips, and he noticed she put her cup down askew again.

'Are you married?' She was looking at her coffee when she asked that.

'Yes. My wife is at the Sorbonne right now, delivering a lecture. Are you married?'

'No.' Her voice barely above a whisper. Juliette looked up at him with wide eyes. Her face became expressionless and looked like porcelain again.

LaStanza took a sip of his café-au-lait.

He was thinking of asking her how old she was, although a good southern boy *never* asked a woman her age. But the thunder boomed again, louder even than before. The picture window rattled and the coffee in their cups made little ripples.

Looking back at Juliette, he saw she was staring at him again. Her face looked different, almost sad now, almost frightened, yet so damn pretty. Her left hand toyed with an oval earring in her left ear. There were four earrings in her left ear lobe, all small and delicate and gold. One appeared to have a diamond in its centre. Her hair, parted down the middle, was drying in places. It seemed a shade lighter now. He could see red highlights in her hair, which looked golden in the quiet light of the café. Her eyes kept staring into his, as if she could look through his eyes, into his mind.

LaStanza reached for his café-au-lait. Juliette did not break her stare. He watched her over his cup as he took one more sip. As he lowered his cup, she said something that made him stop midway between his mouth and the saucer.

She said, 'I think I would like to walk with you. In the rain.' She looked away momentarily, before looking back at his eyes. Behind her, the rain still fell against the picture window.

He felt goose bumps on his arms.

'How long before your wife comes?'

LaStanza shrugged. 'It depends on how many encores.' She didn't get it. It was a bad joke anyway.

Juliette leaned forward slightly, and he could see her eyes were damp. She blinked away the dampness and said, 'I think I would like to make love with you. In the rain.'

His breath slipped away. He felt his heart stammering, racing suddenly, as if it had just been kick-started. The next seconds dragged by, like something from a Dali nightmare. He knew this was one of those indelible moments in a man's life, one of those rivers to cross, one of those magical instants that are so fleeting –

LaStanza felt himself rise and pick up his coat, felt his hand reach into his pants pocket, felt the texture of the money he tossed on the table, felt her hand as he took it and led her out of the café, into the rain where she helped him into his coat.

He liked the way she snuggled next to him, her hands wrapped around his right arm, the faint smell of perfume in her hair. Strands of her long hair brushed against his cheek in the breeze and the rain. Half a block into their walk, the rain began to diminish. Without looking at him, she disentangled herself, pulled his right hand out of his coat pocket and led him into an alley. He could see it was a dead end, with houses lining each side, and two cars parked at the end of the alley. Juliette's heels clicked on the cobblestones as she led him to a spot beneath a balcony.

She leaned her back against the wet wall, ran her hands through her hair and looked at him. He could see her feet inching slowly apart. Her lips were pursed. LaStanza was breathing heavier now.

She pulled her purse off her shoulder and let it sink to the ground. He watched her reach down, place her hands on either side of her hips and slowly, ever so slowly, pull her tight dress up her thighs. The lacy tops of her stockings became visible, along with the crotch of her sheer white panties. They looked soaked, plastered to her mat of dark pubic hair. She continued to raise her dress. LaStanza looked around and felt foolish for doing so.

Juliette ran her tongue over her lips as her hands stopped. All of her panties were visible now. LaStanza felt his heart thundering, felt the stiffness between his legs become rock hard. He moved to her.

Pressing himself against her, he heard her let out a faint sigh as he kissed her ever so softly, savouring the softness of her lips, before their mouths opened and their tongues entwined and pressed against one another. He put everything into the kiss, every bit of unexpected emotion, every bit of excitement growing in his heart.

Juliette seemed to rise as he moved against her. He could feel her hands in his hair, holding his head as they kissed, as he pumped against her crotch. He felt her left leg rising around him, wrapping itself around him. He heard her left shoe fall behind him.

He ran his hands up from her hips, up to her breasts. They were firm, her nipples hard and pointy. He moved his right hand around to the back of her dress and began to work the zipper down. Juliette's hands moved from his head to his belt. They unzipped one another. He felt her hand rub his dick.

LaStanza pulled her dress down and sank to his knees in front of the girl. He worked the dress over her hips. Juliette's hands were back in his hair again, massaging his scalp. He shoved her dress down past her knees. She raised each foot as he slipped the dress from under her. He reached his hands into the rear of her panties and caressed her ass. His face, an inch away from her, took in the beautiful sight of her wet, plastered panties. He licked the front of them, tasting the rain, and then worked them down slowly, his hands stopped to squeeze her ass. He used his right hand to pull the panties off, his left hand roaming over her ass, his tongue working itself into her soft pubic hair. Darker than the hair on her head, her silky pubes had more red highlights.

With his face buried in her bush, LaStanza reached up to unsnap her strapless bra. Juliette helped and the bra tumbled atop LaStanza's head on its way down. He reached for her breasts and kneaded them as his tongue slipped into the soft, sweet folds of her pussy. She was very wet, but not from the rain.

Juliette pulled at his hair and cried out, his tongue working furiously now. She tasted sweet and tangy and hot. She began to yank at his hair, pulling him up. Her hips were already pumping against his tongue. She pulled so hard on his hair, he had to relent and kiss his way up to her navel. Her skin was still wet, but no longer cool.

He stopped at her breasts, kissing each back and forth, feeling each with his eager hands, opening his mouth as wide as he could to take in as much as he could, to run his tongue over her erect nipples. She moaned even louder when he pinched her nipples and gnawed gently on them.

Sinking his tongue into her mouth, LaStanza felt Juliette's strong hands shoving his pants and shorts down and grabbing his dick. She squeezed it gently and rubbed it and pressed its tip against her wet pussy. He felt himself slipping into her. She put her hands on his shoulders and sank down, impaling herself on his dick, moaning in his mouth as they French kissed.

She was so hot. Her pussy felt steamy as it grabbed his dick. He felt himself burning as he rocked against her. He slowed himself and began to move in and out of her pussy in nice long strokes. He loved the way she cried with each insertion.

He had so much trouble breathing he had to pull his mouth away from hers, through the tangles of her hair as they fucked against the wall, in the alley, in the rain, in the city of light. Juliette cried loudly and he began

84

hammering himself into her. He felt her rise and hold him close as she came. He felt her legs go momentarily limp, before she started up again, more fiercely than before.

He wanted it to last as long as he could. He stopped himself twice. Each time, Juliette stopped and, catching her breath momentarily, kissed him again. Their tongues worked and he went back to jamming her against the wall.

When he could hold it no longer, she seemed to know and bucked violently against him. He shot her full, in deep, hot jolts. The muscles of her pussy pulled it out of him until he was wasted. They continued kissing until he had to pull his mouth away or pass out from lack of oxygen. He could feel her vaginal muscles still moving inside.

They did not move for a very long time. When they did move, his dick slipped out of her. Leaning back, he kissed her again, gently. He backed away and looked at her body, examined it, taking every inch into his memory. She was truly a lovely girl. Her face, still flushed, was more than beautiful. Her lips were red, but not from lipstick anymore, but from passion. Her breasts were so white and round, with small nipples. He traced his fingers over the flatness of her belly and the roundness of her hips, down to the thick bush between her legs.

She had nice legs, shapely legs, long slender legs. Sinking to his knees once again, he stared at her pussy. Her legs were still wide and her flesh was still wet and her pubic hair was twisted and matted. To LaStanza, nothing looked more beautiful.

Juliette touched the top of his hair. He looked up and she smiled down at him. He reached around, caressed the cheeks of her ass and kissed her pubic hair once more. Rising slowly, he pulled his shorts and pants up and looked around. A movement caught his eye on a balcony across the alley. There was a bald-headed man out on the balcony, a pot-bellied man wearing a grey tee-shirt and baggy pants. Next to the man was a smaller man, much older, in a wheelchair.

LaStanza looked back at Juliette who smiled up at the watchers on the balcony. So he moved aside, and Juliette let them have a nice long look at her naked body.

He helped her back into her dress and she took his hand again and said, "My room is right here." She pulled him along the wall to a door with the number seven on it. She took a key from her purse and opened the door.

'Come in.'

LaStanza looked back up the alley and envisaged his wife waiting for him in the café. He pulled away and told Juliette he had to go.

'Really?' She tilted her head to the side and seemed hurt.

He leaned in and kissed her again but the passion wasn't in her lips. He backed away and she closed the door firmly.

Moving up the alley, he suddenly felt drowsy. He leaned back against the wall and closed his eyes momentarily because he felt dizzy and hot.

'So, what have you been up to?' Lizette asked.

Blinking his eyes, LaStanza sat up with a, 'Huh?'

His wife stood next to the table in her black skirt and green silk blouse, her long dark hair curled and hanging loosely around her round face, her gold-brown eyes twinkling at him. Instinctively, LaStanza looked over at the table next to the picture window. It was empty.

Lizette moved around the table and sat in the chair to his right. Crossing her legs, LaStanza heard the nylon sound of her pantyhose. It, even more than her voice, stirred him to complete wakefulness. He looked at Juliette's table again. It seemed as if no one had ever been there.

'What have you been doing?' His wife asked again. 'Besides drinking coffee.'

'Uh. Day dreaming.' His mouth was so dry he could barely answer.

'You look wet?'

'What?' He ran his hands over his clothes and they felt damp.

Lizette put an elbow up on the table and rested her chin in her hand and said, 'Did you get caught in the rain? And what were you day-dreaming about?' She scrunched up her full lips in a teasing way.

So he reached down and ran his right hand up her left thigh.

'Was it a nice day-dream?' She ran her tongue over her full lips.

'Yeah,' he said as he pulled her left leg until she uncrossed it. He looked at the picture window and said, 'I thought you could see the Eiffel Tower from anywhere in Paris.'

'Not from every café.'

'You can in the movies.'

She laughed. 'The bad ones.'

'I remember a movie where the couple were strolling through the French Quarter and ended up in City Park?'

'*This Property is Condemned*. Not a bad movie, actually. Natalie Wood and Robert Redford. Play by Tennessee Williams. Screenplay by Francis Ford Coppola.'

'Really? The Godfather guy?'

'Yes, sir.'

'So how'd the speech go? You want some coffee?' He

pushed his fingers down into her crotch and rubbed them against the front of her pantyhose. He knew she wasn't wearing panties today. She let out a small moan and smiled, nodding toward the waiter.

He continued feeling up her crotch as her legs slowly parted. Feeling the outline of her pubic hair beneath her stockings, she felt damp.

Lizette gasped and moved her legs apart, the little exhibitionist. She looked at the waiter. LaStanza could see the waiter placing himself at the end of the counter so he could look up Lizette's skirt. The man pretended to be wiping the counter.

LaStanza leaned over and whispered in his wife's ear, 'Let him look.' LaStanza felt a growing erection now.

She closed her eyes and he felt her up good, gently rubbing her until she was juicy and her chest rising as her breathing increased. Her eyes snapped open and panting, she said, 'Come on, short dark and handsome. Let's get back to the hotel.'

LaStanza held her skirt up a second before pulling his hand away. The waiter certainly got a good look that time.

When LaStanza stood, he felt a little wobbly and sat back in his chair.

'You OK?' Lizette picked up her purse from the table.

LaStanza saw something that caused pin pricks along the back of his neck. He saw two cups at his table. The one to the left sat askew in its saucer. The pin pricks became needles.

'What's the matter?' Lizette asked. 'You look as if you've just seen a ghost.'

'No.' He felt a grin come over his face. 'Better. Much better.'

The café door opened and two armed gendarmes stepped in, each carrying machine guns, each in light blue uniform shirts, dark pants and the classic round police hats.

They scanned the café, their gazes lingering on Lizette as a tall man in a suit followed them in. Obviously a plainclothesman, he had salt and pepper hair and a thin face, deep-set eyes. He barely looked at LaStanza, staring at Lizette as he moved through the café to the portly waiter standing behind the counter.

The men spoke in rapid French and LaStanza heard the word *Sûreté*. He leaned over to tell Lizette that the *Sûreté* were the French equivalent of the F.B.I., when she said, 'National police. They're looking for a woman.'

LaStanza immediately looked at the waiter who was shrugging to the *Sûreté* man, sticking out his chin and rattling at the mouth.

Lizette whispered, 'He says lots of women come in, but not many today and not any in the last few hours. Except me.'

The goose bumps were back. The plainclothesman pulled something from his coat pocket. A picture, he showed the waiter and spoke again, a little louder and LaStanza heard something like *terroriste*. Terrorist!

Like a good Sicilian, LaStanza was used to keeping emotion from his face but Lizette must have seen something in his eyes because she leaned back and narrowed her eyes slightly.

She moved her legs away from the table and uncrossed them and LaStanza saw the gendarmes watching her. They could probably see up her skirt. Lizette noticed and took in a slight breath, a little wily smile on her lips. She left her legs uncrossed as she looked back at the plain-clothes man, then looked away as their gaze moved to her legs. No doubt they were getting a good show, which drew a wicked smile to Lizette's full lips.

The man from the *Sûreté* stepped up to their table and spoke. Lizette answered in fluent French. She'd told LaStanza her Parisian was nearly perfect. The only word LaStanza understood was *Américain*.

'*Oui*, madame,' said the man from the *Sûreté*. 'Have you seen this woman?' He handed the picture to Lizette who looked at it.

'No.' She passed the photo to LaStanza. In the grainy, black and white picture, Juliette's hair was shorter. It was taken from a distance, a surveillance photo.

A movement to LaStanza left caught his attention as the waiter stepped forward, a towel over his shoulder. He pointed to LaStanza's coffee cup but there was something else, a knowing look in his eyes and LaStanza the Sicilian recognized the threat immediately. The waiter backed away.

LaStanza shook his head and handed the picture back to the plain-clothes man who asked Lizette what hotel were they staying at. When she told him, LaStanza saw the eyebrows of the waiter rise slightly. He looked at the gendarmes, who were too busy ogling his wife's legs to notice the exchange of looks.

Lizette told them her husband was also a policeman.

The man from the *Sûreté* said, 'Yes?'

LaStanza pulled his ID folder with his gold N.O.P.D. star-and-crescent badge clipped outside and handed it to the plainclothesman. The waiter's eyes became wide for a moment.

'He's a homicide detective,' Lizette said, finally looking at LaStanza again. She reached for his hand and squeezed it.

'Are there many homicides in New Orleans?' The man from the *Sûreté* passed the ID folder back to LaStanza who told him, 'Every day.' He stood and slipped the folder back into his rear pocket. 'And most nights.'

A sly smile came to the man's thin lips. 'Yes. Everyone in America has a gun.' He bowed slightly and led the other officers out.

LaStanza dug in his pocket for money and turned to the waiter who rattled off an amount in francs and dollars. LaStanza put a ten on the table and caught the waiter's eye again. It was there – that knowing look followed by a slight nod. LaStanza reciprocated with his own slight nod.

Stepping outside, LaStanza spotted the three policemen moving up Rue St André in the opposite direction from the alley. He and Lizette turned the other way and she wrapped her hands around his arm, the same way the girl had done, sending a shiver up his spine.

'Are you all right?' she asked.

'Sure.'

They passed the alley and he looked down it. Empty. They continued to the corner and LaStanza spotted a pay phone across the street. Waiting for traffic to pass, he felt his pulse rising again.

'Actually,' Lizette said as they started across the street, 'my talk went very well. I told you about Professor LeGris, the man who holds the Chair of French Revolution Studies at the Sorbonne, well, he was quite complimentary.'

LaStanza stopped next to the pay phone and Lizette was almost pulled out of step.

'What is it?'

He looked into her gold-brown eyes and smiled weakly. 'I need you to do me a favour.'

'What?' Her voice was lowered, more cautious. The look in the eyes of this police-wife told him she was expecting something. Something not good.

'I want you to call the *Sûreté* from this pay phone. Tell

them the woman they're looking for, the terrorist, lives in the alley just down from Café Degas on Rue St André. The door is on the left with the number seven on it.' His voice rising. 'She's there now.'

Lizette eyes grew wider. 'You saw her?'

He ran his hands up her arms. 'I need you to make the call anonymously. Using that perfect Parisian accent.'

'She was in the café?'

He looked back toward the alley and Café Degas. 'You wanna stand here and discuss it? Or can we talk it out later?'

Lizette opened her purse and reached for change.

LaStanza let out a long sigh. 'I feel naked without my .357 magnum.'

Lizette shook her head as she reached for the receiver. 'I don't believe we come all the way to Paris for you to get in more shit.'

'That's what I do.'

'Cute, LaStanza. Real cute.'

She made the call and sounded a little shaky. As soon as she hung up, LaStanza led her away, quickly. She looked over her shoulder and said, 'What's the hurry?'

'We have to change hotels.'

Lizette huffed and the fire in her eyes told LaStanza he was in deep trouble. Looking around, a freshening breeze flowing over the couple, LaStanza felt pretty good actually. After a week of visiting museums, palaces, dusty bookstores, the Tomb of Napoleon, LaStanza was back in the shit.

About the Story

A CAFÉ IN THE rain, a man alone, a pretty woman enters. Inspiration for a short story as the two sit at different tables and exchange glances. The man's mind drifts to what might happen. The image is indelible and remains in the mind, filed away for use in future writing. A slice of life the writer will expand into a sexy story.

Sitting in another café, on another rainy day, another writer sips coffee as she reads. She's in a short skirt and realizes she's being ogled by two business men who have positioned themselves to see up her skirt if she would only uncross her sleek legs. She does, slowly, opening her knees wider than usual before re-crossing her legs. A slice of life this writer files away for the future, the titillation of flashing the appreciative men.

Paris in the rain. The world's most romantic city, the natural setting for a collaboration of sexy ideas. Drop in characters, let them do what men and women do. There comes some unexpected emotion and steam from writhing bodies, then add a twist.

Sunday
by John Baxter

STEPPING INTO THE CAFÉ Balzac, he was always out of breath. And each time, the same question crossed his mind: what part was due to the effort of walking five blocks from the Métro, and what to excitement?

Was it still exciting? It must be – otherwise why continue? Infidelity demanded organisation; imaginary meetings at unsociable hours, and visits to remote *brocantes* beyond the *péripherique*. Did Bunbury have a French opposite number? More likely, such things fell under the ruling philosophy of most Gallic activities: don't ask, don't tell.

But he did look forward to *their* Sundays; still felt residual shivers of the guilty thrill, so intense during their first hazardous, improvised couplings in hotels, her office after hours, even once at lunchtime in the toilet of their favourite restaurant – and, as she pointed out later, at precisely the appropriate point in the meal; that hiatus where, traditionally, the French get down to business, *entre la poire et le fromage;* between the pear and the cheese.

Even so, what began as an adventure was now, he had to admit, almost a routine.

Or a ritual?

'*Monsieur desire?*' The boy behind the counter was

new, and didn't know him, but the owner, turning from the espresso machine, smiled. *'Deux expresses pour monsieur,'* he told the boy. *'Un pour emporter?'*

'Bonjour, m'sieur. Oui, c'est exact.'

Three months of Sundays had won him the deference due a regular.

As the machine hissed, he stepped outside to make his call. Reception in the café was bad.

He almost collided with a West Indian woman, berating the small white boy whose hand she held. She stopped short, glared, then detoured around him. Judging from her handbag, low heels and hat, and the boy's fresh-ironed white shirt, she was a *gardienne* headed for mass with her employers' son while *maman et papa* enjoyed a lie-in, or a leisurely fuck. Confirming his guess, the bell of the church on the next street tinnily clanged ten.

The boy could have been him at that age – calculating how long he could delay the trial of Sunday mass. Was it still true, he wondered, that, providing you didn't miss the consecration and the sermon, your attendance counted, and you had no sin to admit at Thursday confession?

'Hello!'

Her voice startled him. He'd speed-dialed without thinking. Instinctively, he turned his back on the disappearing woman and her charge.

'Ca va?'

'Ca va très bien,' she said. 'They've just gone.'

'Great. Ten minutes then?'

'Mmm. With my coffee?'

'Of course.'

Through the window of the café, he saw the owner setting out two coffees on the counter; one with cup, saucer and paper spill of sugar, the other in take-away styrofoam.

95

Abruptly, an image coalesced in his imagination, as precise as one of Helmut Newton's *tableaux*.

·'Uh … what would be nice …' he said tentatively.

'Yes?'

'Do you think … maybe … just the heels …?'

'Oh.' She let the thought marinate a moment. '*Just* ...? Not …?'

'Mmm.'

Though two blocks away, he felt her as close as his shoulder. Was that her breath?

'Well, we'll see,' she said. 'Don't forget my coffee.'

At the counter, he gulped his *express*, laid down four Euros, and descended to the toilet, reminded by the rub against his half-hard dick that, as usual on their Sundays, he wore no underwear.

After pissing, he didn't zip up.

What if he let it stay open?

Would the café owner notice?

Would anyone? Some *femme de ménage,* passing him on the street, trailing her wheeled caddy, glancing down, eyes widening, blushing …

This time, the fantasy made him fully erect, and he stood facing the empty urinal for a few seconds, letting it subside, before returning upstairs.

Leaving the small change on the counter, he took the styrofoam cup.

'*Bonne journée.*'

'*Bonne journée, m'sieur.*' The owner smiled – conspiratorially? '*Bon dimanche.*'

Her street was a canyon of six-floor apartments, dating back to the 1890s. The sun reached ground level only between eleven and two, so there were no trees. And no shops either, at least none that opened this early on Sunday, so nobody passed him in the two blocks. He wasn't sorry. For every piquant outcome of his discreet experiment in flashing, he could think of a dozen that ranged from embarrassing to disastrous. But the vision persisted, fanned by the occasional puff of cold air that penetrated as he walked. In one of Kingsley Amis's novels, the hero, to delay his orgasm, mentally conjugated Latin verbs. Would that work in this situation? He improvised, using a familiar succession of digits and letters: *76A34, 76A34, 76A34...*

As he reached her front door, he slowed. In his complicated moral geography, their Sundays, until he entered her building, existed only as a potentiality. As long as he stayed on the street, she remained just one of the thousands of women who'd occupied his imagination since he was old enough to be interested. And to imagine was no sin; or at least no mortal sin. Once, however, he crossed the cracked, uneven tiles of her lobby and set foot on the stairs, a different reality obtained.

But the possibility of walking past didn't survive more than a microsecond. Generations of fingers had almost effaced the figures and letters on the ancient keypad, but his didn't hesitate.

76A34.

The latch clicked.

She lived on the fourth floor, but he always paused on the third landing, to catch his breath, clear his mind.

There were rules to their encounters; that much had been established from the beginning. He instigated the affair, but she controlled it. He could suggest, and she could acquiesce or refuse. Had she disliked what he'd proposed on the phone, she'd have told him instantly. As it was, he knew, as he pressed the bell, what to expect – and what was expected of him.

Even through the door, the click of heels was

enticingly audible.

'*Oui*?'

Her voice came muffled through the varnished wood.

'*Facteur.*' His breath was short, as if he'd run up the four flights.

'*Vous avez quelque chose pour moi, m'sieur?*'

Now he was fully erect, flagrantly excited. If someone should came down the stairs …

He swallowed. '*Oui, madame. Mais vous devez signer, s'il vous plaît.*'

She opened the door just wide enough to admit him to the unlit hall, then stepped back as it shut behind him, the better for him to see her in the dim light from the doors that led to bedroom and *salon*.

Long before she showed herself to him for the first time, he knew how she would look naked: legs – her best feature – slim and straight, breasts soft, larger than they seemed in clothes. Neat bottom, small, well-kept hands with long unvarnished nails. And always, he visualised as he saw her now, hands behind her back, eyes downcast, legs slightly apart – and nude in black patent leather sandals with three inch heels.

He pulled her to him. The first kiss was always too urgent, too hungry. It was a fault he worked to correct. Years ago, in a different country, almost a different life, another woman – like her in many ways – had chided him as his fingers probed and pried the crevices of her body.

'No, not yet,' she had said. 'When I'm more …' She took a moment to find the perfect word. '… *lustful*.'

He tried to apply the lesson now, forcing himself to enjoy the sensations that would exist in this moment alone: the sense of *possession* implicit in his spread palm on the small of her back, pressing her to him, and the surprise of her nudity against his body, clothed.

98

Wait ... wait ... Lacking Latin verbs, he fell back on the words he'd parroted all those Sundays as an altar boy. *Confiteor Deo omnipotenti, beatae Mariae semper Virgini, beato Michaeli Archangelo, beato Joanni Baptistae, sanctis Apostolis Petro et Paulo...*

It won him ten or fifteen seconds of gentle contact, lips to lips, before other thoughts engulfed it.

'Touch me!'

Her cool palm slid unhesitatingly through his open flies, encircling his hardness, but remaining thrillingly motionless; all touch, all promise.

With the other hand, she rescued the coffee he still held, forgotten.

'I hope it's still hot,' she said. Then she dug in her nails.

From what had become, by habit, *his* end of the long black leather couch, he watched her move around the shadowy *salon*.

He didn't mind her not being young; preferred it, in fact. No teenager could walk nude in heels, except with a teeter and a giggle. He liked her stride, her indifference to effect, the unapologetic squat as she retrieved the foil *capsule* peeled from the half bottle of champagne. Today it was Veuve Clicquot – appropriate, since she, too, was a widow – but *marques* mattered less than effect. A jolt of *express* and two glasses of champagne on an empty stomach brought her quickest to the peak of arousal. And *quick* mattered.

'No problems?' he asked.

'Nope. She still loves it.'

She was the daughter, aged nine. *It* was attending Sunday mass with a family friend, followed by a pizza lunch; a luxurious two-hour holiday from parenthood. But though absent, the daughter, like his wife, remained a presence; the two embodied in the mobile phones always placed next to one another by the bed, ready to dispense the excuses that had, by now, become second nature. *'Tell Uncle George he can take you to the park, But no ice cream; I'm having a coffee with X. I'll be home in about an hour.'*

She popped the cork, poured two glasses, set them on the coffee table, and subsided, ankles crossed, onto the couch at the other end. He undid his belt and opened his trousers, easing them off his hips, letting his cock and balls loll out. They drank the wine and looked at one another, enjoying the inevitability of pleasure.

'Doesn't she notice?' she asked.

'What?'

'The hair.'

Not long after they started, he began to shave his pubis. It excited him to do so, drawing his attention at unexpected moments during the day to smoothness or stubble.

'No,' he said. 'Or if she does, she doesn't mention it.'

He liked bodies hairless; would have enjoyed shaving her: warm water, soap, steel, finishing with a shaver. But she refused. "She'd notice," she'd said, meaning the daughter. Did they spend much time together nude? He visualised it as a canvas by Balthus; raised skirts, smooth pussies, a flagrant sideways light.

As she leaned over to pour the second glass, he said 'Show me.'

Taking her time, she sank back into the cushions, sipped, uncrossed her ankles, pushed her hips forward and, letting one foot drop to the carpet, raised the other to hook her heel over the top of the couch.

Her expression was polite? Obliging? Neither, exactly.

100

More like the inscription on Man Ray's memorial in the Cimitiere Montparnasse: *unconcerned but not indifferent.*

The sight left him anything but indifferent. Rather, the pink slit of her pussy, pursed in its nest of almost invisible hair, moved him to a tenderness only partly due to wine and lust.

'You're perfect, you know.'

Narrowing her eyes and making a small *moue,* the French phantom kiss, she said, 'You are not so bad yourself.'

The things one said when one couldn't say 'love'.

They chatted, half listening to *France Culture,* almost inaudible. The sob of a quartet, one of his favourites. *Listy Důvěrné. Intimate Letters.* Janacek. At such moments, he saw life like a bowl filled to brimming; one movement, and it would ripple and spill.

'Well …' he said. Sometimes it was "Shall we …?" or occasionally "Want to play?"

She tipped up her glass to finish the last drops, and placed it on the table.

'Back in a minute.'

While she was in the bathroom, he entered the dark bedroom and dragged the duvet from the low, queen-sized bed, leaving just the two pillows. Peeling off t-shirt and trousers, toeing out of his shoes, he lay on his back in the gloom, idly touching his cock. Awaiting her pleasure.

He mostly knelt at the foot of the bed; at his *devotions*, he liked to think. The folded duvet cushioned his knees, while a pillow drawn under her hips raised her pussy; better for her, he insisted, but thinking as much of himself. Leaning forward too long with his neck at that angle became uncomfortable, and finally painful.

It had taken about twenty minutes, as usual. From the

moment he parted her thighs with his forearms, used his thumbs to spread the lips of her pussy, and lingeringly licked with the full length of his tongue from her anus to her clit, her moans of pleasure and encouragement never ceased; merely, after about ten minutes, rose to a crescendo, and expired.

He never asked 'Did you come?' or 'Was that nice?' The kind ones lied. The unkind thought it was none of his business. 'If I did, it was *my* orgasm,' a righteous little minx had snapped at him in a Finnish bedroom, and after that he never enquired again.

He wiped his mouth, smearing the wetness from his lips and cheeks with his palm before laying his cheek, still sticky with juice and spit, on her stomach. Was it polite to wipe? As a younger man, he'd debated this point of sexual etiquette, deciding that, if the woman noticed at all, she was as likely to take it for relish as distaste.

He pulled himself up onto the bed, glad to lie straight after kneeling so long; the same relief he used to feel at mass when one stood for the *Introit*, then sat for the almost welcome tedium of the sermon. She wriggled up beside him, pulling the pillow with her. In the beginning, he'd assumed she'd want to cuddle, but though she nestled willingly enough within the curve of his arm, he sensed she did so out of politeness. After that, he didn't bother, leaving her to drowse.

At these moments, his mind always wandered to other women – and, more frequently than any other, to the one who'd cautioned him to wait till she felt "lustful". He'd never seen orgasms like hers. Lathered in sweat, she buried her face in the pillow and shrieked her delight until nothing remained, and her exhausted voice petered out in a whimpered 'no more no more no more'.

'Shall I get the sticky stuff?'

'Mmm?'

Her question broke him out of his reverie. But of course it was time. He'd *done* her. Now she would *do* him. It was only fair.

Unfortunately, his options were limited. Penetrative sex, though possible, was complicated. She demanded a condom, which further reduced his already depleted sensations. Then, too, her cunt was tiny – his thumb filled it easily. She loved cock, however, and would come repeatedly, but her body stiffened and reared the moment he entered her, and she signified her pleasure not with moans but a noise between grunt and shout, as if each thrust was a punch. It worked best when he wrestled her under him, trapping her wrists, subduing her with brute weight; something he, who loved compliance and surrender, found anything but erotic.

The compromise was "sticky stuff"; lubricant gel, with the aid of which she administered an inexpert hand job, usually leaving him to finish himself while she assumed the obscene poses he liked. He had no reason to believe they aroused her, a fact that, perversely, excited him more. As he knelt over her belly, hand pumping, about to gush, his last thought was often, *She's whoring for me!*

But today the thought repelled him.

'No,' he said. 'Put something on. Or don't we have time?'

She peered at the big clock on the mantel over the never-used fireplace.

'There's time. What would you like?'

He'd been surprised to find, on one of their first times together in her apartment, that she owned some expensive silk and lace *lingerie;* gifts, she explained, of a previous lover, or lovers – all, from the labels, Italian.

'Stockings, heels, and a bra,' he said. 'The red one.'

'With the suspenders?'

'No. The stay-ups.'

She assembled the outfit silently, with the solemn care he'd seen when, as an altar boy, he'd watched the priest assume his vestments: surplice, chasuble, alb.

Clipping the bra, she settled her breasts with both hands into the half cups of red lace, examined herself briefly and without expression in the full-length mirror, straightened the dark bands of the stocking tops across her thighs.

'OK?'

'More than OK.' His voice was thick. 'Beautiful.'

It was no mere compliment. The moment he saw her in these things, he understood why men bought them for her. Her body welcomed lace; gloried in it, as a bird in air. Stockings, buckles, tapes and straps lay on her flesh as if it had been created for no other purpose. It was only half-naked that she looked fully dressed. How could she not see that? Or perhaps she did, but despised a truth she could not understand.

'Now ... the sticky stuff?'

'No.'

He stood up and put his hands on her shoulders. Did he expect her to flee from what he was about to suggest?

'Something different.'

'*Whip* you?' He'd never seen her startled. 'Why?'

'I'd like it.'

She accepted the statement without comment. That was how it worked. He suggested, and she acquiesced or refused. She did not negotiate.

'Whip you with what?'

He gestured to the wardrobe, the mirror of which reflected her nude back, banded by the red bra strap, and the dark stocking tops. 'You must have belts.'

'Yes,' she conceded. She looked round the bedroom. 'Where? How?'

'Get one. I'll show you.'

He walked naked into the *salon,* scrotum contracted in expectation. Taking a dining chair, he placed it well away from the table, facing the curtained window.

'Like this?' she said from the doorway.

The belt, narrow, plaited brown leather with a silver buckle, hung limp from her hand, like something she'd just killed.

'It'll do.' He was short of breath. His heart thumped. 'Bring it here.'

She did as he ordered, heels clicking on the parquet. He straddled the seat, as if preparing to sit down backwards on the chair, then squatted, resting his forearms on the back. All sensation had contracted to the swing and dangle of his genitals.

He sensed her behind him.

'Play with me.'

Hanging the belt over the back of the couch, she crouched beside him, and used both hands to stroke him as he had taught her, one in front, one behind. Her face was only a few inches away, and they kissed. He was aware, as he hadn't been in the bedroom, of smells; the musk of his arousal, the sweetness of cunt juice on his face.

'Use your nails.'

Instantly they dug into the root of his balls, raked down, while she jerked his cock so hard it almost threw him off balance.

Bitch.

'Now the belt ... and *hard!*'

Some women needed encouraging, teaching, but her

first blow came fast and low, backhanded, cutting across the tops of his thighs and catching his balls, so that he grunted, bowed his head, and clutched the wood of the chair against the pain.

The second, higher, slashed across his cheeks.

Looking sideways, he caught her expression as she drew back her arm for the third.

He had never seen her like this. Eyes narrowed, teeth bared, she *glowed*. A flush lit her face, throat and the slopes of her breasts with a pink so intense that the skin matched the cups of her bra, making the lace seem an extension of her flesh.

As she slashed him again, he reached for her, and inserted his forefinger to the first joint. Ten men emptying themselves in her could not have made her wetter. Withdrawing the fingertip, he ran it between her dripping lips to her engorged clit.

She sobbed, and came.

Twice.

Three times.

Four.

And with each groan of pleasure, another cut of the belt, each more furious, until, untouched, he came himself, ejaculating in air.

Two weeks later, he invited her to lunch, and broke it off. There was no point in wrapping it up in words, nor did any come to mind. He just said 'I think we should give the sex a rest.'

She didn't protest, demand explanations, show emotion. All she said was 'OK. If you like,' and ordered her usual *salade composée* with a half bottle of Badoit.

As they ate, he speculated about what she wore under the plain grey skirt, the neat blouse and jacket. Did she sometimes leave the white bra and pants in their drawer, and slip on, just for one day, those wisps of La Perla?

As he counted out notes for the check, he asked, 'The underwear. Would you have worn it if I hadn't asked you?'

Without hesitation, she said, 'No.'

'And, the other?'

She stood up and wound her scarf round her neck.

'Thanks for lunch.'

After she left, he lingered over a second coffee, watching the office crowd trickle away, back to their desks.

Precisely at 2.30, he speed-dialled a number.

'What's happening?' he asked, keeping his voice low.

'He's got a meeting,' she said. 'Won't be home till six at least.'

'Perfect, then.' He looked around the now nearly empty café. 'What are you wearing?'

She had a soft, husky laugh. 'What would you *like* me to be wearing?'

'Well …'

Et introibo ad altare Dei: ad Deum qui laetificat juventutem meam. And I will go into the altar of God, to God who giveth joy to my youth.

About the Story

THOUGH FRANCE ISN'T NOTABLY religious, the French regard the Catholic Church as important. One of the traditional three estates, with nobility and the commons, it's woven into the national fabric. Even though, these days, its role, like that of the nobility, is more social and symbolic than real, the church flourishes as a repository of guilts and fantasies, often related to sex. In permissive times, bad behaviour becomes more piquant if one dignifies it as sin, and the regalia and ritual of Catholicism lend themselves to mischievous misuse. The Surrealists in particular found rich material there. Salvador Dali would attend mass, but only to sit in the back row and masturbate. Like the legendary young man of Kent, once he came, he went.

Most French men and women enjoy an element of formality and calculation in their sex life, particularly in Paris, where well-paid, attractive and bored men and women circulate restlessly in a culture that places a high value on appearances. An affair is more desirable if it has an element of chic. People dress up for sex as readily as they undress, and a lover may be flaunted as often as hidden. There is even a designated time for infidelity: *entre cinq à sept*, between five, when the businessman leaves his office, and seven, when he actually arrives home. If the Church of England is, as has been described, "the Tory Party at prayer", sex in Paris might be called "the Catholic church on the job".

Paris often seems, like Borges' Aleph: "the only place on earth where all places are – seen from every angle, each standing clear, without any confusion or blending". (He dismisses London as "a splintered labyrinth" – in sensuality, as in most things, uncertain and confused.). Sex becomes interesting to the metropolitan French when it ceases to be just sex, and becomes instead performance, fashion, even politics. This goes some way to explaining their lack of interest in US attempts, like the Kinsey and Hite reports, to demystify the erotic urge. Far from being works of scientific rationality, France's two biggest post-war sexual best-sellers, *Histoire d'O* and *La Vie Sexuelle de Catherine M*, each written by a woman of impeccable intellectual credentials, celebrated closed quasi-religious communities of voluptuaries to which the passkey wasn't desire but style and an understanding of ritual. However style and ritual can wear thin, which is what *Sunday* is about.

Hill of Martyrs
by Kelly Jameson

AIMÉ CLIMBS TO THE highest point in Paris, the Sacré-
Coeur Basilica, a multi-domed Romanesque church built
on grounds traditionally associated with the beheading of
the city's patron, Saint Denis, in the 3rd century. He
crushes out his cigarette with his torn sneaker, marvelling
at the kids below riding the colourful, pumping carousel,
the view of the city, the grids and blocks of people living
out their tiny, spider-webbed lives.

Next he climbs to the top of the dome, more than 200
feet above Montmartre. It's the second-highest viewpoint
after the Eiffel Tower, and the sky is a bowl of brightness.

Once Aimé's sneakers were as blue as the Parisian sky.
Now they are so dirty and worn they are almost grey.
Despite the fact that he'd rinsed his socks yesterday,
they're little oceans of filth. His stomach growls. He
hasn't had anything to eat, other than bread rolls and
coffee, for a day and a half.

Somewhere below him, in the circling mass of
humanity, is Cercle Clichy Montmartre, a place where his
maman spends time when she isn't in the sex joints. She
sometimes plays pool or snooker at 2 a.m. in the place
that had been a gentleman gamblers' haunt in the 19th
century and was used by the Nazis as a military barracks
and horse stable during World War II. That was as

upscale as his maman got. She preferred old cabarets and atrocious, tongue-tying wines. But it wasn't always so.

Aimé likes to climb the Hill of the Martyrs and imagine he is far from his life, a simulacrum of reality. He's only lived seventeen years, but some days he feels like an old deflated man. Here, he feels the world slow down; in this place with its sprawling stone, a frost-resistant travertine that bleaches with age to a gleaming white … this place with its Holy Joe words, its ripples of silent prayer sent up to the sky, the triple-arched portico surmounted by two bronze equestrian statues of France's national saints, Joan of Arc and King Saint Louis IX, and the great bell, the Savoyarde, maybe the world's heaviest bell at 19 tons.

What is it doing here, this church, at the top of the City of Light, in the middle of his murdered dreams? He doesn't know who all these people are. Or why they come here. Week after week. Prayer after whispered prayer. They come. But what does it ever change? His maman still drinks too much. She still fucks strange men on the worn felt of pool tables in the spiritual harness of ill-lit bars. People still get sad and sick and murdered. And whenever he asks his maman about his father, whom he's never known, she always says, "The best thing he ever did was die." And she will not talk about her own family, her own father. They are not French, his family. His mother, his brothers. It's their dirty little secret. He is not allowed to call his mother "mom". He must call her "maman".

Why did Colleen, who now calls herself Colette, drag herself and her three small, red-faced boys to the streets of Paris, where painters and prostitutes still mix? In America, she'd tell the boys the same bedtime story over and over, her voice whispering the truth of what she was: a Kentaurian, a female centaur, half woman, half horse.

111

Born of chaos and unbridled passions. And that, because of her nature, they all had to leave America for France, where with their openness, their love of chaos and passion and art, she would be accepted for who she was.

Later, when Aimé was no longer a child, if he imagined her in America, he could see that Colette was more like one of Picasso's hidden harlequins; a shadowy misfit. A young woman with artistic talent, a sensual nature, and a wealthy, controlling father who wanted her to be an equestrian champion. A father's wishes she denied and who disinherited her when she became pregnant with Aimé.

In France, for a time, Colette was famous, not as an artist as she dreamt, but as an actress in a winter circus of sorts. An equestrian theatre. A beautiful young woman with leaping dreams in her eyes. Who wore stunning costumes on her slender body; who acted in Macbeth, which was performed entirely on horseback.

Aimé liked to believe that somewhere in the sinews and ligaments of the tragedy/comedy of Colette's body was a memory of the *joie de vivre*. Of that time when she stood in a long, black evening gown moulded to her curves, barefoot on the back of a regal horse, woman and beast perfectly balanced, her hair cascading in an elegant braid over her shoulder and down to her waist.

During one performance, a group of animal activists in the city, who believed it was cruel to make horses perform in shows, staged a protest. The protestors startled the horse, and Colette fell from her horse and broke her leg. A wounded female centaur. And then she was only half of herself.

And the circus, her circus, was gone like that. Snapped in two. The gemstone colours, the soft, silky costumes, the carpets, the artistry and magic of gigantic tents, the animals, the loud, rasping music, the scrap metal they used to build the trapeze apparatus. All gone for ever.

Her looks began to fold up too. She drank more then ever. Dabbled in art again but only long enough to complete one sculpture. Aimé doesn't think she ever got back on a horse.

Sex had always been Colette's first language, English her second. She got a part-time job at the Museum of Eroticism (Musee de l'Erotisme) at 72 Boulevard de Clichy. She got to exhibit the one sculpture she made, a six feet tall, moving giant vagina with six legs and feet spread in all directions that twirled and rotated when pushed. No arms, no upper torso, no head, no face. It sat right smack in the centre of a room like a merry-go-round, a room that also contained a chair with a red velvet cushion and a hard gold penis sticking up from the cushion; an old Japanese book about sex; a bunch of chastity belts; erotic snuff bottles; sexual pottery that was 2,000 years old; the bottom half of a naked female mannequin protruding from one wall; a selection of whips in rhino leather; crops for spanking; erotic door-knockers; and a large old-fashioned wooden box fitted with lenses known as a stereoscope that enabled patrons to view pictures of girls on offer.

Aimé was twelve years old the first time he saw the giant vagina, which was at about the same height as his head was. While Colette took tickets at the door and sipped coffee she let him roam and explore all seven floors.

The giant vagina and six legs were made of Plaster of Paris, and each leg wore a different type of stocking. The plastic toenails were painted electric colours. Aqua. Purple. Deep Rose. Tangerine. Plum. Silver. Aimé's favourite stocking was the black fishnet. It felt nice when

113

he ran his fingers along it.

"The French invented sex," Colette would tell the patrons and they would laugh.

But the audience and dreams had galloped out of her life. Turns out she couldn't live without them. Aimé and his brothers always begged her to tell the Kentaurian bedtime story again but she wouldn't; said she couldn't remember it any more. She told Aimé once, while working on the sculpture, that "an additional benefit of the ink wash I'm using is that it creates a pretty tough layer – the wax does, anyway; it helps to keep me from rubbing paint off as I work."

"Do you hate love?" he finally asked her once while he helped her take tickets at the museum. She looked into his beautiful dark eyes. "Did you know in medieval times men actually believed that beavers who were being chased by hunters bit their testicles off? Right. Like any male thing would bite its own testicles off. That'd be the day."

Colette doesn't work at the museum any more. And Aimé is no longer a little boy roaming its floors like a detective delighting in each new fact and find. Now he roams the streets of Paris, its cafés and churches and monuments. Aimé's current girlfriend Brigitte often tells him he is looking for something he'll never find. She will join him soon on the Hill of Martyrs but for now, alone, he watches the city below, its lithe and sensual movements, its startling and abrupt grace, its fat shape like a shimmering body of water that will bubble over. A city of funicular railways, street artists, monuments, churches, hotels, vegetables, flowers, seafood ... and sometimes people who think this is Paris.

Aimé stares at the sun's reflection dripping red-mahogany shadows off one of the tall stained-glass windows. He realizes the blood-buzzing deep within his ears, the metallic pounding thunder in his young soul, is *rage*. Before he can change his mind, he climbs down the dome stairs, finds his way to the Chapelle de la Sainte Famille, and loses himself in thought. At least here he can pretend someone below prays for him.

Aimé is bombarded with ancient smells of stone and dust and perspiration, his eyes flooded with mustard- and wax-yellow light and he thinks of the waxy legs of the vagina sculpture. He takes a seat in one of the pews near the front.

"In the end, God's son went home, Aimé. He went home. God doesn't really care about shits like us." That's what his maman said whenever he asked her to take him to church.

From his first floor bedroom window, Aimé can look up and see the dome in the distance, glistening white, thrusting into the sky. Sometimes he imagines he hears church voices, raised in mad-for-God songs, floating and galloping on the thick grease of the early summer air, and he gets that strange, still feeling inside him. Then it disappears, and for a moment, it's almost like he's changed something in the thick, cruel marrow of his world just by thinking about it. Maman used to call him Andrew. But that was long ago.

He glances at his watch, rises from the pew. Goes outside to one of the neat gardens tucked behind the church, where it is silent as stone, and finds her waiting. The kiss is severe for both of them and neither wants it to ever end. Aimé's fingers slide under her skirt, between her legs. She is hairy. 'Good,' he murmurs. 'No panties, just like I told you.' She makes a sound in her throat that causes his cock to grow even harder inside his jeans; she is so wet, and her musk floats in the air, shameless and

115

demanding, helpless and sacred. She moves against his fingers, sucking his ear lobe with her little white teeth. He backs away and she looks at him with dazed, wanting eyes. He takes her hand and leads her to a deserted nook. 'Get on your hands and knees.' She obeys. 'I want anyone who walks by to see that tight, dripping cunt of yours.' Her ass is in the air, her legs spread. He doesn't want to, but he thinks of the sculpture. All legs. He unbuttons his jeans and kneels behind her. What he likes about Brigitte is that she is not skinny. She is not overly pretty. She is big and warm and soft. There isn't much about their relationship that makes sense except for the fucking. Brigitte smokes and she eats too many chocolate croissants and she is lazy, he thinks, as he pushes his hard cock inside her tight pink lips. Further in now, slippery wet, her belly a little fat, her tits bounce as he thrusts inside her. She does no work, submissive slut, just lets him pound her while she groans and pretends to worry that they may be caught. She could've stepped from an old canvas. Her sad eyes are heavy and dark and she believes she looks best when someone is fucking her. A thin chain of white gold around her plump ankle shimmies as he comes on her bare backside.

Brigitte once had a boyfriend, a seventy-year-old Frenchman who told her she had a "bad" face. She was insulted until she realized he meant "naughty" face.

Aimé keeps her in that position for a while, kneading her buttocks, soft and firm as bread dough, slipping his fingers inside her, studying her cunt. He's thought of himself as Aimé for a long time now.

After a while, he sits down, his back against the sturdy legs of a stone bench, and orders her to suck him. Her favourite fellatio position is on her knees, her wet, semen-spattered cunt in the air, throbbing for more (it takes a long time to make Brigitte come). The harder she sucks him, the less it feels like affection or adoration or permanence. *The actual home of the martyr – across the pink fields and up the hill.* Her lips suck and lick him. Brigitte never tries to make him fall in love with her. She is too lazy, he thinks, as she swallows the first wave of cum and then catches the rest on her face, her cheeks, her lips.

Afterward, she wipes off her face and they sit against the bench, smoking cigarettes; Brigitte's legs open beneath her short skirt, her hand rubbing herself. Aimé likes to imagine she is descended from uncouth Tartans, who lived miserable lives walking around on stilts, raising sheep for their manure, necessary to grow their miserable crops of rye. It is a strange fantasy he doesn't understand.

Eventually Brigitte leaves. She kisses him lightly. He knows she will not exert herself by walking the cobble-stoned streets; she will take the funicular. He continues to sit in the sun, his arm slung over the seat of the bench. This isn't Paris. Paris is the room that's dark, where you can't see your hands in front of your face and it's cold. And rainy. Things are broken and blue-rosed and cubed. That's Paris. Van Gogh colours and Picasso dreams. Hidden harlequins.

The smell of Brigitte, sweet and sour at the same time, lingers on his fingers, his skin. He heads inside, seeking the dark. Finds the same pews and the altar protected by waist-high iron fencing of sorts. He sits in the quiet, trying to feel the ten thousand prayers hanging in the dead, satisfied air. He turns at the sound of rigid footsteps. A young man, dressed in a military uniform, strides down the centre aisle. He doesn't appear to notice Aimé.

The young man places something over the iron-latticed bars, something small. On his way out, he glances in

Aimé's direction. Aimé thinks his face looks a lot older than when he came in. The man's eyes look yellow. Must be a trick of the light.

'Beware the snake eyes,' the man says. 'It hurts to bring someone back from the dead. Bright colours will confuse you. Your open eyes will not focus. And when you can see, you will regret it.'

After the man leaves, Aimé approaches the altar. He doesn't know if he should touch it, but the pull of curiosity is too strong to ignore. It's some sort of choker made with what appears to be old bone fragments and bronze snake-eye beads. It is warm in his cunt-scented fingers.

'I need some good luck,' he says, clasping it about his neck and leaving the church.

Walking home through the crowded, colourful Parisian streets, the people's eyes circling round in their fat heads like the Moulin Rouge, he shields his own eyes. Why had the soldier left the necklace? Would the soldier die now? Everything is much brighter and warmer then when Aimé had gone into the church. He wonders if his maman will be home now. He steals tomatoes from a garden so he and his brothers will have something to eat.

At home, his brothers Dominique and Edgard (formerly Donnie and Eddie) sit on the couch watching television. He sits down next to them, shares the red-gutted fruit. They bite into it like apples. The youngest, Dominique, gets some on his shirt. 'What's that?' he says, pointing to the bone choker circling Aimé's neck, his mouth full of an army of tomato gush.

'Did you brush your teeth today?' Aimé asks.

'Get a new brain already.'

'I don't know what this is,' Aimé says, fingering the beads. 'I found it.'

They turn their attention back to the TV. Aimé gathers up the empty bottles of booze and the rotting bags of garbage and takes them outside. When he comes back, Edgard has changed the channel to some nature show about snakes.

'Hey! Turn it back!' Dominique whines.

Aimé is mesmerized.

'Snakes have rods and cones in their eyes, like we do, though in different numbers,' the host says. 'They have colour vision, but it isn't as broad ranged as ours. They have a yellow filter that absorbs ultraviolet light and protects the eye.'

'Who cares? Turn the channel, butt munch,' Dominique pleads. Edgard sighs.

'Don't change it,' Aimé says.

'Humans need to thank the snake for helping them develop their vision to see inches away,' the narrator continues. 'The ability of humans to have such razor-sharp eyesight resulted from a 'biological arms race' millions of years ago between primates and snakes. The primates eventually won out. Scientists believe primates developed their near-vision to pick hanging fruit and capture bugs.'

The front door slams. Maman's home. She's with someone greasy – a skinny man in a French cap, grungy black T-shirt, ripped jeans. He has limp brown eyes and smells like cheap wine. Colette stumbles into the living room, sets her purse on the scarred table.

'Aimé, I need your ski mask, your knit cap, and Dominique's toy gun.' She has a plastic bag in her hand and removes something from it, puts it on her head. A bright red wig that monkeys to her shoulders. She looks at her reflection in the mirror above the TV. 'I look good, don't I?'

'You look great, like a delicious whore,' sleaze-ball says.

'Wait, I need something else.' She slips a pair of big sunglasses over her eyes.

'Maman, why do you need that shit? I don't know where it is,' Aimé says, feeling something twisted and sick coil in his gut.

'Oh, go get it. It's just a bit of fun, Aimé.'

Aimé gets the stuff and gives it to her. Then she and her greasy pick-up leave. Aimé heats up some water on the stove so Dominique can have a warm bath. Afterward, they eat the last of the tomatoes. Later that night, after his brothers are asleep, Aimé watches TV in the living room. He thinks of his rich grandfather living in America and his horse farms; the grandfather who has never once acknowledged them or tried to help them in anyway. He gets up, goes to the sink, washes the dishes and puts them away, slamming cabinet doors that will soon fall off their hinges. Then he returns to the TV.

Something dark and furry in the corner catches his eye. He tries to ignore it, goes completely still. He pounces and the dancing rodent is in his *mouth*. His upper and lower jaws disengage to further enlarge his mouth so he can swallow it. He can feel the warm blood of the animal, its furry heartbeat, slide down inside him. His vision is fuzzy and his whole being vibrates. The room is a buzzing quadrant of flashing lights and bright colours. He sits on the couch, feeling sick, until his vision returns to normal. His stomach hurts.

He *didn't* just eat a mouse. He *couldn't* have. Thawed, appropriately sized, room temperature mice didn't usually turn him on. He has a sudden urge to rub aspen shavings and damp sphagnum moss all over his body and climb shelves. And he's cold. He rubs his arms and something comes off on the couch. Shiny, iridescent scales.

He clutches the bone choker around his neck, remembers the snake-eye beads, the words of the soldier in the church: "Beware the snake eyes," the man said. "It hurts to bring someone back from the dead. Bright colours will confuse you. Your open eyes will not focus. And when you can see, you will regret it."

He tries to slip the choker off his neck but it won't budge. Later, the door slams again; Sleaze-ball and his maman come in from the slimy night. Sleaze-ball holds his maman's arm; she can barely walk. Aimé thinks she is drunk again until sleaze-ball commands him to help him get her to the bedroom.

'She's been shot,' sleaze-ball says, like this is an ordinary, everyday occurrence for people's mamans to be shot. 'Help me get her to bed.'

'Shot!' Aimé cries. Panics. Sleaze-ball slaps him hard across his face. Aimé feels tears coming but keeps them in check.

'You never saw me today.' Sleaze-ball leaves them there. This is not Paris.

'Aimé? Aimé, is that you, Aimé, my beautiful, beautiful son?' Colette says.

'Yes, yes, it's me, Mom. It's me, Andrew.' He's crying now, brushing the wig hair gently from his mother's forehead.

'We need to get help … what happened?'

'No, Aimé. You're all better off without me. I robbed a store. The money's in my purse …'

'I'm taking you to the hospital …' But Aimé's mouth freezes. His maman's eyes go cold like milk glass. He feels for a pulse and doesn't get one, puts his hand over his mouth. His vision starts to tunnel.

He sits with her for hours, watches the sun come up.

He doesn't know what to do. He gets up, shuts his maman's door, and when Dominique and Edgard get up, he tells them maman isn't home yet. He sends them off to a bakery with some money. He says he found it under a couch cushion.

Aimé shuts off the lights, pulls down the shades, and sits on the coolest part of the couch. Someone knocks on the door.

'Colette? You home?'

Aimé feels threatened. He farts. *Snakes produce a unique scent from musk glands located near the anus when threatened. Copper belly snakes smell like skunks; rat snakes smell like cucumbers.* Why does he have to be good at science? Why does he remember shit like that? And why does it smell like cucumbers? He tries to speak and instead hisses. He opens his mouth again.

'She's not home,' he manages, making sure his maman's bedroom door is still shut.

'Can I come in?'

Aimé gets up and opens the door, then returns to the couch.

Snakes are predators and fussy eaters. Rat snakes eat rats, mice, chipmunks, and occasionally landlords.

The landlord sits down. Aimé does not look at him. He fingers the bone choker around his neck, strokes the smooth white fragments, the rounded, bronze snake-eye beads. *Beware the snake eyes.* He has a sudden desire to crawl under heavy mulch.

'Where is Colette, boy? The rent is due today ...' He licks his lips. He always speaks to Aimé like he's an idiot.

Anger surges inside him in a burst of rainbow-boa strength. His fingers meld with the bone choker as he wishes his maman would come back to life. *All snakes are carnivorous, small animals; they like to eat lizards*

122

and other snakes, rodents and other small mammals, birds, eggs, insects. The room brightens again; he feels another burst of rainbow consciousness. His maman's bedroom door opens; she stands there in her red wig, her eyes like dead dull marbles. Aimé vomits.

After eating, snakes become torpid while the process of digestion takes place. A snake disturbed after eating will often regurgitate its prey in order to be able to escape a perceived threat.

The actual home of the martyr – across the red fields and up the hill.

Colette sits between them, like something out of the movie Frankenhooker. She steps in the vomit but doesn't notice. Aimé gets a towel, cleans it up. The landlord doesn't notice that big chunks of furry rodent have ejected forcefully from his gut? Hair and tiny claws excreted along with uric acid waste? He doesn't see the circus of flies guzz-guzzing around his maman?

Aimé's undead maman is already beginning to stink.

'I'm here for the rent, Colette. God, it stinks in here.' He pinches his nose. 'You should maybe take out zee garbage once in a while.'

'Don't have the rent,' Colette says, her eyes dreamy and unfocused. She puts her hand up, touches the wig on her head. 'I feel pretty. I feel so pretty. Where's my horse? It's a half hour to showtime!'

The landlord's eyes roll over her body. He licks his pasty lips again. 'We can settle the rent in other ways.' He pinches her tit right in front of Aimé.

'Maman, don't. You don't have to do that …'

'Aimé, let me go.' Something about her voice in the music-butchered daylight broke-stomped-splattered his heart. *Aimé, let me go…words hanging like tinsel on the arm of a Christmas tree, glittering for nobody.*

'Take it outside, boy,' the landlord spits. 'Outside.'

Aimé hesitates but goes. He waits a few moments then glides around the back, looks through the first floor bedroom window. He sees the landlord shove his maman stomach down onto the bed, push her green-and-white polka dot dress above her hips. She isn't wearing panties. He knows he should look away but his head won't turn.

'Little fucking slut,' the landlord barks. 'You like this. Only thing missing is a pool table, eh? You dirty American.' He puts his fat cock in the crack of her ass. Then he rises in the air, banging away, his big fat hairy ass a ghostly mountain of flesh, his balls slapping against his maman's curved buttocks, her face tilted up toward the window, blank, but her lips still knifing the tinsel-crisp words, 'Aimé, let me go. Let me go.'

Aimé shakes. *The choker.*

His eyes move back and forth as he tries to focus. He grips the choker and wishes her dead again. He feels it when she dies, her pale flesh unmoving as the landlord continues to bang her.

'Jesus, Colette, some effort? I bang a goddamn corpse.' He looks down, sees her head turned to the side, open-mouthed, her glassy-eyed stare, and screams. 'Oh God! The stupid bitch is dead! Dead!' As he dresses, Aimé slithers back inside and waits for him.

The landlord hurries from the bedroom, closing the door behind him. 'Aimé, we took care of business. Your maman's … sleeping. I go now. Don't worry about the rent.' He is a basket of sweat. Aimé stares at him.

He tries to go but Aimé stops him, bites him, the movement coiled, lightning fast.

'Ow kid! What the fuck!'

Aimé hisses. The landlord clutches his chest and falls dead of a heart attack.

In the dark, shades-still-drawn room, Aimé feels his skin crackle and stretch, his head begin to take an odd triangular shape. Is his imagination choking him? No. Aimé knows his power now, his cobra-like purpose. He looks at the landlord's body. Aimé has the power to reanimate the dead. He didn't realize it until he brought his maman back. And then wished her dead again with the fanged marrow of his thoughts.

Dominique and Edgard won't be back from the bakery for a while. He sits on the couch. Closes his eyes until the room again becomes venomous swirls of colours and bright lights. He concentrates on the landlord's body and hisses rainbow-boa life back into him. The bones in the choker around Aimé's neck tighten, become a little sharper, poke into his skin, draw blood.

The landlord stands, his lips so red now they remind Aimé of bloody steaks. *The actual home of the martyr – across the bruised purple fields and up the red hill.*

'I feel like shit. Like shit,' the landlord mumbles and scratches his ass.

Aimé imagines him walking out the door, like a pilgrim journeying to the graves, looking in vain for the things he doesn't want. Then the landlord actually walks out the door.

Aimé thinks, watches as the landlord acts out his thoughts, walks into the busy street, into the path of an oncoming vehicle. France is very *pro-tenant*.

Later, when his brothers get home, he tells them this is not Paris and their mother is dead. They cry.

'What do we do?' Dominique, who still smells of tomatoes, sobs.

Aimé tells them about the bone choker and his new powers. Then slowly, slowly, Aimé sheds his skin. Dominique claps his hands with delight when he is done.

Edgard doesn't say anything. 'We'll never go hungry again,' Aimé says. 'And no one will ever separate us.'

There are lots of rats in the City of Light. Lots of rats. There are four times as many rats as people. Rat with Chestnut and Duck. Lemon Deep Fried Rat. Sautéed Rat Slices with Vermicelli. Liquored Rat Flambé. Black Bean Rat. Braised Rat garnished with sprigs of cilantro, morsels of rat meat swaddled in crispy rat skin.

'The first nibble of rat exposes a rubbery texture,' Aimé says. 'The skin coats your teeth with a delicious slime. It's like chewing a thick wad of lard. But you get used to it.' *German Black Pepper Rat Knuckle. Rat soup – delicate threads of rat meat mixed with thinly sliced potatoes and onions. Surprisingly sweet. Rat Kabob. Out of love, Aimé bites his brothers so they will have the power to survive, too.*

There are a lot of rats in the City of Light. And he is the king of the Hill of Martyrs, a seeker of heated cathedrals and lazy girls, a music-loving butcher, a boy who dances with thoughts and colors. A pair of spectacles pushed down someone's nose, a black-and-white café where the drinks have a price, the fat tip of a lit, discarded cigarette on grey-black cobble-stoned streets, a boy-snake-man who can roll back asphalt with his big, whalebone thoughts. And this is not Paris.

About the Story

I SPENT A WEEKEND in Paris in 1986. I was a young woman in love. It was the summer before my sophomore year in college. I tried to cram as much of the culture, history, and ambience of the city into that weekend as possible. I was fascinated by the street vendors, the fountains and statues, the grounds surrounding the palace of Louis XIV. The inner quiet and peace of Notre Dame. Walking the streets at night I felt like I was strolling through van Gogh's painting *Café Terrace at Night*, the first painting in which he used starry backgrounds. He went on to paint star-filled skies in *Starry Night Over the Rhone*, and the better known *Starry Night*. I was with people I loved, making new friends, I couldn't speak any French, I didn't really dig French food, but I loved the city. One thing I love about Paris is the mix of people, painters and prostitutes and artists and street performers, travellers, visitors, coffee drinkers, and of course, writers. I wanted to remember some of the sights and smells and fantastic memories of the place and also to write about the things that people martyr themselves for. And the things they don't. So *Hill of Martyrs* was born. When people read this story, I want them to wonder, is it a story about magic? Is it a story about a young man who once had stars in his eyes, but who builds elaborate illusions around himself to survive the abuses in his life? Or is it a little bit of both? Paris will do that. Put stars in your eyes. But not everybody has a romantic view of Paris, even if they are standing on the second-highest viewpoint after the Eiffel Tower, the sky is a bowl of brightness and their ordinary, dirty life is far below them.

Gargoyles and Sidewalk Cafés
by Peter Baltensperger

JACQUELINE WAS SITTING COMFORTABLY on her fold-up canvas seat high atop Notre Dame where the gargoyles watched over the city with their enigmatic stone eyes. She loved the gargoyles. They were such mysterious creatures from so long ago, such distorted and grotesque beings from a distant era of architecture and popular beliefs that they inspired a deep feeling of awe and wonder. She loved sketching them, trying to capture their essence, attempting to derive some universal meaning from their existence, some personal insights from their bizarre faces, their misshapen bodies.

For a while, she just sat there on the balustrade, leaning against the ancient stone wall. She was content just looking up at them through the early afternoon light, waiting for the sun to come around a bit further and produce the patterns of light and shadows she wanted to capture on this particular day. Her carrying case stood on the stone floor beside her, her sketch pad balanced on her knees, her charcoal ready in her hand.

It was a perfectly pleasant spring afternoon, not a cloud in the sky, the sun still quite low and soft, the perfect conditions for plying her trade. All she had to do was to sit there for a while, wait for the light to change, and gather her thoughts, imagining the four gargoyles perched in the corners above her the way she wanted them to appear on her sheets of paper.

Then the light was just right and she started sketching with quick, determined strokes. Her eyes flitted back and forth between the gargoyle in her field of vision and the paper in front of her. Her charcoal danced over the paper as if on its own, as if independent from her hand, from her mind. Yet she knew exactly where she wanted the outlines and the shadows to go, how she wanted to delineate the stark profile, how to present the object of her fascination in the best light and to the best of her artistic ability.

Her strokes with the charcoal and the smudging of the black substance with her agile fingers seemed automatic and rehearsed. In actual fact, she concentrated so hard on her task that her hand sometimes trembled with the effort. Her heart and her mind raced inside her with the artistic impulses flooding her as she poured her soul, her very essence, into her work.

Curious tourists had begun to gather around her, watching her in amazement as she brought the piece of paper to life until the figure took on a three-dimensional look, an almost life-like shape. She was barely aware of them. She had become used to admiring onlookers over the years of her artistic career and wasn't fazed at all by the growing crowd. She knew by now that she was very good at what she was doing and that she could please even the most discerning aficionado with her art.

She applied the final lines to her sketch, emphasized a shadow here, a curve there, scrutinized her creation carefully by holding it up at arm's length to get the full effect. When she was completely satisfied with her sketch, she signed her name at the bottom, and wrote the words *Gargoyle, Notre Dame* at the top. As a final touch, she sprayed the charcoal sketch with lacquer to keep it from smudging. Then she pulled the sheet of paper from her pad and held it up, calling out the price of her latest piece of art.

A foreign couple standing close to her practically snatched it out of her hands, handed her the money, and detached themselves from the group, smiling proudly at their acquisition and admiring it together in the brightening light of the sun. They appeared extremely satisfied with their morning outing and their valuable purchase from a real Parisian artist, signed with her name and all. Most importantly, they had been there when it was created, and they had obtained it from the artist herself.

Jacqueline had learned a long time ago, back when she was in art school and trying to make money any way she could, that the tourists delighted in her work, even her earliest sketches. It gave them something very tangible, very real, very uniquely Parisian that they could take home with them and show to their friends. She was flattered by the attention she received, by the ease with which she could sell her sketches, and she made sure she continually improved her techniques. She had to be proud of every piece she sold and signed her name to in front of curious crowds.

The foreign couple with her first sketch of the day in their hands were still standing on the balustrade admiring her rendition of the gargoyle, when she focused her attention on the next figure and immediately began sketching again. She knew that the tourists surrounding her would be buying her sketches as long as she produced them and she had become very quick and secure with her charcoal.

As she had expected, she sold every piece she drew of

130

the gargoyles at a good price, and she kept sketching until the sun was getting low on the horizon and the Cathedral was near to closing. Her body was beginning to ache and her hand felt as if it were going to fall off at any moment. She titled and signed her last representation of the fourth gargoyle, sold it to an older man who had been standing behind her looking over her shoulder for quite some time, and closed her pad.

The crowd sighed with collective disappointment, but she pointed to the time and the trembling of her hand. They dispersed gradually and reluctantly, looked out over the city once more, and started to head back downstairs, the lucky ones among them carefully carrying their masterpieces in their hands. Jacqueline packed her sketch pad and charcoal into her carrying case, rose from her canvas seat, and stretched her aching body voluptuously in the slowly cooling evening air.

She was alone by then, and she allowed herself the luxury of leaning against the balustrade and looking out over her city, the Seine a black vein traversing the city below, the Eiffel Tower at a distance silhouetted against the darkening sky. For a brief moment, she was tempted to get her sketch pad back out and capture the quiet evening over the city, but she was really too tired to do anything else. Besides, the attendant would soon be coming to order her downstairs and lock up the building.

She was still leaning against the balustrade, lost in thoughts, when she heard footsteps behind her and turned around. To her surprise, and pleasure, the attendant was a handsome young man she had never seen before.

'You must be new here,' she said.

'My first day,' the young man replied. 'Summer job, you know. I'm Jean-Claude.'

'Jacqueline,' she replied, holding out her hand.

131

Jean-Claude took her hand into his and squeezed it lightly, looking intently at her. 'I'm supposed to tell you to leave now so I can lock up the building.'

'I know, I know,' Jacqueline sighed. 'I just always enjoy the last few moments after everybody else has left. It's so quiet and peaceful up here, and I love looking down over the city when the light starts to fade. It's as if the city belonged just to me, in a strange sort of way.'

'Of course, I could let you stay for a while,' Jean-Claude suggested. 'I'd just have to go downstairs and lock the doors.'

'Can you really do that?' Jacqueline asked, genuine surprise in her voice.

'Nobody told me that I couldn't,' Jean-Claude replied. 'Besides, I'm the one with the keys, so it's highly unlikely that anyone would come and check.'

'That would be really wonderful,' Jacqueline enthused. 'I've never been up here at night. Could you really?'

'Just give me a few minutes,' Jean-Claude said. With that, he disappeared down the stairs and Jacqueline found herself all alone atop Notre Dame again, free to wander around the balustrade. She took in everything she could, imprinting as many details as she could on her fertile, ever-active, mind and storing everything away for a possible painting when she was working in her studio.

She didn't just sketch. That was basically her bread-and-butter. She also painted, and that was her passion, the real expression of her soul, that which was giving true meaning to her life. She was quite successful with that as well, selling her work at a small art gallery on a regular basis and getting better known all the time.

Footsteps coming up the stairs interrupted her reverie. Jean-Claude stepped up beside her and they stood in silence for a while.

'I saw you sketching this afternoon,' Jean-Claude confessed. 'I was up here a few times to make sure everybody was all right and there weren't too many people on the balustrade. You're very good, you know.'

'Why, thank you,' Jacqueline replied coyly. 'I like what I do. And you? What do you do, when you're not working at a summer job?'

'I'm at the Sorbonne,' Jean-Claude confided in her. 'Philosophy.'

'I love philosophy,' Jacqueline enthused. 'I took a couple of course a few years ago. I love Kierkegaard, in particular. I was really able to get into his writing. He has some really wonderful things to say about the stages on life's way and the process of individual growth and development.'

'He does, indeed. He's one of my favourite philosophers, too, for much the same reasons,' Jean-Claude agreed. 'And Jean-Paul Sartre, of course.'

'Of course,' Jacqueline said. 'If you're studying philosophy. He was always too difficult for me, so I didn't learn an awful lot about him.'

'He is difficult,' Jean-Claude agreed. 'But well worthwhile once you get past the basics and really get your teeth into his work. Maybe sometime we could get together and talk existentialism.'

'Maybe we could,' Jacqueline said. She turned towards the city again and leaned on the balustrade with her arms folded in front of her.

Jean-Claude tentatively put his arm around her shoulder and gently pulled her towards him. Without hesitation, she leaned against him and put her arm around his waist. For a moment neither of them moved, Jacqueline mulling over in her head just what she wanted to do and what might come of it. He was quite a bit younger than she was, and she usually preferred somewhat older men. Yet the idea of being way up here above the city and in complete solitude and silence was definitely very tempting. And she did love sex, sometimes to a fault.

She had a long-standing relationship with a man considerably older than her and she liked that a lot, but she didn't feel any kind of deep emotional connection with him. His name was Luc and he was out of town on business quite a bit, so she didn't see him all that often. When they did get together, they always had a lot to talk about and they always cooked sumptuous suppers together, in her apartment or in his, and usually shared more than just one bottle of wine.

Afterwards, they always had excellent sex, in a comfortable and familiar sort of way. He was an experienced lover, always treating her with great tenderness and respect, and knew exactly what she wanted and wanted to do. It was he who showed her how to become a multi-orgasmic woman way back, when she first met him in an art class, and he was the teacher, in more ways than one, as it turned out.

But she needed more. She needed variety and excitement. She needed short-term relationships that provided her with good sex, stroked her psyche, and made her feel good about herself. Now she was faced with one of those decisions again, but she simply told herself that sex was sex and she wanted it now. It would certainly be a first for her, way up here where they were.

No sooner had she formulated her last thought than she turned to Jean-Claude and put her arms around him. He smiled, pleased with the development, and wrapped his arms around her, pulling her close. From then on, it wasn't a matter of thoughts or ideas or decisions any more. It was simply a physical coming together of two people who wanted each other and delighted in each other's bodies.

Jean-Claude proved to be a surprisingly good kisser, nibbling her lips expertly, probing her with his tongue, sucking at hers until her knees wobbled and she had to hold on to him so as not to buckle in his arms. She loved being kissed like that, forcefully and with determination and passion, and she thoroughly enjoyed the time he spent on their initial kiss.

She gasped with delight when he put his hand on her breast and started rubbing and stroking it through her blouse, fondling her nipple until it stood out from her round breast. Before she knew it, he had unbuttoned her blouse, sliding it off over her shoulders, and reached behind her to undo her bra. She sighed when he put his hands on her smooth, soft breasts, held them for a while in his palms as if weighing them, caressed them with expert fingers and palms, tracing their outlines and contours like a real connoisseur. To her delight he suddenly seemed much older than he really was.

She felt incredibly good, being fondled like that high above her city, high above in the darkness with the city below bathed in light, the gargoyles perched ominously above them. She was sure they were watching them and delighting in their activities. The knowledge of their silent presence and their stone eyes only served to heighten her arousal. She quickly pulled off her jeans and undid his shirt while he unzipped his trousers. Then she reached for his shorts and pulled them down over his legs, releasing his stiff penis. He, in turn, hooked his fingers into her briefs and pulled them down over her legs as well, then went on his knees to kiss her pubic hair and send delicious shivers up and down her spine.

They quickly spread out their clothes on the stone floor and were lying naked beside each other in no time. They were breathing heavily, excitedly, sighing and moaning as they grabbed hold of each other and pressed their hot bodies together. Although they could hardly wait to get to the real thing, they kept fondling and caressing each other at great length. His penis was growing and hardening against her legs, her pussy tingling with excitement and getting wetter by the minute, her breasts aching with desire.

The gargoyles watched in silence when he went down on her. She spread her legs as wide as she could and pulled up her knees to give him the best exposure and access to her quivering pussy. He worked wonders with his tongue on her swelling lips until she thought she could no longer contain herself. Obviously enjoying himself immensely, he continued licking and sucking her. When he reached her clit with his tongue, he pulled her lips apart with his fingers, and worked his magic until she shuddered and screamed with her first orgasm came under the open sky, shaking her to the core. And still he licked her and sucked her until her second orgasm rushed through her, tantalizing her mind, her soul, setting her already hot body on fire. She screamed her intense pleasure into the night air and dug her fingers into his back.

Only then did he emerge from between her legs and climb up on top of her to penetrate her with a forceful, determined thrust that sent more delightful tremors through her body. He thrust in and out of her with his youthful exuberance until she trembled through yet another orgasm and he gushed into her at the exact same time. Lying lifelessly on top of her, he groaned his own pleasure into her ear, making her feel exceedingly good and proud of herself.

She dropped her legs back down onto the stones and flung her arms out in pure ecstasy, crucifix-like under the stars and the rising moon. She hadn't felt quite like this in a long time, probably, she thought, because she was out in the open and the whole situation was so forbidden and just dangerous enough to provide her with a special thrill.

'Wow!' Jean-Claude exclaimed as he rolled off her. 'That was the best sex I've ever had. You were fantastic!'

'You were pretty good yourself,' Jacqueline moaned. 'I'm really glad you suggested this. I wouldn't have wanted to miss this for anything in the world.'

'I'm glad,' Jean-Claude gasped, trying to get his breath back.

They lay quietly beside each other, basking in the afterglow of their orgasms, lost in their own thoughts.

'We probably should be going soon,' Jean-Claude finally broke the silence. 'I have to be here again in the morning to open up.'

'It is getting late,' Jacqueline agreed. She stood up and put her clothes back on.

'Will you be back?' Jean-Claude asked as he put on his own clothes.

'I'm always back,' Jacqueline replied cryptically, winking at him conspiratorially. She picked up her carrying case and her folding seat and waited for him to lead the way.

They kissed once more when they stepped out of the cathedral, then went off in their own directions to get to their respective abodes. Jacqueline walked leisurely along the familiar streets, letting the evening's event play itself out in her mind, smiling all the while. She wondered whether she would really see him again and, if she did, whether she would want to repeat their encounter. But it had been a most enjoyable and liberating experience, and maybe, just maybe, she would want to repeat it at some other time. She would give it some more thought before making up her mind.

Taking her time on her way home, she finally reached her spacious flat on the top floor of an old building in Montmartre. The building was fairly high up on the hill and afforded her a panoramic view of the city. Large curtainless windows provided her with ample light for her painting, and she could move her various easels freely around the room to get the best illumination for whatever she happened to be doing. She had been lucky to find an ideal home like it for herself and considered herself very fortunate to be living in a place like this.

Coming home so late after a busy day of sketching, she decided to let herself sleep in the next morning and stay at home for the day. When she was feeling more energetic again, she started to work on a large canvass of various gargoyles in black and gray against a background of a red sky with ominously dark clouds. She wanted to capture the mystery of the sculptures, balancing the positive and the negative, imbuing the monstrous creatures with mystery and intrigue.

It rained for the next couple of days and she made good use of her inability to be outside sketching by working on the painting until she had all the elements and the colours exactly the way she wanted them. It was a lot of work, but she managed to finish the painting to her complete satisfaction. As soon as the paint was completely dry, she would take it to the art gallery where her other paintings were on exhibit and enjoyed considerable success with tourists as well as with local buyers.

When the rain stopped and the city was cleansed and

sparkling again, she took her carrying case and headed down the hill to one of her favourite streets. It was an old, narrow street, with several sidewalk cafés on both sides. She found herself an empty table, ordered a coffee, and placed her sketch pad and charcoal on the small round table she had selected. Then she focused her attention on the sidewalk café across the street and started to sketch.

Sometimes she liked to pick out individuals on her own side or across the street to add to the collection of portraits she later used in paintings. On this particular day, she decided to sketch the whole café with all the patrons sitting in the sunlight. She was busily sketching away, capturing the atmosphere and the personalities, when she noticed out of the corner of her eye that a young man had sat down a couple of tables away from her and was watching her intently.

She looked up from her sketch. The young man smiled at her.

'May I see?' he asked, quite bluntly, she thought. 'I'm a bit of an aficionado and I'd really like to see what you're doing.'

'It's not finished yet,' Jacqueline protested. 'I only started a little while ago.'

'I like seeing works in progress,' the young man countered. 'I won't say anything negative about it.'

'Oh, all right, then,' Jacqueline relented.

The young man rose from his table and came to sit at hers, across from her.

'I'm Henri,' he introduced himself. He seemed nice enough, probably a bit older than her but not by much, dressed in a smart business suit with matching tie and shoes. And he was very attractive, with a striking face and obviously professionally styled light-brown hair.

'Jacqueline,' she replied, holding out her hand.

139

He took her hand in his and pressed his lips against it. '*Enchanté*,' he smiled.

She couldn't help laughing. Nobody had ever done that to her or greeted her like that, but she quickly covered up and shoved her sketch pad across the table. There was something very likeable and intriguing about him, something that stirred up deep feelings in her. After all, she hadn't had sex since Jean-Claude, and she found herself starting to get very turned on by his presence.

He looked at her sketch for the longest time, glanced across the street at the reality, looked at the sketch again.

'Excellent,' he finally said. 'You're very talented.'

She liked him better by the minute. 'You're too kind,' she smiled coquettishly.

'What are you planning to do with it?' Henri wanted to know.

'I'm not sure yet,' Jacqueline replied. 'I'll have to see what it looks like when I'm finished with it.'

'Yes, of course,' Henri said quickly. 'I didn't mean to pry.'

'You're not prying,' Jacqueline protested. 'I'm just not sure what I want to do with it. Some of my sketches of street scenes I take home and make them into paintings. Others I sell to the patrons. There's always somebody there who wants to buy an original sketch with them in it.'

'I can believe that,' Henri acquiesced. 'I would certainly buy it if I were in it.'

'Why don't you go across the street, then,' Jacqueline suggested. 'I'll sketch you in, if you'd like.'

'Would you really?' Henri enthused. 'I'd like that very much.'

He found an empty table across the street, waited for the waitress to bring him a cup of coffee, and struck a pose, smiling broadly at her.

She laughed gleefully. Her morning was progressing much more interestingly than she had expected.

Moving her sketch pad to her side of the table again, she finished the backdrop of the café's façade and the other patrons on Henri's sides, then concentrated on him and his appealing features and demeanour. She ordered another coffee to keep her going, but it didn't take her nearly as long as she had thought it would. Or maybe she just lost track of time, being able to look at him freely across the street as much as she wanted.

Then she was done. She waved to him and he quickly came back to her table. He picked up her sketch pad before even sitting down and studied it intently. He held it up at different distances from his eyes, turned it into various positions in the sun, studied it some more. Jacqueline was getting rather impatient. She could hardly wait to find out what he thought.

Henri sat down, put the sketch pad on the table in front of her, and looked at her with his sparkling blue eyes.

'This is just excellent!' he finally exclaimed. 'You really are good. And you said you sometimes make these into paintings?'

'Sometimes,' Jacqueline agreed. 'But, as I said, some of them I sell as soon as they are done. Would you like to buy this? I'll sign it and date it for you.'

'Actually,' Henri said, leaning across the table towards her. 'Actually I think I would prefer to have a painting of this. Do you think that could be arranged?'

'Anything can be arranged,' Jacqueline replied. 'A painting it going to be much more expensive, you realize that.'

'I didn't ask about the price,' Henri simply said. 'Where do you live?'

'I have a studio up in Montmartre,' Jacqueline offered.

'That's not very far,' Henri stated. 'Why don't we go there now and I can watch you paint. I'll pose for you some more, if you'd like, so you can get some more detail.'

She hadn't expected this. She usually took several days to work on a painting like that, and she had never had anybody watch her doing it. Nor had any of the patrons ever offered to pose for her. Her sidewalk café paintings were more general views of the cafés with the patrons more suggestions of colour than distinct individuals. She wasn't very sure at all about this, yet she couldn't help thinking how nice it would be to spend the afternoon with him and working on the painting with somebody watching who seemed to know what he was talking about.

'All right, then,' she answered after a moment's hesitation. 'If that's really what you want to do.'

'Yes, I really do,' Henri answered firmly. He put some money down on the table to pay for the coffees and rose from his chair.

Jacqueline packed up her things and they walked up to her flat. Henri was quite impressed with her living quarters when she led him inside. He walked around the whole place, looked out the windows with great interest, and finally came to her paintings. She was a bit embarrassed. Some of the paintings she kept around were experiments that hadn't quite reached their final state yet. Others were half-finished because she didn't know yet what to do with them. All her good paintings were either sold or waiting to be sold at the gallery, with the exception of the gargoyle painting from a few days ago.

Henri looked carefully at everything, nodded now and then, went back to something that seemed to have caught his eyes, ending at the gargoyle painting.

'This is fabulous!' he exclaimed. 'I've never seen

anything quite this powerful and persuasive. You must really like gargoyles and admire them a great deal.'

'They mean a lot to me,' Jacqueline admitted. 'I've done several in the past, but they've all been sold. I think this is my best one so far.'

'No doubt,' Henri agreed. 'Would you let me buy this from you?'

Jacqueline's mouth dropped open. She'd never had an offer like that for any of her paintings. She brought them to the gallery and they looked after everything. She didn't even know what she could ask for something like that without going through the gallery.

'I don't know,' she said weakly. 'I've never done this before.'

'First time for everything,' Henri quipped. He reached into his pocket, pulled out a wad of bills, and started counting them out on the table. Jacqueline couldn't believe her eyes. 'Do you think this would be enough?'

'Oh, I would definitely think so,' she said. 'But why this? And why me?'

'I really like the painting,' Henri said. 'And I really like you.'

He stepped away from the table, walked towards her, and put his arms around her. 'Shall we seal the deal with a kiss?'

Jacqueline was too overwhelmed by the unexpected development to say anything. She just knew that she had made a big sale, perhaps the biggest in her career, and that a very attractive and sexy man held her in his arms and wanted to kiss her. She leaned into his embrace and closed her eyes.

His lips were firm and determined against hers. She gasped, then reciprocated the pressure, opening her mouth to let his tongue slide in, and flung her arms around him in a sudden flurry of emotions. Her whole body went limp in his arms, but he kept her pressed against him and kept kissing her deeply and passionately while she rubbed herself against him and tried to keep up with his probing kiss.

When he let go of her, she led him into her bedroom. They immediately began to undress each other, very slowly and meticulously so as not to miss anything. As the garments fell to the floor one by one, they let their hands glide over their bodies, discovering each other, learning each other. Henri took her breasts into his hands and methodically, carefully, massaged them for her until they were full and round and the nipples stood straight up. He definitely knew what he was doing.

Not to be outdone, she reached for his penis and started rubbing and stroking it lightly, pulling the foreskin back and exposing the damp head. He groaned, deeply, passionately, then reached for her pussy and began to let his forefinger travel along the lips, between the lips, up to her clit, but just for a delicious moment, then down again to her opening and the freely flowing juices. He removed his hand, brought it up to his mouth, and licked her juices off his finger.

Then he put his finger back into the wet opening, brought his hand back up, and held his finger out to her to lick it herself. She was ecstatic. She couldn't stop moaning and sighing from the way he played her body, found all her most sensitive spots, lingered here, lingered there, and they weren't even in bed yet. He reached around her, took her buttocks into his strong hands, and practically lifted her off the floor in his attempt to get her body closer to his.

And then all the clothes were on the floor and they stood naked in front of each other, finding great pleasure in the visual delight of seeing each other like that.

'You're very beautiful,' Henri whispered. 'And very sexy, too.'

'You're very handsome,' Jacqueline replied, whispering herself because that seemed the right thing to do. 'And,' she smiled, 'very sexy yourself.'

'Well,' Henri said. 'Now that we have that established and out of the way, how about going on the bed instead of standing here beside it?'

They climbed on the bed together and made themselves comfortable beside each other. Henri slid one arm under her back to hold her close to him, then put a hand on her breast to caress and titillate it some more. Tracing her contours and her lines with his fingers, he described concentric circles on her breast, working his way slowly towards the centre and her jutting nipple.

Jacqueline was just lying there, basking in the detailed attention he was paying to her body, enjoying every caress, every movement, every touch. Without letting go of her breast, he bent over her and started to kiss her soft white globe, licking her smooth skin with his tongue, working towards the nipple again. She gasped when he took it into his mouth, ran his tongue around it, and began sucking at it greedily, hungrily, until it was big and hard in his mouth.

Then he moved his hand down to her pussy again, parted her lips with his fingers, and sent them on a detailed exploration of all her wonderful, exceedingly arousing parts. She could only moan and groan as his ministrations sent currents of electricity up and down her body, into her mind, into her soul. She was flooded with the most incredible sensations, he was so good at manipulating her and managing her body. She felt reduced to a bundle of extremely sensitive nerves, floating on the wonderful rush of orgasmic delights surging through her and filling her every fibre, every nerve.

Her body was trembling uncontrollably by the time he finally let go of her, climbed on top, and slid into her effortlessly and calmly yet with purposeful force and determination. Her orgasms were still surging through her when she felt him coming inside her and she felt she would never have enough of him.

Yet it all did come to an end, amid yelling and screaming and groaning and moaning and they knew that they had satisfied each other on the deepest level of their beings, that they had touched each other in the most hidden recesses of their psyches.

They finally fell apart and stretched out on the bed, feeling luscious and satiated through and through. They didn't talk, only gasped for breath and waited for their hearts to slow down. At one point, Henri turned on his side, put an arm around her, and took her burning breast back into his hand. She sighed contentedly as he smiled at her with a deeply satisfied look on his face.

Jacqueline briefly thought of Jean-Claude and their escapade on Notre Dame, but as satisfying and pleasurable as that had been, being with Henri was a far deeper and much more emotional experience. It was definitely better, she thought leisurely, than being with Luc. Yet she also knew she would never stop seeing him and being with him, any more than she would stop going to the gargoyles, to the sidewalk cafés, and perhaps even to Jean-Claude. All the men in her life and all of those things were integral parts of her life and contributed in no small measure to her continued growth and development along the path she had chosen for herself.

She couldn't wait to start on the painting, with Henri

sitting among the other patrons in the sidewalk café. Perhaps she would do a portrait of him as well, one she would keep for herself, to remember him. It might well take her a few days of having Henri in her studio before she would be able to complete everything. She was already delirious with anticipation, and they weren't even out of bed yet. Life was definitely good, and progressing much to her delight.

About the Story

ONE OF THE MOST memorable experiences of my young adulthood, when I was still living in Switzerland, was my weeklong visit to Paris with my girlfriend. Having travelled extensively in other European countries and cities, and having heard and read so much about my latest destination, I was thrilled to finally see and experience the queen of all cities in all its splendour for myself. It was a beautiful summer, ideal for a leisurely visit, and the city was alive with tourists as well as with plenty of Parisians who chose to spend the summer in the city. We made the best use of the relatively short time we had available by visiting as many landmarks and attractions as we possibly could, including, of course, the Eiffel Tower, Montmartre, the Marché des Puces, the promenade along the Seine.

The definite highlight of one of our days in the city was the visit to Notre Dame and its famous gallery of ominous gargoyles carved of stone and surrounding the top of the cathedral. We could see the whole magnificent city spread out below us, just as the gargoyles in their infinite silence could and have for hundreds of years. Gargoyles as symbols of ancient wisdom and constant vigilance have held a special place in my life ever since and they keep creeping into my writing every now and then. I still have a black-and-white photograph I took with one of my first cameras during that visit hanging on the wall beside my computer desk. I managed to capture one of the more striking gargoyles crouched atop Notre Dame in the foreground and overlooking the Seine with two of its bridges down below and the Eiffel Tower in the distance. It was that photograph that I have kept over all these years, together with my still very vivid memories of the romantic atmosphere and the ancient monuments and buildings and streets, that inspired the setting and prompted me to write this story about the beautiful city of love and light.

Some Virgins Learn Quickly
by Toni Sands

AT LE BOURGET I claimed my suitcase as if greeting an old friend. The arrivals hall was an ant heap as I faced the next hurdle of the journey. My first real live gendarme walked by, dressed exactly as I'd seen in pictures, but face flushed and shiny as if he'd been somewhere he shouldn't.

That certain smell would for the rest of my life remain the French smell: a mix of tobacco, garlic and hubbub. At the time it was exciting and also scary. I was just eighteen years of age. Teenager or young woman? I thought I was a young woman. I'd have scorned anyone who suggested anything else but now I look back I realise how gauche I was when I flew to Paris Easter '67 to meet my pen friend.

There was no sign of Jeannine in the concourse. I'd scrutinised her photograph so many times I imagined the pretty, plump girl with dark eyes, mischievous grin, and scribble of curly black hair would be unmissable. I raked the crowds with my eyes. My hands were clammy and I was a little queasy from my first ever flight. My ears still felt stuffed with cotton wool as I searched for a scarlet jacket.

'Mademoiselle Carr?' A tall man approached. 'Are you Helen Carr?' His words were softened by a polite smile.

Then he held out a photograph. The slender teenager captured by the camera smiled back at me from beneath the lilac tree in our garden back home. Suddenly I didn't want that person to intrude on the moment. But the anxious-not-to-look-anxious, crumpled child-woman, dressed in a trench coat and marooned in the soulless surroundings of an unfamiliar airport must have had something about her for the Frenchman to recognise. I wasn't as fashion-conscious as Jeannine and hadn't decided what clothes to travel in when I wrote that last letter, confirming travel details.

I smiled back at the stranger but, uncertain what was going on, made no move to greet him, shake hands or even speak. Jeannine had said she would meet me then we'd go into the city for lunch and a little exploration. She wrote of taking the Metro to her uncle and aunt's apartment which was where we would stay two nights before the long train journey south. *Mon oncle Emile et sa femme Adrienne*, Jeannine wrote, are *sympathique*. I knew this meant they were likeable, pleasant people.

Her uncle was certainly patient. 'I bring papers to identify myself.' He handed me my own photo and fumbled in a pocket. 'I am Emile Clement. The uncle of Jeannine.' His passport revealed no particular likeness to my pen friend but the name fitted. I wondered why this man had my photo in his possession.

'But where is she?' I asked. 'Where is Jeannine? I don't understand how you have my photograph.'

He nodded. 'My niece is what you English call scatter-brained. I think her parents insist she send it to us, in case of any problem.'

'Does this mean my holiday's off?'

'Of course not. Jeannine missed her connection to

151

Paris. She does not arrive until eight o'clock tonight at Gare de Lyon. I know you have journeyed from Oxford to catch your flight from Heathrow. Let me take your suitcase.'

He bent to pick it up. I caught a whiff of cologne. The unexpected fragrance hit my nostrils and I was startled by my reaction. My father always smelled of carbolic soap. My brother smelled like an apprentice mechanic unless my mother made him wash. My Latin teacher's aura was that of old tweed and leather.

A man who smelled delicious was uncharted territory. I had read of so many things still not experienced, but this was an erotic moment. There was no mistaking the jolt I felt. It was at the same time disturbing yet exciting.

I remembered my manners. 'Thank you, monsieur.'

'Emile. Please call me Emile. I hope I may call you Helen?'

We walked to his car. It was my first time on French soil. Every step I took seemed to distance me further from home and closer to the throbbing heart of Paris. How many times had I read about the city? How many books by French authors had I studied? How many occasions did I wish the language would slip from my lips as effortlessly as it did from the lips of the mademoiselle attached to our school to improve our oral skills? She pronounced my name the French way, but it was the first time I'd heard it spoken by a man whose first language wasn't English.

Emile stopped beside a black Citroen. Took out his key and unlocked the boot to stow my case. Then he went round to the front and opened the door, waiting for me, beaming. I hesitated then realised of course the driver's seat was the opposite side from cars at home. My cheeks burned and I felt stupid. Emile said nothing. I settled myself into the passenger seat, tugging my skirt over my knees. As he drove away I shot swift glances at his profile. He didn't look as old as I'd imagined he'd be.

The apartment was in a tall house with dark green shutters. The residential row overlooked a park in an area my parents would have called a nice neighbourhood. Emile unlocked the front door and gestured for me to enter.

'We are on the first floor,' he said. 'Pardon. I go ahead of you.'

I followed him up the stairs. He might have been a stranger to me but he was part of my pen friend's life. Yet I still felt slightly disorientated. Wished Jeannine hadn't missed her train. His manners were beautiful, but he made me feel edgy. Not that there was anything in the least alarming about him: far from it. He was clean-shaven and wore a dark suit, tie, and white shirt. Just as if he'd abandoned his desk in some anonymous officc or bank in the commercial quarter to come and meet me. He was broad-shouldered yet lithe. Looking back to that first day in the city of my dreams, I know now it was not just his Frenchness that fascinated me.

'I hope I'm not interrupting your day too much.' I waited for his wife to appear.

But Emile put down my case and shook his head. 'Not at all. Make yourself at home. Shall we have coffee?'

He opened one of the doors leading off the tiny hallway and I walked into a sitting-room. The window overlooked the trees opposite and I gazed down at an ornamental pond in the park and benches with people sitting on them. It was a mild April day. Old men played boules. It was everyday Paris for everyone except me.

The chair I chose to sit on was so soft it sighed around

me. A polished table stood on a circular black rug in the middle of the room but the floor beneath my feet was bare wood. Faded wallpaper peeped from behind a collage of framed pictures, most of them city scenes. I recognised the Arc de Triomphe and the Eiffel Tower. There were prints by Degas. There were pen and ink sketches, achingly simple. They seemed to me to contain the soul of the city I already loved. Paris was a siren, calling me to explore its scents and sounds. I was ready for adventure and, although I didn't acknowledge it, my body was calling the shots as surely as the mantelpiece clock ticked away the seconds.

The smell of coffee drifted from the kitchen. Emile returned, carrying a tall pot and a jug of milk. He placed both on the table and retraced his steps to collect a tray of food. '*Voilà*,' he said. 'A picnic. I am sorry my wife is not returned from her work yet. Tonight she will make delicious dinner for us all.'

I joined him at the table. There was a dish of what appeared to be wizened sausages.

He saw my expression. 'Garlic sausage. Tastier than it looks.'

The crisp French stick and dish of creamy butter appealed more, though the black olives were alien. I pulled out a chair and Emile placed before me a glass containing a measure of colourless liquid.

'Calvados. It is apple brandy. You look a little fatigued. This is your first time in an aeroplane?'

I nodded. Picked up the glass and sniffed. The smell stole my breath but I wanted to savour everything about France.

Emile nodded encouragement. '*A la votre*,' he said.

I repeated the toast. Mademoiselle had taught us this one. But she hadn't prepared us for such a kickback. My first sip crackled down my throat. Fiery fingers clawed at every part of my body.

Emile chuckled. 'Two firsts in one day,' he said. The words seemed to hang in the air.

He sat down opposite me. I took another swallow of the spirit and this time the hit was a gentle buzz. Suddenly my angora cardigan was too warm. I undid the few buttons I'd fastened and wriggled my arms out of the soft wool. I hung the garment on the back of my chair and turned to pick up my glass again. Emile seemed frozen. He'd been buttering a chunk of bread when I began removing my top layer. Now, looking at him across the table, I saw how his eyes had changed colour ... changed from light grey to granite.

I tried to ignore the throbbing between my thighs. I'd had crushes on boys and been kissed by a few but I was still a virgin. No one had ventured above my stocking tops though there'd been attempts. At bedtime, my own faltering efforts at masturbation were always self-conscious and left me yearning, feeling there must be something better. If anyone had asked me how I felt at that moment I would have had to say I felt excited not just by the alcohol but by the realisation that this man found me attractive. All of a sudden I wasn't just an English schoolgirl treading the traditional path to improve her examination grade. All of a sudden I was on the brink of something. I didn't know it at the time but I was empowered.

He passed me the dish of olives. I bit into one and shuddered. He laughed and poured me a glass of water. I drank it greedily. He cut a sliver of Brie and placed it on my plate. He got up and went over to the sideboard, returning with a bunch of black grapes. He stood, broke off a cluster and bent to put them beside the cheese. His proximity was almost unbearable. I felt his masculinity as something tangible, something to push away or something to welcome. As I struggled with my emotions, he plucked a single grape from the sprig and held it to my lips. His fingers brushing my cheek sent an electric shock straight to my core.

We ate in silence. My taste buds were stimulated as never before. The Brie tasted wonderful and the fruit luscious and sweet. I drained my glass then sipped coffee darker and stronger than anything I'd drunk at home.

'Would you like to take a walk?'

'I could go to the park. Really, I can quite easily amuse myself if you have things to do.'

Those granite eyes didn't meet mine this time. They were focused elsewhere. I remembered that without the pale blue cardigan the outline of my bra was obvious under my white blouse. My mother always frowned when I wore this particular garment. But, I took a very deep breath, conscious of my breasts rising and pushing against the sedate fabric. The pulse between my thighs was really quite strong now.

He got up from the table. Abruptly. Cleared his throat. Reached for the cigarettes he'd placed on the mantelpiece. 'Do you mind if I …?'

'I don't mind.'

When I pulled my cardigan back on, this time I turned my back to him. He picked up my coat and helped me into it.

We walked towards one of the bridges crossing the Seine. I don't remember which. I was counting the hours until this torture was over. I was a shy eighteen-year-old with an imagination too vivid for her body to contain. My mind was painting pictures of something which I'd wondered about for so long, but had not dreamt would ever taunt me so. Emile seemed preoccupied. He stopped near an ice cream kiosk and asked me if I'd like a cornet.

My eyes wandered over the sweet biscuit cones and I wondered if he was trying to ground me in childhood. I didn't want to blur the strong coffee and tangy schnapps with vanilla or strawberry flavours. So I refused but thanked him nicely in French.

We walked towards a row of shops. The first window contained works of art. There was a painting of a man and woman, naked. Her leg shielded the part of the male anatomy that fascinated me. Embarrassed, I looked away. Emile took my arm and my heart seemed to pound against my ribs.

'Look, what do you see now?'

But he wasn't looking at the paintings. It was within view: the Eiffel Tower thrusting skywards, angular, and to my surprise a little rusty. I was seeing it for real and all I could think about was the way his knuckles grazed my breast when he grasped my arm.

I pulled myself together. 'It's a dream come true, seeing something I've always wanted to see. This whole trip is dreamlike.'

He didn't immediately reply. He seemed almost to struggle for words. 'Tomorrow you and Jeannine can spend all day sightseeing.'

The sky had been steadily darkening. Now raindrops splashed on the pavements. I pulled the belt of my coat tighter. My mother's words returned to me. *You should have travelled in something with a hood.*

'Come on. I know a short cut.'

Emile held out his hand and I grabbed it. We ran down an alley, rain bursting from the sky, hitting our faces and drenching our hair. The bridge was within view. We pounded across, ran until I got a stitch and cried out for him to stop. I bent double and when I stood up again, he lifted his hand and brushed my dripping fringe from my eyes.

'Two minutes and we are home,' he said. I wanted to suck his voice inside me and keep it there.

The apartment seeped garlic-laced warmth. Emile hung up my coat in the kitchen and brought me a towel so I could dry my hair. I kicked off my shoes and wished I could peel off my stockings.

He seemed to read my mind. 'Use the spare bedroom. I will show you. This is where you and Jeannine will sleep while you are our guests. And I shall bring you a gown.' He hesitated. 'Paris has not been very hospitable today. You should get out of those clothes so we can dry them in front of the gas fire.'

In the bedroom with the pink ruffled counterpanes and the gaudy-faced rag dolls perched on pillows, I began to remove my clothing. My shoes and stockings were sodden. The front of my slip and of my skirt was damp but my cardigan and cotton blouse were fine so I hung them on a chair back. I kept on my pants and bra, but bit my lip as I looked down and saw how prominent my nipples were. I picked up the towelling gown and pulled it on, securing the belt so the fabric tightened over my breasts, heightening my feeling of longing and not knowing quite what to do about it.

I unwound the towel from my hair and ran my fingers through the tangled blonde curls. I was going to look such a mess. Suddenly I felt shy. Did Emile mean that I should stay in the bedroom until my clothes were dry? I had plenty of spare things in my suitcase.

My thoughts were interrupted by a discreet knock.

'Come in,' I called.

He left the door open behind him. His eyes were troubled. 'I am so sorry to have got you caught in the rain. I hope you won't catch cold.'

'I'm used to getting caught in the rain. I'm British.' My nervous giggle died in my throat.

Because Emile did something I shall never, ever forget. He walked towards me and took one of my hands between his. He turned my hand over, hesitated a moment then bent his head and kissed my palm, right in the centre.

I trembled. I didn't know how to deal with this man. But my instinct was to wait and see what happened. He raised his head then he put both hands on my hips and drew me towards him. I moved as if wrapped in satin. My body and brain were lulled in a delicious stupor, bathing me in its rosy glow.

His lips on mine were cool and soft. He didn't let them linger long before he began scattering tiny kisses over my throat so I threw back my head, arching my back. One of his hands moved, pushing gently inside the towelling gown, his touch soft as swansdown on my skin. With his other hand he loosened my belt and his lips moved lower still so they kissed the swell of my breasts.

'It is good?' His voice caressed me.

I must have made some small sound. I was incapable of coherent speech.

He crooned as if reassuring me that if I should tell him so, he would immediately stop. But I didn't want him to stop. His hands unclasped my bra. His mouth moved to my left nipple. As his lips and tongue sent tremors through me, I thrust myself closer, as if trying to disappear inside him. He chuckled. *'Ma belle petite,'* I think he said.

Looking back, I realise how skilled he was. Just one

159

finger of his other hand touched my right breast. With just one finger, Emile circled the aureole relentlessly, round and round until I cried out, unable to bear the delicious agony. At once his tongue latched on to my hungry nipple, licking and flicking and sucking before he took it between his lips, gently nibbling the swollen bud with his teeth.

I shuddered then, giddy with wanting. He swept me up in his arms and laid me gently on one of the narrow single beds. I still wore my pants and my borrowed gown though it gaped open.

'We should remove these,' he whispered. But he waited for me to do so. At no time did he force the pace. There was an unspoken acceptance that I was in command and I knew that should he go away from me, I would be bereft. I wanted this to happen.

I wriggled out of my knickers and robe. He turned away from me then and I closed my eyes, hearing the rustle of clothing. Then he was beside me, pushing a towel under me, murmuring something, teasing my mouth with his tongue and making me feel as if all my nerve endings were aflame.

When he began stroking my thighs I was floating somewhere outside myself. But the feel of his fingertips drumming my warm wet place, marooned me in a magic circle where only he and I existed. He murmured something in his own language but I missed it. My body seemed to have taken over from my brain. My eyes were closed and my hips moved, rhythmically grinding my bum into the mattress. If he had asked me whether he should stop at that point, he would surely have realised I was beyond stopping. If he had sudden scruples about whether or not I was a virgin then that was of no account. I trusted him totally and utterly to finish what we had begun.

His hands were busy elsewhere now. I heard him open the packet. Curiosity opened my eyes as he sat on the side of the bed. Then he was astride me. The touch of his mouth on mine was urgent. His tongue probed as his hand moved between my legs and I felt one then two fingers slipping inside me. I moved against him and he groaned.

'You are like velvet. I'll be gentle. I promise.'

He moved his hand away and I felt the silky tip of him nudge me. Inexperienced as I was, I reached for him, marvelled at this rock-hard thing smooth in my hand: about to enter my intimate regions. It wasn't too late if I decided I didn't want this. But suddenly the scenes in *Lady Chatterley's Lover* that we sixth formers had giggled over and discussed at great length, curious about size and sensation, suddenly they made sense. I too knew desire. I too needed to feel a man inside me. And it was happening.

Emile was working me. The tip of his shaft probed then progressed a little further. His body was angled so that as he moved, he massaged my flesh. The sensation was warm and I was aching down there; a dull, sweet pang. But there was a barrier. He retreated slightly and I sensed his hesitation.

'No, no,' I clutched him, pulling him closer. 'Go on, Emile. I want you to. I want you to take me.'

He gasped as he penetrated further. I tried not to tense myself against what was about to end my girlhood but as the gateway yielded and the sharp pain sliced, I cried out. Then as he filled me utterly and entirely I relaxed beneath him, feeling his excitement mount. It seemed I need do nothing other than wait. I felt slippery. I felt a kind of triumph. But I also felt a kind of disappointment. Was this all there was?

His movements quickened. His breathing changed and there was an urgency I couldn't match. The thrusts were shorter now. Rapid. When he cried out, I wondered what, if anything, I should do next.

Emile raised his head, smiled at me and gently pushed my hair back from my face. He whispered, 'Wait a moment.' Then he left me for only moments. When he returned, he held a tube of something which he unscrewed. Kneeling beside me, he parted my pussy lips. After the first shocked moment of coldness I relaxed, moaning and writhing; closing my eyes; arching my back as he pushed some kind of gel inside me. His fingers circled, circled and stroked, caressing and rubbing my swollen lips and my clitoris, finally focusing on that tight concealed bud whose potential I hadn't quite mastered.

I was tightening my muscles, riding the spasms, calling out to him. If there were neighbours listening behind the walls then I could not have cared less. All I cared about was reaching that magic pinnacle.

As I shuddered against his hand, joy and accomplishment closed my eyes and I could not keep myself from smiling.

'*Ma petite*,' I heard him murmur. 'I have unlocked your treasures. You do me a great honour.'

I was in my mid-thirties when I returned to Paris, this time with a special boyfriend. Rob was nothing if not a romantic. We'd held hands in the taxi, watching the lights of the city slide by. It was his first visit to the city. I kept pointing out places to him. My excitement mounted and I wondered why I'd stayed away so long from a place that attracted me so. And yes, as Rob got his first glimpse of the Eiffel Tower, I did wonder whether Emile still lived in that shuttered house overlooking the park.

Champagne on ice waited in our room. I was delighted by the en suite bathroom. And I was already almost up to High Doh. The sounds and smells of Paris recreated that sense of wonderment, that mix of fear and desire that led the eighteen-year-old me to give herself to the uncle of a girl she'd yet to meet.

'What is it about you and Paris?' Rob handed me a glass of bubbly.

'Paris is so sexy.'

'Like you. So, tell me more.'

He loved me to talk dirty to him. It's a skill I've developed over the years. I find it a total turn on both for me and for the man I'm talking to. There have been several lovers since my, shall we say, initiation into the sensual arts. And, on lonely nights when my vibrator has come some way towards filling that ache, I've played out that first time with Emile again. I was so very fortunate that my first lover was thoughtful enough to teach me how to orgasm.

'The first man who ever fucked me was a Parisian.'

'Hussy. How old were you?'

'Just eighteen. My bra and knickers were white cotton aertex. Don't smirk! And I hadn't a clue what I was supposed to do.' I kicked off my shoes and relaxed into the couch beside him.

He began massaging my right ankle. 'Can we pretend you're a virgin tonight? I just might have to fuck you before dinner.'

A frisson of excitement travelled down my spine and centred in my cunt. This was the kind of thing I wanted to hear more of. 'Are you playing the virgin too? Or, the sophisticated Frenchman?'

Rob's fingers massaged my leg. They were warm against my skin. That special sensation was taking over.

163

And my panties were damp. Whether it was at the thought of my boyfriend making love to me on French soil or the thought of that distant seduction by a Gitanes-smoking Frenchman who must have thought Christmas had come when that sudden downpour pasted my clothing to my teenage body, I really don't know.

'Did he talk dirty in French?' Rob breathed more rapidly as his fingers found my damp crotch under the lacy fabric of my knickers.

'You needn't say anything. Just pretend we got caught in the rain. Tell me to take all my clothes off.' I swallowed. 'You have to act concerned. Be a gentleman and hand me one of those big towels. Then start French kissing me.'

'Why don't you get in the shower? Leave your bra and panties on so I can peel them off when they're stuck to you.'

He was keen, I'll give him that. And I liked the image.

I gave a little wriggle. 'Let me finish my champagne first.'

'Tease.' He moved my hand to his groin. Rob's luscious knob was worth any amount of role play. He was worth any amount of dirty talking. He just needed to dominate a tad more.

'You mustn't frighten a shy virgin like me.' With some reluctance I moved my hand away from temptation. I leaned back and began touching my breasts. The nipples were already fighting the soft stretchy fabric of my dress. 'Mmm,' I crooned.

Rob's hazel eyes were turning into melted toffee – the look that tells me he's turned on. But the guy had stamina. He needed to, with me around. If only I could lift him out of his comfort zone.

I drained my glass. Stood up and began a slow

striptease. When I stood in front of him in my underwear, he was looking at my already damp knickers, snowy white but lacy, clinging to my contours. He reached out to me and stroked a finger between my thighs so cleverly that I shivered. I wanted to scream at him to fuck me. It was all I could do not to go down on him. But that would have spoilt the show.

'Top up our glasses,' I told him. 'I'm going to take mine into the bathroom. Then we'll turn the clock back. But don't forget, I hardly knew anything about sex when I was eighteen.' I lowered my voice. 'I definitely remember telling him not to stop ...'

Rob closed his eyes briefly then opened them again. 'Dirty, horny little bitch – longing for prick in her tight blonde pussy.' His voice was husky.

I gnawed on a knuckle. Stared at him. 'You have to use a French letter.'

He stared back. 'I'll need to go down to the lobby. Better use the lift.'

I dragged my eyes off his crotch. 'When you come back, we'll drink a shot of Calvados.'

'That stuff you bought in the Duty Free?'

'Trust me.'

We opened the Calvados. That fiery jolt startled me again. I was already relaxed by the Champagne and the anticipation of how this role playing might develop.

Rob knelt at my side. I was spread-eagled on the bed, on top of a fluffy towel, my wet underwear a heap on the carpet. I was hardly able to keep still. All I could think of was that big, beautiful cock Rob was encasing in the tight rubber sheath. I wished it was me squeezing myself around it. I remembered being eighteen years of age, hearing Emile rip that packet open; lying on that single

165

bed, imagining what it would be like to feel a man inside me. Taking his cock in my hand that first time.

'What will you do to me?'

'I want to lick you everywhere and anywhere you'll let me,' Rob whispered. 'I want to get inside your mind, inside your cunt and inside your prim little ass.'

This was very promising. Especially as he began with my ears. I loved it when he did that. I always trembled and wriggled and couldn't get enough. Then when he pushed his tongue, hot and wet, inside my mouth, I had to suck on it, taking it into me as if it was his stiff, hot rod. He was doing that to me now. I couldn't help it. I sucked back ... hard. Some virgins learn quickly.

He groaned. Moved down my body and flicked his tongue around my tummy button. It was no longer Rob caressing my body. It was Emile with his long, lean, male unfamiliarity. Rob's duty-free after shave I'd treated him to, became Emile's cologne that to a naïve English girl seemed as foreign as the territory I was now about to enter.

I was more aroused than I ever remembered being before. My brain and my body seemed to be in synch. After all, I'd played out my solitary fantasy many times since that satisfying encounter in Emile's apartment. But this time I was back in Paris. And I had Rob to help. I felt my guy's fingers parting my pussy lips, felt his tongue flick across my frills. He pushed his tongue inside my slit. I began to pant. And writhe.

'You're so wet. So gloriously sticky. So, little honey cunt – you want me to stop?'

'Don't stop. Please don't stop.'

'Turn over for me then. Pretend I'm him. Your Frenchman, I mean.' His voice was hoarse again. As Emile's had been at the thought of pushing his cock into a virgin pussy.

Just as I had travelled beyond my boundary that rainy afternoon in Paris, I was on the verge of something unknown now. Rob had sensed my need. I turned over, got on my haunches and knew he was about to perform something I'd never before allowed any man to do. What's more, he told me precisely how he would achieve it. He talked about my velvety pink nipples swelling like raspberries as he pinched them. He described how he knew I was creaming and how my tight cunt would stretch to let him push his fingers inside as far as he could go, making me scream for more and more. Making me beg him to let me come.

Then he talked about finger-fucking my forbidden place. He said I would tell him to stop. And he'd pull out. And make me long for him to keep going. He told me how he'd grease me with one inquisitive finger then slip right in and ride me. When I came, I would cry out.

'Remember … I want you to come like you came for your Frenchman.' He was issuing an order. And I loved it.

I felt him gently nip my bum. I whimpered. I longed to come almost as much as I was greedy for the sweet torture of waiting to come. I imagined Emile's pale face, those high cheek bones and sensual curved mouth: the face that figured in my fantasy sessions. Now 'he' was here. It was Emile rubbing my clitoris with fingers slippery with my own juices. He was behind me: pushing cold, smooth gel inside my secret place … gently prising first with a finger of his other hand. When that erect cock nudged my bum I cried out. The thought of what was about to happen next lifted me into an unknown place.

This was where I wanted to be. As my man hesitated on the brink, my own eager hand took the role of Emile sliding one, two then three fingers inside my slit. I found my sweet spot and worked it. All the time I could hear myself panting. I writhed and wriggled my taut tunnel around Rob's cock as he entered. Could this really be me? Taking a man into me this way?

'Oh my God, I mustn't let you ... but, oh don't stop. Please ... don't stop.' I wanted him to tip me over the edge. I closed my eyes because I needed my own hand to become Emile's, bringing me to climax while Rob fucked virgin territory. I gasped at each short sweet stab.

And then Rob did something strange. He cried out in French. I heard him call me 'ma petite.' I was right on the edge as he pulled out of me. I was frantic. Until I felt the palm of his hand spank one bum cheek, then the other. Hard. The shock and the hot sting unleashed a juddering, shuddering rush of pleasure that engulfed me just as the rain engulfed me that distant afternoon. We had travelled inside and around and outside each other's most intimate places. And I knew Rob was drowning amidst splintering darkness and light, just as I was.

Neither of us needed to speak. I knew this had been awesome for us both. And my naughty little mind was already planning another three in the bed scenario for tomorrow. Rob was going to need all his powers of imagination for this. And another pot of gel.

He seemed to read my mind. 'Not bad for a shy virgin on her first night in Paris. Tomorrow we buy you a little souvenir of the city. A pair of handcuffs, I think, ma petite.'

About the Story

CAPITAL CITIES ARE MULTI-FACETED, reflecting the enticing cleavage and the dirty linen of the nation whose essence they reveal. City noise comes in layers. Some cities are underpinned by tube train networks. Like Paris. Some cities are divided by a river with its own allure and detritus. Like Paris. It's a city that rocks.

I've always known it as the city where lovers linger beside the Seine. I know it as the city where ecstatic businessmen straddle expensive mistresses on satin couches. I know it as the city where honeymooners' heartbeats race simply by osmosis.

Could I have woven my story elsewhere? Yes. But I believe Helen deserves her sexual awakening to happen in her dream city. She's bound by the constraints of a conventional middle-class upbringing. Her body dictates her needs. Her conscience inhibits her. She's out of her comfort zone and a combination of circumstances dissolves her schoolgirl inhibitions. She's no precocious nymphet: the sixties are perceived as the permissive era, but for many young women there was still an expectation that 'nice girls didn't'.

Sophisticated older man Emile tries his best to fulfil his avuncular role. If his niece, Helen's pen friend Jeannine, hadn't missed her train, there would be no story. But by catapulting gauche Helen, achingly aware of her sexuality but still pure, into a position where temptation and opportunity exist, desire can engulf both characters. I imagine Emile being similarly 'unable to bear the delicious agony'.

The story concludes with the adult Helen in the

driving seat this time, feeling that her guy Rob needs a little roughing up. Paris pushes him to greater heights. And Helen's real-time fantasy could turn into a real threesome.

I built upon personal experiences when crafting my story for *Sex in the City*. But my own pen friend met me on arrival and escorted me to her uncle and aunt's Parisian flat. My taste buds still flinch at the memory of eating stringy garlic sausage. A Gitanes-smoking Frenchman was cool beyond belief. And the Eiffel Tower wasn't as alluring as the silken underwear and kid gloves glimpsed in boutique windows.

I might just have to revisit the city. Maybe write a sequel ...

Paris Passion Patsy
by Michael Hemmingson

I

PARIS WAS COLD AND grey when we arrived in September, 2005, and there was something ugly in the air. I could feel it like a demon hand at the back of the neck: a gentle stroke before tearing into the flesh with demon claws. I did not like the city and I don't think the city cared much for me. I didn't belong here and my blood was estranged to the land. Still: here I was and I was determined to make the best of it. Dominique and I had about $5 between us when we got off the plane – we had depleted our combined resources for the coach class tickets from Los Angeles to Paris. We had left school. She was an exchange student at UCLA and I was a bum taking literature courses and writing pretentious critical papers on American writers.

Broke in Paris and we were hungry but optimistic. Her younger sister, Sabine, took us in. It seems Dominique's parents were not very happy with her stay in America; she'd dropped out of college and been cohabiting with an American guy while abroad. They probably wouldn't have allowed me to set foot in their house.

Sabine was nineteen and a student at the Sorbonne. Dominique introduced me as her 'American boyfriend'.

Sabine looked me up and down and did not shake my hand when I offered it; she was a smaller version of Dominique, with shorter hair and a rounder face. Dominique was twenty, five foot eight, skinny with long black hair and pale skin: just the way a French girl should be.

Sabine lived in a tiny one-room apartment on Avenue Georges Mandel in Poissy, the usual fare for a common student. There was a single mattress on the wood floor, the rest of the apartment was stuffed with books in four different languages. Dominique and I laid some blankets down and slept in a corner, using our bodies to keep warm.

Sabine could read English but she didn't speak it well; it didn't take long for me to understand the younger sister did not like me, not one bit.

'Are you sure this is OK?' I asked.

'All is fine,' Dominique said.

'But your sister …'

'She is an odd one, yes?'

'She hates my guts.'

'No.'

'She does.'

'It takes her time to warm to new people.'

'I didn't know she was warm at all.'

'In time, you and Sabine will be very good friends.'

'Oh?'

'I believe so.'

'You're too sanguine.'

'I am, yes,' Dominique said. 'I have to be, if we're going to survive here. Now I want you to smile.'

I smiled.

'Très bien, baby.'

II

Dominique and I would fuck in our little corner when we could; Sabine didn't seem to mind; she was asleep or pretended to be asleep or acted like she wasn't aware of the copulation going on so near and under her roof, but I wondered how she could deny the deep smell of fuck that permeated the air. Either way, Sabine would sneer at me when she could; she would look me up and down and shake her head in disgust and after a month of this I started to get really pissed off. Who the fuck did this little French bitch think she was? I was determined to show her who the superior one was – maybe being cooped up in the tiny space was getting to me (it was too cold to go outside) – and so one morning I did. Dominique had found a part-time job at a market and left for work at 7 a.m. We usually had a quick fuck before she went, but there was this one morning we did not; my cock was hard and I was alone with Sabine. The little sister was lying on her stomach wearing a shirt and panties, the panties hiked up the crack of her ass. I went over to the mattress and got on top of her. I pulled the panties down and shoved myself inside her. She wasn't very wet so I had a hard time, but she started to juice up as she woke up and struggled under me, cursing me in her language – and then, in English: 'What in the damn hell do you think you are doing, Maurice?'

'I'm fucking you,' I said softly, 'I know you want it.'

'Go to hell, bastard!' she cried. 'I do not want any part of you like this, you bastard!'

I was holding her arms down, keeping my cock inside her. 'Maybe so,' I said crazily, 'but you need it.'

'Quoi?'

'You need a good hard fuck,' I told her, 'It'll do you

good.'

'N'importe quoi!'

'Hold still, girl,' I said, 'Hold still and enjoy it.'

She stopped fighting and lay there. I fucked her. She didn't make a sound but her pussy was contracting.

She said, very softly: *'Encule-moi.'*

'What's that?'

She turned her head and said: 'Fuck me by the ass. Fuck me like I was a *boy.* Fuck me like two men fuck. *Encule-moi!'*

I did what she asked and stuck it up her tight little French asshole.

'Oh yes, *oh yes,'* Sabine breathed, *'Fuck* me like I'm a boy!'

'You like it up your pooper, girl?'

'I'm a boy!'

'Your sister sure doesn't like it this way.'

'It feels so good, Maurice.'

'It's so goddamn dirty,' I said. I felt sick and horrible and came inside my lover's sister's ass. That orgasm moved up and down my body like a happy whale in the big ocean. I turned away from the girl but she grabbed me and kissed my nose and lips and asked me to do it again to her, when I was ready. 'Let us engage in this sex matter all the time,' Sabine said, 'It is so marvellously marvellous.'

III

At first, Dominique didn't appear to mind sharing me with Sabine; I can't say I didn't mind having these two sisters (ensemble or solo) taking turns from one hole to another. Oh, we had some memorable moments there in that Lilliputian and benumbed apartment, all right, but

174

Dominique wasn't fooling me: she was simply 'going with the flow', acting 'cool', still trying to be the hip-chick she left back in California, still acting like she believed in 'polyamory' and that Sabine's new-found affection for me was 'a good thing' *blah blah blah*, but I knew this train was going to hit a wall soon, this balloon was going to explode. So I let it.

IV

Sabine held my limp, sticky dick in her hand: examining it closely with a wry and attentive smile on her pretty round pale French girl face; jiggling it to and fro like the neck of a turkey, rubbing her thumb from my curled-in balls to the discolouration caused by the early removal of the sacred foreskin. 'I *do* wish I had one of these,' she said in strained English (which, I'd like to think, was improving with my influence). 'I do wish I was a *boy,*' she said with a growl at the back of her throat. 'Then I could live my life as I should be.'

'You are a funny one.' And I patted her on the head like I always did when she did her weird talk before, during, and after sex.

'There is no "funny" here, Maurice,' she said, looking up at me, and she looked *sincere*. She said, 'I am a homosexual man trapped in the body of a girl.'

This was the first time I realized how earnest she was.

'Would you still love me if I was a boy?' she asked.

'But you're not.'

'One day you may wake up and wah-lah! a boy with a penis will be at your side, and his name will be Saul.'

'What?'

'Saul Bean.'

I said, 'Cool-io.'

175

V

'You didn't *know?*' said Dominique with a small laugh, covering her lips with a gloved hand and rolling her eyes. 'How could you *not* know?'

'I'm an idiot,' I said.

We were at a café down the street from the Sorbonne, drinking cognac before sundown.

'You are dense,' Dominique said, rolling her eyes more. 'It is your most endearing quality, Maurice.'

'Has she always wanted to be a man?' I asked.

'Always,' said Dominique, 'always and always.'

I rubbed my temples.

'But she doesn't care to fuck women,' said Dominique, 'she likes to be fucked by men.'

'She sure does,' I said.

'In the anus, like a boy.'

I smiled. *'Your* sister.'

'You care for her.'

'Of course I do. So do you.'

'I love her – always and always.'

'What about your parents?'

'They love her as well.'

'Do they know?'

'I'm sure they suspect,' said Dominique as she looked away, 'But, like many parents, they pretend the reality doesn't exist.'

I sipped cognac.

She said, 'Do you love Sabine?'

I said, 'Do you need to ask?'

She said, 'Don't answer a question with a question.'

'I love you both,' I said.

'Tell me,' she said, 'now that you know what you know about my sister, do you still wish to fuck her in that

176

special way she likes? To play her little game?'

'What about you? Do you still want me to fuck her?'

'Why do you ask, lover?'

'Don't answer a question with a -'

Dominique sighed, heavy and loud. 'If she wants your cock inside her … so be it.'

'Do you even care?'

She sighed and rolled her eyes.

'If you do that thing with your eyes again,' I said, 'I will pluck them out and you'll live the rest of your life as a blind woman.'

She laughed.

I laughed, and sipped cognac.

'*So* violent,' she said.

'I'm a man of my times.'

'Things are changing, lover.'

'Hey, those are some nice clothes you got on there, *lover.*'

Why hadn't I noticed this before?

I was the blind one.

I always am.

What the hell.

Her long leather jacket, her cashmere sweater.

'My clothes,' said Dominique. 'Thank you.'

'Where did you get them?'

'What do you mean?'

'How did you *buy* them?'

'With printed notes called currency,' she said with a pronounced Parisenne huff.

'You don't make that kind of money, Dominique.'

She crossed her legs and wagged a finger at me. 'Oh you are *impossible* sometimes! Do you know that? *Do* you?' she said.

I said, 'How about them gloves, baby? Those are some

nice leather gloves, baby. How did you afford them, baby? Gloves like that would cost you a week's pay, baby.'

I smiled because I was seeing clearly now in my cognac-induced drunk.

'Shut your dirty mouth,' was her response, 'And you have a real *dirty* mouth, don't you? You *cretin.*'

'Talk to me.'

'I am talking to you.'

Silence.

I sat back and said: 'So … what's going on, Dominique?'

'Things are changing,' she said.

'"Things" don't,' I said, *'people* do.'

'The world,' she said, raising an eyebrow, *'is.'*

Silence.

'Back to my inquiry,' she said, 'do you still desire to fuck my sister who covets, in her tainted heart, to be a man hole?'

'Right now, at this moment,' I said, 'I want to fuck *you,'* because I had a feeling it might be the last time my cock would connect to her.

'Very well,' said Dominique, standing up, 'let's go home and make love.'

It was the best, and the last.

VI

So this is what happened:

Dominique went her own way, the beginning of October, a cold fall. I suspected there was a man who was buying her things and clothes and good food and this turned out to be true; he now wanted her all to himself; he was a forty-two-year-old doctor who spotted Dominique at her market job and said to himself, 'I shall covet that *jeune fille.*' She was resistant at first, but reality took hold of her senses like Ernest Hemingway reeling in a marlin; she knew she needed to get serious about her life and find a good man to marry and, well, the doctor wanted to marry her! 'Imagine that,' said Dominique, 'I, *moi*, a doctor's wife.' Sabine accused her sister of wanting to bring babies into a crowded, violent world. Dominique said: 'Yes, I do want children. I shall be a wholesome mother.' I wished Dominique good luck, gave her a kiss on the forehead and sent her off to a new life.

Sabine said, 'So be it, I'm relieved.' This was not true. I could see the distress in her eyes, feel the anxiety when I held her body to mine; when I fucked her and said into her ear, 'You are my good little boy, Saul Bean ...' Gradually, Sabine showed signs of depression: she wouldn't eat, wouldn't sleep, wouldn't go to her classes, and she wasn't interested in sex.

Then, a change: she'd close her eyes and sleep and wake me up with my cock in her mouth and be the girl/boy I knew and was growing very fond of. 'When I get an operation and have a penis,' she asked once, 'will you still want me?' I told her I was willing to try anything and this pleased her. A few days later she'd get depressed yet again; this was making me insane like a character in Ken Kesey's *One Who Flew Over the Cuckoo's Nest* (which I read that week); I told her she should look into getting some kind of medical help at the university; this was a socialist country so surely that was available, but Sabine merely turned up her nose and told me, 'Mindfuckers are assholes.'

October 27: the Muslim riots happened. Hundreds of Muslim young men took to the streets, destroying property, fighting with the police, setting hundreds of cars

179

on fire. Sabine was gleeful and ready to mutiny with the masses. I followed along with her although we were in danger because our skin was too white and we didn't worship Allah: we were possible targets; on the other hand, the police ignored us. I was an outsider in many ways but I understood what was happening, I felt what the kids were experiencing, all the years of perceived repression and racism. Word on the street was that the police had murdered two Muslim youths, but later the truth (or what we were told was the truth) came out: the young Muslim males ran away from the authorities checking papers, they hid in an electrical sub-station and, apparently, accidentally electrocuted themselves . The memory of 9/11 and the London attacks was still fresh, and there was a war going on in the Middle East that France did not support, but that did not mean the French government was pro-Muslim. A great change *was* in the air. Dominique was correct; it was intoxicating and made Sabine and I fuck for many sweaty hours, whispering *let the city burn* orgasms. And the city did burn, for nearly two weeks. It was the French Revolution all over again! It was 1968 redux, with a different agenda but a similar spirit: a distrust in the powers that be, a need for violent expression. A new era had dawned and it made me want to fuck the crack of that dawn! When it was all finally over, Sabine was disappointed; she didn't go to her classes for a week, she didn't bathe or eat and she didn't want to fuck; it was the worst of her bouts with dejection.

We stopped playing our lovers' game. I don't know what we were. She refused to say a word of English any more. I could get by on the French I had now acquired, and was taking odd jobs washing dishes and cleaning up the mess the riots left; mostly to get away from that tiny fucking apartment and Sabine's depressing shit.

And one cold day in late November, I returned to that apartment after a hard day's work and found Sabine in the tub, her wrists and neck slashed open. She left a note, it was brief. *Farewell*, it said. The police questioned me for a day, trying to coerce me into a confession: that I had murdered my girlfriend and tried to make it look like a suicide.

I said: 'She was not my *girlfriend*.'

They asked: 'So what was she?'

'She was a person.'

'Why did she kill herself?'

She'd had problems with 'moodiness' all her life; this is what Sabine's mother told the police.

'My daughter never said she had a beau,' the mother told the police.

'You are free to go now,' I was told, and I quickly left the station and found a cheap room to rent on the other side of the city.

VII

Dominique blamed me for Sabine's death. I met her and her husband for lunch, but no one had much of an appetite. 'You should have *stopped* her,' she said, 'you filthy bastard!'

'How was I to know?'

'I told you!'

'You left out the details, lover.'

'There must have been signs! You *knew* what was in her heart, you *knew* her secrets.'

'I didn't know her at all.'

'You loved her!'

'No,' I said, 'I fucked her.'

Her middle-aged doctor husband took Dominique's

181

side. 'You should feel shame,' he told me, holding his wife close.

'I feel bad, I feel sad, I feel like a piece of dung,' said I. 'But shame? Guilt? No. No. *No way*, man. I'm not taking the fall for this. I won't be the passion patsy. Your sister had some major problems in her noggin and there was nothing I could do about it. She wanted to be a *man*. She was a *freak!*'

'I hate you!' Dominique screamed. 'I hate you! You … you … sonuvabeetch!'

'You are a sorry excuse for a man,' said her husband. 'I say this with conviction.'

'Fuck you,' said I. 'You don't even know this woman here, this tramp you call a wife. Oh, there are stories I could tell you, Monsieur.'

'Kill him!' cried Dominique to her husband. 'Murder him like he did to my sister!'

Her husband said, 'I admonish you to leave Paris.'

I replied, 'Great idea,' and that's exactly what I did.

About the Story

MARLON BRANDO SAID IN *Last Tango in Paris*, "There are more rats in Paris than people." I've had some strange and wonderful and memorable and sad and happy tangos the three times I've been to Paris. I lived there for nine months in 1992. It was grey and cold, or so I recall. Some of my best memories are going to the Sorbonne to listen to Jean Baudrillard guest lecture, and sex in a cold damp cellar. The two are not related but may have happened in the same week. There was this great white wine I used to drink there; I think it was called Georges Messengy or something like that. I once found it in a Farmer's Market in San Diego and have not been able to find it since. It was the only wine I ever had that tasted good at room temperature.

The Poetry of Pigalle
by Savannah Lee

'YOU ARE OBVIOUSLY AMERICAN,' said the intolerably sleek woman in intolerably precise English to the intolerably rumpled man whose mouth was intolerably wide open for his next bite of food.

His name was Lawrence A. Pinney, and he was showing off his fillings under the tattered awning of the Café de la Chance, one of the less favoured sidewalk establishments of Pigalle.

'I suppose you came to Paris to visit the Louvre, like everyone else,' snorted la femme.

'Guilty as charged.'

'So what are you doing here in Pigalle?'

Lawrence A. Pinney thought about it. 'Maybe I feel sorry for the place.'

'Oh do you! And why?'

'Well, imagine when it goes to a cocktail party and the other neighbourhoods ask it what it does for a living!'

Lawrence A. had been experiencing some problems with that question himself. He was too old by now to bring out his tales of taking a few months to learn fibre arts or backpack the Himalayas. He was starting to have to take a deep breath and say, 'I'm living off my trust fund.'

In other words, he was starting to have to admit that he

was a cliché.

So he felt for Pigalle at that imaginary party as she tugged on her dress and sweated into her drink. 'Well, I'm about sex, really,' she admitted, 'but please don't confuse me with one of those booths on 42nd Street back in 1987 – please?' He could see her hopeful eyes, her tender …

'Are you listening to me?' demanded the tiny, steely woman in front of Lawrence A. 'I asked you whether you considered that ridiculous remark to be whimsical in some manner.'

Lawrence A. Pinney merely shrugged.

His affable indifference only seemed to enrage her more. 'Look at your appearance, you look as though you spent two hours walking in a rainstorm. And you come to a café in such a state? To say nothing of your large ears, your rough cheeks and your thick eyebrows. What do you have to say for yourself?'

Lawrence A. barely heard her. He was busy doing a visual inventory of his own. 'You,' he told the woman, 'are a 32E with a 25-inch waist or I'm not a former tailor's apprentice. And despite your tiny dimensions,' he continued, 'your suit is just a little too tight.' He put a twinkle in his eye. 'Have you gained some weight in the hips?'

'A mouth like that deserves a muzzle!' the woman cried.

'A muzzle, eh? If you're not careful, I'm going to get the idea that you're trying to seduce me in some bizarre way.'

'What on earth makes you think you deserve to be seduced by me, you upstart? Look at yourself! *Vous n'avez pas honte*? Are you not ashamed? You are holding your fork in a bear's grip, your elbows are presumptuous and without discipline, and your giant bites of food make your gums gape like the over-used flaps of a whore. Only Americans eat in this horrible manner. And *occasionnellement les Australiens*,' she added.

Lawrence A. Pinney sighed. 'Madame,' he replied, '*je m'interesse à la question de pourquoi vous devez me dire ces choses dans un lieu comme celui-ci. Nous ne sommes pas*,' he emphasized, '*dans le restaurant Pierre Gagnaire.*'

For those not acquainted with the tolerable foreigner's French employed by Mr Pinney, he was asking the steel hourglass why she felt the need to bring these matters up in this particular location. It was not, after all, the highly exclusive restaurant of Pierre Gagnaire.

To the contrary. This sidewalk café would never make it into a guidebook, except perhaps as an example of what to avoid. There was much to un-distinguish it, ranging from its statistically improbable rates of escargot explosion to the sub-Moldovan calibre of its *chocolat* (a serious matter even in this neighbourhood).

And the service would have embarrassed an Uzbekistani hotel staff of 1973. The waiter was one of those who had better things to do than serve people. Or at least, he had better things to do than serve Lawrence A. Pinney.

He knew Lawrence A. Pinney was there – he'd stood there for quite a while, in fact, staring at Lawrence A. with huge eyes full of backlogged opinions – but had ignored him completely. Lawrence A. was only eating now because this same waiter had mysteriously set a plate of *croque-monsieur* down on an empty table and walked away. (Lawrence A. had taken the sandwich but left the plate where it was).

But the main problem with the café would have to be

the lamppost. Positioned only a few feet from Lawrence A.'s table, the lamppost turned the space in between into a needle to be threaded by pedestrians. Which frequently included bicyclists riding home from the market. Before the table-manners police made her appearance, Lawrence A. had been struck by baguettes no less than three times.

Given all this, he hardly expected that his problem would turn out to be one of excess visibility.

But here this woman was, fixated on him and his appearance.

And she would not move.

She was causing a bottleneck, too, yet the increasing numbers of outraged Parisians piling up on either side of her ('*Salope*!' '*Imbécile*!' '*Allez, enfin ALLEZ*!') budged her not an inch. She was intent on giving Lawrence A. Pinney the tongue-lashing she felt he deserved. It was almost, he thought, as if she were looking for something.

'Do you call that 'French' which you were speaking just now?' she demanded.

'*Bien sur que non*!' he cried.

She failed to be mollified. 'Then why did you attempt it at all? Did you think I would be impressed?'

'Why would I care what you think or not?' he asked, but more in the manner of an advanced Buddhist than a defiant prisoner or angry stranger. It was reasonably impressive. Even the most aimless lives do make us masters of something or other.

'All right then,' conceded the woman, and roved him with her eyes to find new weaknesses to attack. It didn't take long. Pointing, she demanded, 'Is that an Ungaro tie?'

Lawrence A. Pinney did not, in fact, remember which tie he was wearing, and drew it out to have a look.

'Oh for heaven's sake, you foolish man, put that thing

187

away. Of course it is Ungaro. Now why does it look so hopeless? Did you throw it into the washing machine? To say nothing of that suit. How does a Caraceni arrive in such a condition? You could not be so stupid as to have ruined these clothes by mistake. I can see that just by looking at you. So it was deliberate. But the question is why. Tell me, do you hate your origins? The wealth which belongs to your family? Not to you, of course. You surely didn't earn it yourself, your eyes are not so cruel.'

Lawrence A. Pinney could only laugh. 'My eyes are poetry,' he said, hoping to move the conversation back in what he considered a more flirtatious direction.

'Poetry!' spat the woman. 'If you want poetry, go further up into *le vrai* Montmartre, go to the Marais. This is Pigalle. There is no poetry here.'

Lawrence A. Pinney shrugged. 'All right. Whatever you like.'

The woman's lips drew tight enough to fire bullets. 'Fine! Then tell me this. Your battered tie, is it really your cock? And what you hate is yourself?'

At that, Lawrence A. Pinney had had enough.

As was his way, he under-reacted, but differently this time. Something new invited itself into his voice. 'Why don't you try me and see.'

To his surprise, the woman's eyes lit up like the devil's Christmas. 'There it is,' she breathed. 'At last.'

Whereupon she spun on her high-heeled toes and parted the tiny crowd around her as if she really were made of steel to their flesh.

In her wake, they all pushed and shoved to make it through the needle. Lawrence A. Pinney was hit with baguettes again.

As he knocked the crumbs off himself, he seemed to hear people behind him. Two voices. Murmurs. 'Mildly interesting.' 'That combination of qualities ...' 'Not much, but worth spending some time on, perhaps.' He wondered what it was all about. Maybe they were businessmen discussing prospective hires. He wondered what it would be like to have a job. A real one.

The most astonishing pale scent distracted him, a bouquet of orchids and thin ice.

It heralded the approach of a blur of white and blonde. In her hands he saw the plate from which he had taken his stolen *croque-monsieur*.

'Is this yours?' she asked.

'No,' he said.

She set the plate down on his table regardless and seated herself across from him. 'I hope you don't mind,' she whispered. 'I'd like to pretend we're together. Women alone can be harassed sometimes.'

Lawrence A. looked around in case any potential harassers had followed her here. He didn't see any. 'Are you all right?' he asked her, just to make sure.

'You're so kind,' she said, looking right in his eyes. 'Thank you.'

That extraordinary scent took over his senses again, beguiling and almost frightening him. Silver violets – had he thought they were orchids? – silver violets trembling.

The grateful lady's eyes were dark as secrets.

It seemed like he ought to say something now.

'Funny,' he said. 'I spoke to a woman a few minutes ago. Or she spoke to me. And ...'

The lady raised her eyebrows. 'Yes?'

'Well, she was very rude ... shocking, really ... but I didn't lose my head. Or not very much. Yet here, with you, I ... I don't know what to say.'

At that point something odd happened. He could have sworn that the lady replied, 'I have an idea. Why don't you tell me exactly how you would possess me if you had the chance.'

Obviously it was his imagination. She wouldn't have really said such a thing.

Nonetheless, Lawrence A., previously too flummoxed to talk, now became too flummoxed not to. 'That woman, you know, I'm realizing that I never did get a good look at her eyes. I wonder now what they were like. I do remember her suit. It was custom-fitted or I'll eat my poor old tie (it is an Ungaro but I did not throw it in a washing machine, I jumped in a pool) … anyhow, her suit … Dior from the look of it … English woollen, a menswear feel … gunmetal gray.'

'I see you have an eye,' mentioned the lady, 'as well as a heart.'

Lawrence A. waved the compliment away, as was his habit, then continued, 'Her hair was auburn. It was piled on her head in curls that looked like metal shavings. They matched the rest of her, which was all steel. Poured steel. I can remember all that, as clear as day. But I can't remember the colour of her – Watch out! Baguettes!' It was another bicyclist, and bearing down hard. Lawrence A. lunged across the little table to shield the lady and took three fresh-baked, extra-crusty tips full across the face.

'My goodness!' cried the lady. 'Thank you so much! Oh dear. Look at you. Scrapes like that would have broken my own skin, it's so much softer than yours.'

'Well, yes, I, I was worried about that,' admitted Lawrence A.

'So you took the blow in my place! You sacrificed yourself for me.'

'Well, I …' blushed Lawrence A.

'You're not just kind, you're chivalrous! And here you are in the birthplace of chivalry. It is perfect.'

190

Lawrence A. developed a sudden problem with his shirt collar. He fumbled and tugged at it. 'Does it seem hot to you?' he asked.

'So now,' the lady announced with great satisfaction, 'I can tell you how you would possess me. Exactly how. I've learned what I need to know. And,' she whispered, 'I like it.'

Lawrence A. Pinney's mouth unhinged itself to a degree that would have provoked violence in Madame Steel. His eyes went full goldfish.

The lady stood. She took a moment to write his helpless look onto her heart for safekeeping, then floated away like dreams.

He heard the voices again.

'A romantic, then.' 'But of the stern, old-fashioned kind.'

How strange; what would romance have to do with job qualifications? Were they perhaps computer professionals dreaming of the mainframe days?

'... Colour of that tie is perhaps a bit tragic.' 'Yes, that will have to go. At least it's linen rather than silk.' 'Either way, pale blue is pale blue. Well, then. Are we going to proceed?'

Lawrence A.'s veins turned colder than the lady's flowers.

His ruined Ungaro retained a poignantly optimistic cerulean hue. In other words, you could call it 'pale blue'.

As the implications of this began to unfold in his mind, a hand fell on his shoulder.

'No!' he shouted.

But instead of male attackers, he heard the voice of a woman, deep as earth and warm as cinnamon. 'You're all right, dear,' it reassured him. 'Now how can I help you?'

She sat down across from him and he looked in her

face. It was a triumphantly middle-aged face, one which came right up into the strong lines and grooves of its years. In this way, it was masculine, since men are the ones who wear the scars of time with pride. But the effect was lovely.

Lawrence A. Pinney immediately confessed all to her. 'Ma'am, I've been having some truly strange experiences. Women have come up to me … people have been talking about me … I ate a sandwich from an empty table … and the baguettes …'

'Not to worry, not to worry,' said the woman, patting his hand. 'You are far from home. That's all. Now, tell me about yourself.'

This was certainly a pleasant change from what had gone before, seeming to put him in control at last. But having been granted control, he found he didn't know what to do with it. So he asked, 'What do you want to know?'

'Suppose you tell me why you came here.'

'There really isn't a reason.'

The woman shifted in her chair and her eyes became a bit more grey and searching. 'I see. Was it just a vacation, then? Or were you perhaps trying to find something?'

'That would be nice, wouldn't it?' he smiled. 'But I think life is going to have to find me.'

The grey of her eyes now sparkled like a winter evening. 'You may be right about that.'

'Not so far. Life hasn't gotten the memo. I've been drifting,' he confessed, 'for an awfully long time.'

The woman – he suddenly thought of her as 'mother' – tilted her head. 'What do you think being found by life would be like? How would it unfold? How would it feel?'

To his own utter shock, Lawrence A. blurted out, 'It would feel like sex. From the other side. Like being

192

penetrated. More than that – like being taken and entered, deeply, totally … Pardon me,' he apologized. 'I'm so sorry. I don't even know you …'

'Do I look uncomfortable?' asked the woman with some amusement. Indeed, she didn't. There was nary a blush on her. It was as if random men unburdened themselves to her about fucking all the time.

Lawrence A. thought, 'She must not be very motherly after all, to be so calm through all this,' and then he thought, 'No, it means she's the perfect mother. A mother for grown-ups, a mother who really can hear anything you need to say.'

And this made him ask the woman something even more embarrassing than talk of penetration: 'Do you believe in goddess?'

'The one or the many?' she replied. 'Western or eastern? Historical or conceptual? Avatar or essence?'

'My god, you're an intellectual!' cried Lawrence A.

The woman heaved a great sigh. 'Too late, you remember you are in Paris. So sad. I'd hoped for better from you.' She stood up.

'No, wait! Don't go!' Lawrence A. at last felt like he was being tested – and like he was failing. Worse, he already felt lost at the idea of not having this woman near him. He needed her. 'Give me another chance,' he pleaded.

But she was gone.

For the first time in his life, Lawrence A. felt a sense of consequence.

He leaped to his feet. 'Come back! Come back! I need you! I want another chance!'

The wide-eyed, silent waiter appeared and clapped a surprisingly large, heavy hand on Lawrence A.'s shoulder. With immense but invisible force, he shoved

Lawrence A. back down in his chair, then held him there as if to make sure that Lawrence A. got the point. In all this he remained silent and his eyes refused to divulge their many secrets.

When the fight at last went out of Lawrence A., the waiter let go of him, took the plate off the table and disappeared.

'Well,' said Lawrence A., to no one in particular. 'Does it get any worse?'

He shouldn't have asked. Here came the voices again.

'… Michaud just do what I thought he did?' 'Looks like … but we haven't … decision yet!' '… Take it up with him later. Meanwhile, let's …' 'Yes, let's.'

Let's what, exactly?

It was right at that moment when Lawrence A. remembered the Louvre.

He kicked over his chair and started towards it like a rocket with an onboard guidance system.

The Louvre! The Louvre! Symbol of all that was right and good and normal and ordinary and totally clichéd! If he hurried – he checked his watch – he could get in line in time for the last group to see the Mona Lisa.

Several times he looked back to make sure the sinister café was not following him. Clearly it had been a mistake to come into Pigalle. Why had he done it? He didn't remember now. A sense of wanting to go someplace without pretensions, without false charm, yet recognizably Parisian in a way which perhaps some of the other arrondissements no longer were, not because of globalization but because so many other places in the western world had become unashamed. The sidewalks had stopped peeking up skirts and storing up scandals to whisper in the night. With the way things were these days, there was no point to that anymore.

But still no place was quite, quite, like Pigalle. (What had she said? There was no poetry here?)

So he had come here, but now he regretted it. Maybe Paris itself had been a mistake. Maybe he should go back to the apartment in Massachusetts, or that retreat on Puget Sound. There were a thousand non-things he could do to keep himself not-quite-busy. He knew how to live his life. He knew how to find women. Well, not women like Madame Steel with her small frame and large breasts and slightly mis-cut suit, or women like the lady of the icy lilacs ... or ... or women like the sacred mother, proud of her years and thus untouched by them.

No. Not women like them. Women, but ... not women like them.

Lawrence A. Pinney stopped dead in the street in total despair.

Madame Steel had been right. When she said his battered tie was his self-hatred, when she said that it was everything he couldn't do to the long strip of flesh between his legs which was its analog, she'd been right. He wished he'd listened.

Damn cock. Damn self. Damn tie. He was going to throw it in the gutter. Throw it in the gutter, that's what he was going to do. *Jerk* and *yank* it *off* his -

His exertions knocked something out of his suit. It fluttered to the ground.

Lawrence A. Pinney went after it to see what it was. From the dirty speckled asphalt he picked up a business card. Odd; he didn't remember anyone handing him anything like this. Odder still, it was engraved, "Mistress,' 'Damsel,' and 'Mother': The Three Graces Severes.'

English words but French grammar and construction.

Lawrence A. now saw that, underneath the engraving,

there were lines of precise and tiny handwriting. He had to squint to read them: 'The school of the Graces – *deuxième étage* – back of the building which you will see on your left if you first exit Café de la Chance heading ...'

Café de la Chance, that was where he'd just been.

The waiter. The waiter must have slipped it to him while holding his shoulder. The waiter was telling him how to find those women again: the Mistress, the Damsel, and ... and the Mother.

He remembered the Louvre. The safety. The reassurance. If he didn't go now, he'd never get in. He'd never be able to keep hiding from ... from what had found him.

Legs shaking, Lawrence A. Pinney set out to follow the hand-written directions on the card. He turned left, he turned right, he cut through this alley and over to that one, he walked through this sex shop and that dirty movie theatre, he found the fountain sticking oddly out of the side of a building on a tiny un-named sliver of street and ritually washed himself in it (ruining his poor tie even more), and at last he came to the fire escape on the back of the promised building.

Struggling inside through a window, Lawrence A. Pinney found himself in a hot and stuffy hallway which smelled like damp woollens and French pride.

There was a half-open door. Lawrence A. Pinney heard odd, leathery creaking sounds coming from inside. He crept closer and peeked in.

It was the waiter, stark naked and secured by heavy straps at his elbows and knees (leaving his hands almost ominously free). The straps affixed him to a rough wooden slab. Currently the slab was cranked into an upright position, but there was plenty of machinery to enable this to change if the waiter's diabolical dominants should wish.

Lawrence A. Pinney now understood the appearance of the waiter's mouth and eyes back in the cafe, because here the waiter was wearing a tight muzzle. This was obviously his natural state; his face, in retrospect, had looked more naked back at the café than his cock did now. Many sessions like this must have formed him, made his eyes so huge and full of unexpressed words, made his mouth so flat and useless-looking.

A stern woman's voice, familiar-sounding, interrupted.

'<u>Yes</u>, Michaud. You will.'

'Mmmm, mmmmm,' protested Michaud, neck turning red and eyes rolling up in his head.

'You have only produced for me three times today,' objected the strict speaker, 'and your output has furthermore been pathetic.' A well-manicured hand thrust a ceramic bowl into Lawrence A. Pinney's sightline and the direct vicinity of Michaud's cock. 'Get to work. I want some fresh, and I want it now.'

There was a clink of knives and china beyond Lawrence A. Pinney's line of sight. A lighter, gentler voice said, 'It may not be much, Agnès, but you must admit it's tasty.'

Lawrence A. Pinney was insatiably curious to know what they were talking about. He slipped past the doorway and hid against the opposite wall. He peeked into the room from this new angle.

There, he saw the belligerent 32E (holding the bowl) and two of her friends sitting at a tiny table, balancing their demitasses and their plates.

On their plates were slices of baguette, with some sort of white jelly or jam spread upon them.

... Oh.

Lawrence A. Pinney zipped back across the doorway so he could see Michaud again. The poor waiter had now taken his red, tired cock in his hands and was working it to hardness over the bowl so he would soon be able to come and give the ladies more special jam.

Lawrence A. Pinney immediately forgave Michaud his seeming laziness at the café. This was a hardworking man!

One of the friends said, 'Oh, Agnès, look at him, he's struggling. Let us help him.'

'Oh, very well. Hold the bowl, Minette. Come with me, Chloe.'

Heels tapped. Lawrence A. Pinney watched Michaud follow the sound with his huge, and at the moment rather nervous, eyes.

Heels tapped again. Agnès and Chloe returned with two wide-end riding crops.

Michaud's eyes had quite a lot to say about that. He added some very meaningful vocalizations: 'Mmm! Mmm-mmm-mmm!'

While Minette knelt with the bowl, Agnès and Chloe stationed themselves on either side of the wooden slab and began patting Michaud smartly on the thighs and stomach with their crops.

'Mmm!' shouted Michaud, but this time neither his voice nor his eyes needed to say anything; his formerly tired cock, now shiny and full, did all the talking needed.

Lawrence A. Pinney's own cock decided to have some words of its own with the seam of his pants. He reached down ... closed his eyes for one brief -

'Mmm!' sounded Michaud in a new and alarmingly different tone of voice.

Lawrence A. Pinney opened his eyes and saw to his considerable alarm that Michaud, in his struggles, had turned his head. As a result, Michaud's huge, expressive eyes were now focused right on him.

He didn't wait to see what would happen, but fled down the hall. Around the corner he hoped to find some sort of safety, but he only found another door.

Inside he saw a man kneeling on the hard floor.

Lawrence A. knew he shouldn't look any further; he knew he should keep running. But he couldn't help himself. He drew nearer.

The man kneeling in the room had a shiny bald head and enormous meat-cleaver hands. Like Lawrence A. Pinney, he was dressed in a custom suit (Gieves and Hawkes as a matter of fact), but unlike Lawrence A.'s, his was sharp and proud – lending his humility a poignant air.

He also had a pained expression on his face. Lawrence A. quickly saw why. With the way the man was kneeling, his suit pants functioned as a chastity harness, restraining his cock. And as Lawrence A. could clearly see, the man's cock was in no position to tolerate such repression without considerable suffering. Yet the man bore it with an air of patience, even thankfulness, as if he considered it a tribute to the beautiful legs at which he knelt.

Lawrence A. realized now that he'd always believed that this was how it should be. Men should, maybe not serve, but certainly suffer for women. What was the point of all that strength otherwise? And women, when they commanded, commanded with pity and love, turning their words into nectar and wine.

'Now take the bread, Antoine,' came a sweet voice as case in point.

'Yes, my lady,' said Antoine with fervent devotion. He reached out of Lawrence A.'s sight line and came back with a scarred baguette. 'What shall I do with it, ma'am? Take it as far into my mouth as I can for you? Rape myself with it? Tell me what would please you.'

Tell me what would please you ... those words, spoken with such yearning, pushed Lawrence A. from mere arousal to an unprecedented state of frantic need and transcendent joy. They began repeating themselves in him like a mantra: *Tell me what would please you, tell me what would please you.* In his mind he saw his grey-suited inquisitress, his icy lilac, his spiritual mother, his actual mother, God, Goddess. He begged them all to tell him what would please them.

Judging by his subsequent actions, their answer was that he should sneak into his ruined pants (the zipper only stuck a little), take out his cock, and cradle it so lightly as to only increase its heavenly agony.

'... into me,' the lady of the moonlit legs was saying.

'Yes, ma'am. Yes, ma'am.' Tremblingly, Antoine took the staff of bread and laid it between the soft, dimpled thighs of his female master. He twisted it, and, with a gentleness born only of true force, he fitted the head of it in her.

'Ahhh. Now tear it off, Antoine, so that only a bit is left. And eat your way up into it. Eat your way up into me.'

'Ma'am!' groaned Antoine. 'Thank you, ma'am, thank you, ma'am, my lady, my wonderful lady, thank you, thank you. But, ma'am, I beg you for one favour. I need this, I need it in order to do what you've told me, I need it not to die. Ma'am, I beg you for permission to touch my cock, ma'am.'

'Yes, Antoine; in fact, take it out for me.'

Antoine began to weep with joy. Lawrence A. Pinney heard – he had eyes only for those thighs and the very strange intruder between them – a zipper.

'Very good, Antoine. Oh, look how hard it is. Look

how it's straining and silently crying out for release. Look at that. It's so beautiful. Beautiful in lovely ways, but beautiful in terrible ways too. Yes, beautiful as death and dark and hell. All the hells. There are so many hells. Hells of fire and hells of snow and hells in the blackness between. That's where we forge ourselves, Antoine, in the hells between.'

Lawrence A. Pinney's whole body jerked the way it sometimes does in sleep. He'd forgotten, again, where he was. He'd forgotten that he was in this city where words like that seemed to grow up through the cracks. Yes, like weeds, stubborn and tough. Poetry was fragile everywhere else. But not here. Here, in Paris, poetry was strong.

'And *this* poetry, out of all poetry,' he said to himself, 'is the poetry of Pigalle.'

'... hear something, ma'am?'

'Yes, Antoine, I did hear something. Would you please look? Then come back and eat the bread from me. It's soaked up my juices by now.'

Lawrence A. Pinney dearly wanted to watch that happen, but he retreated before the advance of Antoine and slipped around another corner like a ghost.

And walked right into a faceful of baguettes.

A bicyclist – *the* bicyclist, Lawrence A. realized; there had only been one – turned. From under his regulation helmet, he looked Lawrence A. up and down.

'Here you are at last. It certainly took you long enough.'

Baguettes rustling in his shoulder bags, the bicyclist came right up to Lawrence A., violating every rule of personal space without even so much as a smirk.

'Now let's get that cock stored away properly,' he continued. 'We don't want to try Madame Maman's patience.' With wind-chilled fingers he seized hold of Lawrence A.'s swollen cock (Lawrence A. stifled a yell) and stuffed it back in Lawrence A.'s briefs. His impersonal, commanding roughness almost made Lawrence A. pee with shame.

The bicyclist acted like grabbing a man's cock and manhandling it with such force was nothing out of the ordinary, and therefore any shock Lawrence A. might be feeling was entirely Lawrence A.'s fault. He simply said 'Zip up. Come with me.' Off he trudged in his strange bicycle shoes.

Lawrence A. Pinney, still shocked at having been handled so, wandered after him like a forlorn duck. 'Where are we going? What's going to happen to me? What does it all mean? If this is my destiny, how come I feel so confused? Can I have some of the bread? Were you hitting me with it on purpose?'

The bicyclist approached a particularly shabby door and, with an oddly courtly gesture, waved Lawrence A. inside. (His two loads of baguettes shifted as he moved.)

Lawrence A. knew, of course, what awaited him in this room: the cinnamon-voiced woman, and the third man. The other one who had been discussing Lawrence A. at that back table.

What would the seasoned goddess be doing to this man? Making him lick her floor clean with his tongue? Might Lawrence A. get to help? Would the man be assigned to treat Lawrence A.'s cock with the same familiarity and disrespect as the bicyclist just had? Would it stop there? Or would it go further?

He went inside and …

'You're alone,' he told the woman. (She was draped in russet pashmina.)

'Of course I am.'

202

Behind Lawrence A., he heard the bicycle messenger clop away in his strange bicycle shoes. The woman's eyes softened as he went. 'Ah, Pierrot,' she said. 'Such a nice boy.'

Lawrence A. protested, 'But there should be a man with you!'

'Nonsense! How could there be? I've been waiting for *you*.'

'Me? But I displeased you! I failed you!'

'Yes! Of course! That's why you're here. You could never belong to Agnès or Cerise, because you passed their tests.'

'Tests?'

'But of course. They were testing you. And you passed! You passed naturally. What more did you need from them? What could they teach you? But I, I have much to instill in you.'

Lawrence A. Pinney felt absurdly proud and hopeful – then, afraid. 'Ma'am, I ... I've never ... I've never had to *work* like that. I'm not sure I can.'

She arched her brow. 'You will,' she said, and her voice both terrified and heartened him.

Then he thought of something. 'But, ma'am,' he objected. 'Watching the others ... I was so hard. Here, with you, I ... look, I've gotten soft.'

'Yes, exactly,' she said.

He waited for her to say more, but she did not. She merely sat there in turn, waiting for him to understand.

He did, then, or thought he did.

There was one last question. 'Ma'am?'

'Speak.'

'Ma'am, tell me, please – who was the third man? The one who's not here.'

She tapped her fingers. 'Explain.'

203

'Well – the waiter at the café downstairs – it *is* downstairs, isn't it, Ma'am.'

'Yes … my son.'

At that word, Lawrence A. Pinney felt his toes curl in a pre-arousal fear and finality unlike any he had known. At the moment, he was still soft, but slowly, slowly that would change, and when the hardness reached him this time, it would never leave.

There was nothing to do but go on. He took a breath.

'Ma'am. The waiter, Michaud … I saw him down there, and I saw him up here. He was the first man.'

She smiled to her feet. Her soft, sensible shoes hushed past Lawrence A. Pinney to the door.

'And Antoine,' Lawrence A. Pinney continued, 'was the second. I saw him up here, but I *heard* him downstairs. Didn't I. Well, didn't I? He must have been one of the ones sitting behind me in the café.'

'You can begin to undress now,' mentioned the woman.

Lawrence A. Pinney, fingers shaking, slipped off his loosened tie. 'So I wondered – who was the third man? The other one who was talking about me with Antoine?'

His grown-up, second-chance, pretend-Maman held out her hand for the blue Ungaro.

'Ma'am?' faltered Lawrence A. Pinney. 'Ma'am, are you going to tell me who he was? And … and where he is now? What awaits me from him?'

Madame-Maman pulled the tie menacingly straight between her hands. 'Do you think stories are like that here? So simple? So easily resolved?'

Too late, he remembered that he was in Paris.

She closed the door.

About the Story

AH, PARIS, AS THEY say. So many memories. Sidling up to my sister-lover in the bloody dark and murmuring '*Solange*?', my ecstasy and terror only assuaged when she replies, euphonically, '*Mon ange.*' ('*Les Bonnes*')

Struggling down the street with my basket of *linge sale* only to feel that beautiful blond man's lips against my ear: '*Ecoute, Gervaise.*' Or is my mind playing tricks on me, and it's my brutish but compelling husband trying to pull me back from my already-late work? ('*L'Assommoir*').

Speaking of brutish but compelling mates, how can I forget gasping out '*Crois-tu que cela est sage?*'- you have to admire my composure – as yet another one penetrates me a few inches up (since I'm on my stomach) from where I'd been expecting. No consent, no prior discussion of mutual fantasies, not even any warning, none of those *choses americaines*, just *lui voila*, because this is Paris: where de Musset triumphed in his tears and where Desnos still follows us in shadows. Where orgasm is death, pleasure an executioner, and regret is a smile. (*Baudelaire, bien sur.*)

I have never been to Paris. But of course, I have also never left. Not since the moment in 1985 when I first had enough French to pick up Voltaire – which I must say I managed quite capably, *quoique je ne puisse me tenir que sur une fesse.*

That's from '*Candide*,' and the *sang-froid* in the face of unexpected anal sex is from, I think, Malraux. Search as I might for it, it refuses to answer me; it refuses to be simple.

If Sartre and Camus were dramatically wrong and

Therese de Lisieux right, and we really are bound for a heaven, then these things will be among my treasures there. And more: Courbet, Redon, Toulouse-Lautrec and Brassai, showing me the present all the more clearly through the lens of the past, showing me what does not change by way of marking what does: these things will be among my treasures.

There's a distinctive feeling to the French and specifically the Parisian consciousness. A flavour. It demands first your respect, then your tender protection, and finally everything. What else could I write for this anthology but what I wrote?

An Unreliable Guide to Paris Hotel Rooms
by Maxim Jakubowski

IT WAS IN PARIS that he first slept with a woman.

No wonder that, for the rest of his life, he would entertain a love and hate relationship with the Paris capital. Often, when asked in social circumstances why his view of Paris was so ambiguous, he would mostly answer in jest that he loved Paris, but wasn't actually too enamoured of the French.

He once lived there, but it had now been many years ago. He still returned on two or three occasions every year. Usually because of a woman. Seldom the same one. And, unsurprisingly, they weren't always French.

HOTEL DE L'ODEON, rue de l'Odeon, Paris 6
She was German and had red hair. They had agreed to meet at the Gare du Nord, co-ordinating their respective arrivals from London and Hannover on separate trains a quarter of an hour apart.

She was taller than he expected and the buttons of her tapered white blouse strained against the opulent swell of her heavy breasts below the thin cotton fabric. Her brown boots reached all the way up to her knees.

They embraced.

Smiled at each other.

Maybe this would work, they both thought.

They made their way to the taxi rank, and exchanged small talk while they waited for the queue to shrink ahead of them. Neither had much luggage. It was just going to be a couple of nights. Their fingers touched fleetingly.

The first floor room was small and cramped and at the end of a long and dark corridor. The adjoining bathroom, though, was of a decent size.

As soon as she had set her case down on the bed, Claudia said she needed to take a shower. Her train journey had been much longer than his.

'No problem.'

She slipped out of her loose skirt first, then her knickers. He noted how big her thighs were, the luscious roundness of her arse and then the unnatural, artificial tan she sported. She turned her head towards him.

'You looking?'

'Of course.'

'You like?'

He smiled. 'I like'.

She quickly unbuttoned the shirt, unclasped her bra and briefly swivelled so he had a full view of her naked body. As she had written to him, she was fully shaven. Her mound looked plump, like a warm fruit intersected by the darker line of her opening.

'I still like,' he said. She took a few steps into the bathroom and closed the door.

Later, they fucked.

She was a hungry lover. Sucked him with an eager appetite and once she had fitted him inside her, her cunt had the raging warmth of a furnace. Noisy too, demanding, pliable.

Still embedded within her, both relaxing for a while, he distractedly began pulling out the hairpins from her raised hair, allowing the blur of long flowing flames to pour down over her hard breasts. He had already extracted more than a dozen, and there were still as many left. Her eyes looked mischievous. He took one of the liberated hairpins and implacably tightened it around one of her dark nipples. She sighed loudly, and he felt her cunt muscles contract and surround his cock like a vice. He pressed the hair pin branches together harder and watched as tears formed in the corner of her eyes.

'Yes,' she said.

Encouraged, he fished another pin from the jungle of red-hued branches now surrounding her face and took hold of the other nipple. Her whole body shivered with pleasure, as he squeezed the pain out of her.

Still, she did not ask him to cease the torture. He thrust hard into her, the tip of his penis reaching new depths, hitting her inside walls, scraping fiercely inside her. She shuddered and screamed.

'That was good,' she would later say.

'Did I hurt you?' he asked.

'No,' Claudia answered. 'I like it hard. It's the way I am.'

And suggested he take a digital photo of her right then and there.

'Naked?'

'Of course,' she delved into her bag and took out her small camera.

They took a bath together after their first fuck, and, after she had dried herself, she asked him to rub some cocoa butter creme all over her body. Now he knew why her pale brown tan was so even. But he hated the smell. Then Claudia dressed and informed him she had made arrangements to meet up for drinks with a friend, to take advantage of the fact she was in Paris again. He asked whether he could join them, but she was against it.

'I'll be back in the room in two hours at most. Jean-Claude is just a friend, you know.'

While she was out, he read in bed and dozed off. He woke in the middle of the night and Claudia still hadn't returned. He rang her on her mobile. She sounded drunk when she picked up the call, loud café noises in the background.

'I won't be long,' she said. 'Oh, I'm having so much fun …'

By the time she crept back into the room, he was asleep again.

They fucked three times the next day, but he felt used and was no longer attracted to her. Between the sex, they had a couscous on the Boulevard St Germain and saw a movie on the Place Saint Michel. Seeing her off at the Gare du Nord the following morning, he had little to say to her.

HOTEL HENRI IV, rue Saint-Sulpice, Paris 6

The Italian woman came from Padova. Her name was Annarita.

She had written him a fan letter following an exhibition of his paintings in a Venice gallery, and they had flirted amiably for several months through letters and e-mails, until he suggested they finally meet. She was a lawyer. They agreed on Paris. He took the Eurostar and arrived on a Thursday, with some business to be dealt with on his first afternoon. Annarita was due to fly in the following day.

He took the RER train from Luxembourg and arrived at Roissy to greet her arrival.

He didn't have to wait long, as she only carried hand luggage.

She had jet black hair and brown eyes and looked

exactly like her photo, which was a relief. Her English was as tentative as his Italian, so communication was halting and hesitant. He was never sure if Annarita fully understood what he was saying – she just kept on nodding, smiling, acquiescing in an emotionless manner – or even caught the gust of his feeble jokes or his possibly hopeless hints at the sensual nature of their burgeoning relationship.

She had left her shoulder bag in the hotel room he had booked for the tryst. The window looked out on a flower stall. She wanted a coffee. They walked down the road to the Café des Editeurs, an habitual haunt of his. He always felt comfortable in any bar with bookshelves full of volumes across its walls. And they did a great citron pressé, he had to admit.

The afternoon lingered on as they sipped their drinks, and then ordered again.

Finally, he suggested they leave. It was too early for supper.

'What do you want to do?' he asked her.

'I don't know,' Annarita said.

He suggested they return to the hotel.

'It will be easier to talk,' he said. 'It's getting a little noisy here.'

'OK.'

The room was too small, and there was little space on either side of the bed. Just a small shelf en lieu of desk and a metal chair facing it and then the door to the bathroom.

They both sat on the edge of the bed.

He didn't know what to say.

He slowly put his arm on her shoulder. Annarita shuddered. Drew back. His hand retreated. He looked her in the eyes. 'No?'

'I don't know,' she said. Her new refrain.

'I'd like to kiss you,' he said.

'I'm not sure.'

'Why?'

'I don't know,' again.

'We've both come a long way,' he added, hoping his face reflected kindness. 'You look lovely.'

She didn't reply for a while. Standing there, her back straight, her features a welter of simmering emotions he couldn't fathom.

Then, suddenly, she stood up and said: 'I don't want to be another fuck, some anonymous *scopatta*. I don't know you ...'

'Well, you agreed to come to Paris,' he added pleadingly, 'you knew we'd be sharing a hotel room ...'

'Yes,' she agreed, 'but this is now reality, not just words ...'

She lowered her eyes. Looked away from him.

'You don't like me?' he asked.

'Not enough,' she replied.

'Oh. I see that makes it awkward,'

'Yes. But ... there is another thing, you see ... Since we began writing to each other, I've become friends with someone else back at home and, just last weekend, we ... sort of happened ... you understand?'

He sighed. Bad timing. Oh well ... Said nothing in response to her revelation.

'It's another woman,' she then added, still avoiding his gaze and sitting upright on the far right end corner of the bed as if an invisible wall grew between them. 'She works for the same legal office but in our other branch, some kilometres away in Mestre ...'

'I didn't know that you ...' he enquired.

'Neither did I. It's the first time I have been with a

woman,' she indicated. 'But I do like her a lot. Her name is Barbara.'

He nodded.

They had a meal nearby in a small, student-like, Japanese restaurant where most of the meal came on small skewers, even the cheese. And the silences between Annarita and he grew more strained as night fell and the prospect of sharing the room loomed. There was only one bed and no prospect of either of them sleeping on the floor due to a distinct lack of space in the small hotel room, a common feature to the majority of hotels in the Latin Quarter.

'I'll behave,' he promised. 'No need to place a cushion between us,' he feebly jested. She changed into a long night gown in the bathroom while he slipped between the covers waiting for her. He hadn't brought any pyjamas, and always slept in the nude anyway. In deference to the situation he kept his underpants on.

'Can you switch the lights off,' she called out.

She made her way between the sheets and turned her back to him.

They tried to sleep.

It proved a difficult night. On occasions, almost out of primeval instinct he would regularly awaken and one or the other had moved closer to the other's body, in search of warmth, like magnets drawn towards each other. On one occasion, he heard her quietly say 'No' when his hands, out of mere tenderness, drifted towards the hard flesh of her rump without him even being aware of the fact. He remained hard throughout the night. Wanting. Balls heavy. Hoping against hope. Trying to control his frustration.

She woke up before him and made a beeline towards the bathroom to take a shower.

She returned to the bedroom wrapped in a large blue towel, her hair still damp, her eyes surrounded by black shadows from the lack of sleep. He was sitting back with his arms behind his head, watching her.

What could he say? What could he do?

She interrupted the heavy silence.

'I'll just grab a hold of my clothes and go change in the bathroom,' she said. 'I think later I'll go visit the Musée d'Orsay. There's an exhibition there I'd like to see.'

'I won't be joining you,' he told her.

'I understand,' Annarita said.

'I'll go out on my own,' he added. 'Probably will stay out until the evening.'

'That's fine.'

She was now holding a set of clean clothes and was about to turn back towards the bathroom.

'Annarita.'

'Yes?'

He hesitated.

'I want something to remember you by,' he said.

'What?' Thin rivulets of water were still snaking down from her hair onto her smooth forehead. A legal Medusa. His stomach tightened.

'At least show me your breasts.'

'Why?'

'Because.'

She stood still. Outside the window he could hear the rubbish collectors orchestrating their early morning cacophony.

Finally, she pulled the towel down to her waist. Just a few seconds before she turned silently and disappeared back into the bathroom where she changed into her day wear.

For years, he would recall the spectacle of her exposed breasts with fondness and a gentle tremor in his cock. Small, high, untouchable, so close, so soft in his imagination. But would never remember Annarita's face. That evening when, after catching a couple of movies and haunting bookshops and art galleries to kill time, he returned to the hotel, she had already checked out.

HOTEL DU PARACHUTE, Montparnasse, Paris 4

Mimosa and he had once worked together in the same office, but their brief affair had only begun once they had both moved on to other companies. The sex was pleasant, convenient. They were not in love. Fuck buddies, long before the expression even became fashionable.

She wore glasses and looked prim.

He was accustomed to spending an evening or so a week at her South Clapham flat, and they both needed a change of scene, a different bed and, in his case, none of her bloody cats lurking around the room, slyly spying on them while they fucked. They decided to go to Paris. It felt more attractive than Birmingham and Brighton. Less sordid. The food at least would be better.

At short notice, because of some fashion week or a trade fair or another event, his usual hotels in the familiar areas were all full, so they ended up in a small, unfamiliar joint south of Boulevard Raspail.

Their window overlooked an avalanche of tile roofs, and in the far distance, the very top of the Eiffel Tower could be glimpsed on a clear day. Not that either of them had any wish to go visit. They'd both done the deed with previous partners on earlier occasions. This time, they'd just come here for sex.

He loved her pubic hair; dark, thin, sparse, silky. She loved to let his tongue linger over it, brush it, travel and laze amongst this intimate vegetation while he splayed her open and licked her out or fingered her to orgasm, in between lengthy sessions of penetrative sex. He even liked that on regular occasions, in the throe of the moment, she kept her glasses on. Without her spectacles, Mimosa always appeared quite lost, like a tourist in a strange place, unable to understand the local language or the lay of the land. Even more so when she was naked. He even reckoned that she could not see him properly in that particular state of total nudity and might even mistake him for another. A doe in headlights, tall, pale-skinned, dark-tipped breasts at attention, standing legs apart, always impeccably scentless, he noted. Which somehow didn't concord with the flower of her name. She also happened to be a botanist.

On the second morning, their limbs still exhausted from the previous night's over-exertions in the hotel room's narrow bed, they took a walk across the Seine, through the enclosed courtyard of the Louvre (this was some years before the glass pyramid was built) and emerged onto the Rue de Rivoli, where Mimosa insisted on visiting a Prisunic store just a hundred yards or so south of Brentano's, the now much-missed English language bookshop.

She purchased a simple white tee-shirt, which she had changed into inside the store.

'All the way to Paris and just a tee-shirt?' he queried.

'Oh, my dear,' she said, 'French tee-shirts fit me so much better, don't you think?'

It was tight and nicely emphasised her slim figure and pert breasts, but then he thought any old tee would have.

'I suppose so,' he concluded.

Later that afternoon, she suffered the initial pains and within a few hours knew she was having another cystitis outburst. They never made love again in Paris on that trip and spent the next morning, their last in town, scouring the city for an open Pharmacie where he had to explain what the problem was as she spoke no French and ended up with a bottle of pills that would make her proudly pee blue for days.

Paris, city of romance …

HOTEL ST THOMAS D'AQUIN, rue du Pré-aux-Clercs, Paris 7

Jeanne had taken the train from Arles in the South of France and they agreed to meet at la Rhumerie on the Boulevard St Germain.

She had sent him a pleasing black and white photograph long beforehand but the moment he set eyes on her that morning as she gingerly walked up the bar's raised steps he realised years had flown by since the photo had actually been taken. Not that she wasn't attractive any more. Elfin-shaped, delicate, smiling lips, wild dark hair and all, but all he could think of watching her approach clutching her backpack under one arm, was that she now looked too much like his sister.

'Fuck', he swore under his breath.

She swiftly apologised for her subterfuge, bombarding him with explanations: lack of self-confidence, the fact that she had three children and not the single one she had previously admitted to, errant past husbands and boyfriends, financial difficulties …

'But you look exactly the same,' she said and took hold of his hand. Her grin was quite disarming. For the next couple of hours, he truly believed that once they were together in the hotel bedroom and facing each other in the glare of their nudity he would prove incapable of having sex with her. Right body, absolutely, but wrong

217

face, utterly. Would he even manage to get hard?

When the time came, however, the chemistry of lust reasserted itself and they did make love. She proved both voracious and tender, hungry and demanding. But every time he raised his eyes to her face, he had to catch his breath and quickly banish images of his own sister. Mostly he rode her from the back, and her hourglass shape took his breath away when, following each fuck, she would raise herself from the bed and tip toe nude towards the bathroom to clean up; every curve almost perfect, every shadow on her skin like a target for his cock. 'Don't turn round. Ever,' he felt like whispering. Half the ideal woman …

Apart from the sex, they had little in common and, out of bed, they rapidly found they had little to say to each other, beyond tired and familiar tales of past sexual encounters with others, whether casual or serious. Silence quickly took root.

For years after that brief encounter, he would always remember the unforgettable vision of her bare back, her arse in motion as she would step out of the crumpled bed sheets, poetry in motion, a ballet of bare flesh, soft geometry and would invariably feel his cock stiffen. But he quickly forced himself to forget Jeanne's face.

After two nights together as total strangers who indulged in sex with each other because the flesh was weak and there was little else to do in that damn hotel room, he summoned a taxi to take her to the Gare d'Austerlitz and her train to the south coast back to her children. They never corresponded again and carefully ignored each other when they crossed paths in the same Internet chat rooms.

HOTEL BERSOLYS, rue de Lille, Paris 6

Tabby was half-Lebanese, half-English and lived back in Milton Keynes with an undertaker.

The hotel was an equal stone's throw from St Germain des Prés and the Seine, one street away from the Rue de Verneuil where Serge Gainsbourg had once lived.

She had the wettest cunt he had ever encountered in a woman. Or would even come across later in his life. Maybe it was a Mediterranean characteristic? And he knew it had little to do with him. He wasn't that good. She was permanently wet between the legs, even when sex was not involved. It didn't cease to amaze him. He would slide into her so effortlessly, no friction, no resistance, as if gliding down a moist, waxy river towards her heart of dark lust.

She would practice her yoga in the nude first in the morning and again in the evening before they went to bed. Her body had the suppleness of an animal, and he stroked himself idly while she stretched into unimaginable contortions; her cunt often gaping so wonderfully open and visibly humid as she forced her sinews into compromising positions and extended her legs in impossible directions, her small milk chocolate-nippled breasts jutting proudly ahead. The room had the barest of curtains and he was certain anyone living in the flat immediately facing their hotel could see everything. It tickled his pride.

Sweating profusely, tangled in sheets and blankets, leaking, panting, his left hand distractedly travelling across her skin, as they caught their breath between fucks, he reached her arse crack on an aimless journey through her intimacy and Tabby shuddered.

'You OK?' he whispered in the midnight darkness of the Bersolys room.

'Yeah,' she said. 'For a moment there, I thought you were going to slip a finger into my arse hole.'

'No, I was just aimlessly touching your skin. I like it that you're so soft.'

'I'm very sensitive there,' she advised him.

'Really?'

'Hmm … my boyfriend likes to ride me there, back at home,' she added.

'Oh.'

He had never had anal sex with a woman, back then.

'Would you like to?'

'Maybe.'

'Come on. It's fun, it's good, it's not dirty. Please.'

'You sure?'

'Don't worry. I'm still quite tight.'

She disentangled herself from the bed's battleground and placed herself on all fours in readiness.

But they had been having sex for several hours already and he couldn't get hard again that night, even with the radiant pucker of her arse hole almost leering at him, at the heart of concentric circles of darker shades of skin, and the glaring humidity of her ever wet and fertile cunt just below, dominating his field of vision.

The next morning, he had to leave Paris, but Tabby stayed on for 48 hours as planned when she moved to another hotel.

HOTEL DU PARADIS ET DE LA FICTION, Faubourg St Antoine, Bastille, Paris 4

The hotel's annex was situated at the back of a courtyard.

Christel was already in a bad mood because the hotel he had booked was not on the Left Bank or, failing that, near the Champs Elysées. She'd always wanted to stay at the Hotel Costes, as she'd always enjoyed their music compilations, but the Costes was too expensive, and all his familiar haunts around Saint Michel, Odeon or St Germain des Prés happened to be fully booked since this visit had been arranged somehow at short notice.

They'd unpacked in silence. He'd given her a cuddle, but she was unresponsive, claimed that she was hungry and they found a Korean barbecue place just off the Place de la Bastille. She protested that the food was too spicy, although he judged it was nothing of the sort. He knew what spicy could be. By the time they returned to the room, her mood had settled into a permanent state of simmering disquiet.

They were sitting together on the edge of the bed and he pulled her closer. Christel sniffed. His hand grazed over her breasts. They had always been magnificent and she was in the habit of wearing her tops too tight, buttons straining under the pressure of the opulent flesh beneath.

'Come on,' he said. 'We're in Paris. It's us. Relax a little.'

Her green eyes softened.

She extended an arm towards him.

'OK,' she said.

She lowered herself onto the bed, pulling him down with her.

Their lips met. He could still smell the cigarette she'd smoked back in the taxi queue at the airport.

His tongue advanced, probed, circled hers. His free hand readied itself to slide inside her blouse, or her skirt.

'Fuck!' Christel cried out, disengaging from him in one swift movement. 'Look at that shit!'

He looked at the direction she was pointing towards.

In the far corner of the room, where a tired wooden cupboard stood, small drops of water were falling from the ceiling onto the top of the cupboard.

He tried to reach reception on the phone next to the bed, but there was no answer.

'Tell them I just can't stay in this room,' Christel screamed at him.

He made his way down the stairs, then down the length of the courtyard. The woman at the desk was busy dealing with a coach arrival of German tourists. When she finally had time for him, he reported the problem and she promised that the hotel's handyman would be there to investigate within a quarter of an hour. It took him more than half an hour to attend. By then, Christel, still furious, had left the room and walked over to the Faubourg to have a coffee. She couldn't face that damn drip drip drip any longer, she said.

The workman swore.

They were given another room, further down the landing.

When Christel returned, she gave the new room one look.

'It smells,' she said.

No more than the ghostlike tobacco fumes that still surrounded her in an aura of nicotine, he reckoned.

'I can't stay here any longer,' she complained. 'It's not working. You and me. This weekend. I want to leave. Give me some money for a taxi,' she asked.

One hour later, she'd taken the first train back home and left him in Paris on his own.

That evening, he ate alone and treated himself to a seafood plateau at an expensive restaurant on the Place de la Bastille. Maybe food was sometimes better than sex, after all.

HOTEL DES ECOLES, rue Monsieur le Prince, Paris 6
The hotel lift was the smallest lift in the whole of Paris.

Maybe in the whole world. Two people of average size could barely squeeze in, what with the metal ashtray digging into your stomach if you faced the wrong way. With two bodies fitted in, there was not even any space for a single piece of luggage, and it had to be expedited onwards before or after, on its own.

The room itself was no ballroom either.

She had no name but her hair was brown and she displayed a bird tattoo on her left shoulder. He didn't quite recognise the species. She also wore a thin gold chain around her right ankle.

Her eyes were mauve and her breasts felt thin and hollow to his touch.

He thought she was Australian but he couldn't be bothered asking her. Conversation was not an art they practised much.

Their fingers did all the talking, as did their lips and bodies, the orifices probed and drilled, licked and forced, the skin caressed and slapped, the secretions poured in the give and take of lust.

Between the sex he would watch her retreat to the bathroom where, behind the thin wall, he could hear her wipe her face and sniff cocaine from whichever flat surface she had found there. On his own visits to the toilet, he allowed the water from the sink's unique tap to pour out loudly to cover the sound when he was taking a shit. Intimacy, after all, had its limits.

And then they'd fuck again. Like strangers. Like beasts.

She would squeeze his ball sack while she sucked him, hard enough to make him wince or even his eyes water. He would bite her nipples hard in the course of improvised embraces hoping to make her cry. There was no tenderness, only anger.

They would both emerge from the room the following morning to share a croissant and coffee breakfast in the lobby in silence with their bodies bruised beneath their clothing, skin scratched, torn in places, a respective geography of desolation.

He kissed her. Her lips were dry. They parted. He watched her tall silhouette and her endless legs walk away along the Rue Racine away from the hotel. He walked up the stairs back to the room to pack.

Another encounter ending in silence.

This was Paris, this was yesterday. He sullenly now reflects on those past days of epiphanies and pain and sex. Of excess and emptiness.

And can't help thinking of the only woman who never came to the city with him. *'Je t'aime,'* he whispers in the morning dawn on yet another day when he wakes alone. The breeze carries his words away towards the South. He wonders idly if she will ever hear them.

About the Story

MY PARENTS MOVED TO Paris when I was only three years old. As a result, I was brought up there and, apart from one final curriculum year at the Lycée Francais in South Kensington, London, have never been to school in England. As a result I have always had a curious relationship with France and the French. After all, I was the little English kid (despite my Polish name on my father's side) who was accused of burning Joan of Arc and was on occasions beaten up in the kindergarten school yard for his imagined inherited sins. Needless to say I got my own back in later years when by virtue of being fully bilingual, few people around me even suspected me of not being French, and I could operate like a spy in the house of love, to paraphrase Anais Nin.

What this French side of me is grateful for is that I quickly learned to appreciate the art of erotic fiction, a literary discipline so much better appreciated by the French.

Sadly and inevitably, Paris has changed a lot since my teenage, and beyond, years. And even though, on my frequent return visits, I still haunt my old Latin Quarter patch, the charm has long dissipated. But then you can never revisit the past. I reckon it's not only the city that has changed, it's me too. But I still look forward to every new occasion I walk on to the Eurostar train and, two hours or so later, come in to the Gare du Nord, and the distinctive smell of Paris tickles my imagination. And I of course also invariably remember the naïve youth I once was and his awkwardness with women.

Naturally, whenever I am in Paris, I stay in hotel

rooms. Most often in small establishments dotted between the Odéon area and St Germain de Prés. Which doesn't mean this story is autobiographical. Well, I would say that, wouldn't I?

The Red Brassiere
by EllaRegina

OUTSIDE PASCAL'S BEDROOM WINDOW, erect nipples pressed against the glass. They shivered in the early hour crisp, waiting for him to awake, bucking towards the white duvet rectangle with a gentle persistent knock. Pascal's fingers, curved around his morning hard-on, idly synchronised their rhythm to the odd staccato.

As the sun rose over the *quartier*, a shadow edged across the stone façade of the grey building overlooking Rue de Ménilmontant, then fell through the panes into Pascal's room on the top floor where the patch of darkness landed on his face like a cloud blocking a piece of blue sky.

Pascal opened his eyes and looked towards the sound coming from the window. Paris was always grey to him, even though it was in colour. Now, suspended over the balcony and breaking into the black and white image, was a red brassiere – a buoyant arrangement of lace curves and negative space, alert and fastened, as if enclosing a body. The garment was animate, not clothesline-limp; it appeared to be levitating, like the velvet top hat hanging from invisible fishing line above his bed.

Pascal considered himself a fine magician though he had yet to make a woman disappear. He glanced around his bedroom. Everything was in order. The dove was quiet in its cage, under a canvas night cover. His props were in place near a battered green suitcase -scarves, card decks, a pile of rings. Near the door an arm emerged from the wall at the elbow, dressed in a navy blue suit sleeve, hand extended as if to shake another, its fingertips holding his velvet cape and black cane.

His performance the previous night had gone without incident; he had been onstage as usual, standing in the dank ancient dimly-lit Marais subterranea, twenty-five metres directly below a vitrined jelly-donut pyramid in a Jewish bakery, correctly guessing the identities of female audience members, prompted by spontaneous appearances of their names – a moving rash of lines on foreheads – written slowly in his loopy handwriting.

Pascal got out of bed and opened the floor-to-ceiling window. He squinted up the next building – a hand and forearm shaking out a grey rag. He looked down at the cobblestones – a black cat curled on the sidewalk, licking its genitals. The red brassiere moved aside. It was free-standing, apparently, not a snagged runaway specimen from the nearby weekly market.

Pascal stepped onto the balcony. The red brassiere bolted out of reach in a wide arc, then came closer, tentatively. It rubbed up against Pascal as if locked in his embrace. When he lunged for a shoulder strap it pulled away again. Not much for teasing, Pascal returned to his bedroom and closed the window, the red brassiere quickly following in a silent swoop, slipping inside before it shut.

Pascal returned to bed, unaware that the red brassiere was behind him. It flew up to the rafters, under the skylight, and angled downwards as if worn by a woman on a ladder. Pascal's erection resurfaced and he closed his eyes, resuming his morning routine, stroking himself with more than the usual intensity. The red brassiere descended from its lofty perch to investigate, placing itself squarely above Pascal's hidden hands. A perfume filled the room – that of Geneviève, an early love; the pungent grapefruit and cumin of her armpits, the private spices between her legs – and with it a distinct vision occupied Pascal's imagination: Geneviève, on all fours, his full cock in her mouth, her wine-stained lips encasing him.

As he pulled at himself the smell grew stronger. Pascal opened his eyes. The red brassiere swayed at his face, emitting a heat along with the unmistakable scent. It did a bob and a bounce. The duvet rolled back into a croissant and Pascal's pyjama pant buttons undid themselves one by one. His cock sprang out, shaking off his gripping hand, and disappeared into what felt like a mouth but was just empty space above a quivering piece of lingerie. The length of his penis came in and out of view as unseen lips slid over him. It was as if he were a figure drawing being erased and then re-sketched with the mouth's advances and retreats. His palms grazed the red brassiere's pebble-like nipple bumps. The fabric felt warm, inhabited. Pascal's head flushed as if wrapped in a feverish blindfold. His eyelids burned. The invisible mouth took him deeper, containing him completely. He rubbed until his magic lamp released its oil then relaxed all muscles, spent. The red brassiere collapsed for a moment, folded at Pascal's feet. He observed the silk and lace. On a shiny white label, flattened at the inside, near the underarm area, a size number and style name were written in his loopy script: *90C Geneviève*.

As Pascal's empty cock lay in repose the word vanished from the satin tag along with any traces of Geneviève's fragrance. The red brassiere hovered motionless above the bed, as if waiting for a sign, a signal, an instruction.

Pascal enjoyed the company of women. Many many women – each one, one at a time. He was a sexual cartographer, leaving semen imprimaturs in bodies across Paris like inkblots on a map of the city. He had bedded women from every arrondissement, *in* every arrondissement, several times over. His erect cock had been a directional pointed throughout Paris as frequently as a *Vous Êtes Ici* map indicator. He could summon the chronicle of his roving carnal travelogue at will. Its various destinations were also the settings for his fantasies, both daydreams and nocturnal reveries.

To Pascal's highly developed sense of smell each woman was a snowflake – there were no two alike, even when they wore the same perfume. And of all the characteristics women presented to him their personal scent was the thing he found most arousing and the feature most indelible in his memory. He could recall the specific melodies of each one the way a gourmand has the ability to catalogue a history of refined meal courses. And, despite the esoteric differences between them, they were linked by an irrefutable underlying aura of femininity as a given, an aroma which also varied but was fundamentally and ultimately similar, exhibiting the entire olfactory spectrum, from highly pitched to low and broad.

Pascal eyed the red brassiere intently and re-wrapped his fist around his rigid cock. He closed his eyes and concentrated. The first woman to enter his thoughts was Delphine, the private tour guide who had fellated him in the artificial lake pooled beneath the Paris Opéra. Delphine liked to have sex in public or nearly so. She enjoyed being stripped naked except for a pair of high heels and a string of pearls. She favoured wearing a chef's toque during intimate relations and bought them by the half-dozen at a uniform store on Rue Turbigo. She wore

Mitsouko – he could always smell her before he saw her.

Pascal tugged at himself with ferocity, conjuring Delphine from puffy hat to pointy toes, filling in more of her details with each hard stroke. He raised his eyelids. He was face to face with the red brassiere, its cups enlarged as if supporting Delphine's abundant breasts, the bedroom smelling like a Mitsouko tornado.

In that moment Pascal understood that the red brassiere was both a tabula rasa under his control and an object that could hold him simultaneously under its spell.

Pascal spent the entire day in bed with the red brassiere as his travel companion. He plugged and played, repeatedly. With each change of character the red brassiere assumed specific dimensions and offered Pascal a particular scent; the label changed its size and name information accordingly. He journeyed the entire city without leaving his bed:

Noémie had persuaded the man taking tickets for the Eutelsat tethered in the Parc André Citroen to let them up alone. Once the dirigible halted 150 metres above Paris she bent over and Pascal entered her derriére. Noémie's dark hair smelled like roses. Pascal watched as the red brassiere showed its back to him – a narrow band of hook and eye – as he imagined Noémie. The odour of rosewater filled the room.

He and Agnès had visited the Panthéon forty-five minutes before closing. They'd positioned themselves against a column where Pascal could slide himself unseen inside her from behind and fuck her to the rhythm of Foucault's slow-swaying pendulum. All the while Agnès kept a straight face, so as not to belie what was happening. The red brassiere tilted almost imperceptibly from side to side like a slow metronome wand as it gave off Agnès's personal fragrance, a mixture of sex and tea tree oil.

Octavie was – appropriately – an accordionist who played beneath the arcades of the Place des Vosges. She and Pascal spoke about the perfect acoustics of the space then went for a pastry at Sacha Finkelsztajn on the Rue des Rosiers. Afterwards, Octavie played Pascal's organ in private. She wore perfume made for babies. The red brassiere seemed to heave as if taking deep breaths while it replicated her bouquet.

Pascal went through his personal index of intimate sights and smells. He thought of the dark-skinned Sidonie (lilacs), whose long thin nipples echoed the dome tops of the Sacré-Coeur. He recalled Irène, into whose patchouli-cloaked nakedness he tunnelled until the houseboat on which she lived drifted away from its moorings. He remembered Odile, who had welcomed him inside her on all of Paris' thirty-six bridges (Chanel No. 5, thirty-six times). There was Eugénie, whom he had balanced on his cock for 15 minutes in an automated street toilet, at her insistence (savon de Marseille with a hint of bleach). Clementine gave Pascal a handjob at dusk one summer night in the centre of the labyrinth at the Jardin des Plantes. She smelled not of clementines but of lemons. Vignette took him in her mouth on a rented boat in the Bois de Boulogne, lying flat so that he appeared to be the sole passenger, rowing as slowly as he could to keep the craft – and Vignette – going. She liked the smell of his semen in her hair.

Pascal dressed and left his apartment. The red brassiere followed him down the building's spiral stairs in a corkscrew blur like a thrown party streamer. He stopped at the Bar des Sports for an espresso and a brioche. The red brassiere clung to his back, protected from onlookers, as he leaned against the zinc bar. He watched the twin peak line of red strap tops, like a child's drawing of mountains, reflected in the mirror. A boy of twelve or so was playing a noisy game of flipper, head down. Pascal paid for his breakfast and a few loose cigarettes and was on his way, the red brassiere at his shoulder. He picked up a newspaper at the kiosk.

As Pascal walked the red brassiere played with him, evading his grasp when he tried for a strap, pulling a storey above, then falling down like a torpedo to reclaim its place beside him, each time smelling like someone else, a woman whose fleeting image had just made an appearance in his head because of something he noticed on the street, some *je ne sais quoi* suddenly noted, which struck him, awakened him, moved him – an object, a sound, a memory.

It began to rain. As its fabric soaked up the drops the red brassiere got richer in hue. Pascal unfolded his newspaper in an attempt to shield the garment from the elements. Before he could fully succeed a series of umbrellas opened like black flowers, clutched in fists at the ends of extended male arms left and right, one after the other like a choreographed dance, offering the red brassiere dry passage. It hopped from the shelter of one to the next, for the three-block duration of the cloudburst.

They passed a lingerie store where the red brassiere stopped for a moment of camaraderie with the black and white models in the display window, worn by silently laughing mannequins, until Pascal sensed its absence and walked back for retrieval, firmly hooking his fingers around the elastic straps.

At the flea market the red brassiere admired its own reflection in an antique mirror, its nipples brushing the hard surface as if kissing itself.

Back at his building Pascal tapped in the entry code and opened the heavy green wooden door. As he pushed inside the red brassiere broke free and flew to the top storey, hanging outside Pascal's bedroom window until he arrived himself.

The next morning there were already several people waiting at the bus stop near the Rue des Pyrénées. An old woman bumped headlong into the red brassiere as if it were invisible but the men stared at it, unblinking, and stepped out of its way.

They boarded the 96 which would deposit Pascal in front of the magic club. The bus driver made him pay two fares. It was standing room only. A man with a white cane occupied the handicapped seat near the door. The red brassiere loomed above his shoulder in the last available wedge of space, overlooking a blonde woman in a blue trench coat flipping the pages of *Paris Match*. The red brassiere appeared to be reading over the woman's shoulder.

'Marie-Blanche?' asked the blind man, arching his head in the direction of the red brassiere, '*est-ce que c'est toi*?'

The blonde looked at him quizzically. 'We do not know each other,' she said curtly.

'Non – pardon,' replied the blind man, 'I was talking to *her*,' again motioning his eyebrows towards the floating garment.

'*Qui? Il n'y a personne là, monsieur.*'

'*Oui!*' he insisted. 'Marie-Blanche!' he continued in a singsong, 'I was just thinking of you!'

'Idiot!' huffed the blonde, vacating her seat and pressing the red request button for the next stop.

Several women jostled the red brassiere as they left the

bus, as if they did not see it. But Pascal sensed the sure and steady gaze of every male passenger – sitting or standing – their eyes, young and old; blue, green, grey, brown and hazel, uniformly fixed on the red brassiere, surrounding it from all spots in the bus. Pascal could see their erections, in various stages of angle development like a progressive geometry diagram, pointing at the red brassiere from their trousers, a collective of anatomical radii, as if the red brassiere were the Place de l'Etoile and the fleshy arrows radiating spokes of the surrounding streets – avenues Victor Hugo, Kleber, d'Iena, Marceau, the Champs-Élysées … Pascal felt cornered. There was a quick change of plans: he would not go to the magic club today. At the next stop Pascal swiftly grabbed the red brassiere by a shoulder strap and hurried off, several pairs of men's hands trying unsuccessfully to snatch the delicate fragrant gossamer as it passed – like sticks thrusting at brass carousel rings in the Jardin du Luxembourg.

'Françoise!'

'Adèle!'

'Lucienne!'

'Mignon!'

The men followed Pascal off the bus in pursuit of the red brassiere, and with each block more added to the mob, the mass of hands and shouts expanding like a bubble. A dozen Chinese men practicing Tai Chi in the Parc de Belleville got wind of the red brassiere, each man smelling a different woman. They tracked their noses and joined the rumble. Pascal broke into a sprint, the red brassiere an angel's wing above him, just clear of the men's grasps.

The Boulevard de Belleville was crowded, the market stalls taking up the shaded pedestrian median. The sidewalks on either side were filled with young women in hijab and shawls, men in kuftis and caftans – some of them shopkeepers in long blue smocks over their street clothing lounging in front of their stores, suitcase-sized bags of rice at their backs. Pascal ran in and out of traffic, on and off the sidewalk. He passed an Algerian patisserie, a Cambodian sweet shop, a Kosher restaurant, a halal boucherie, le Marché Franprix. A laughing teenage boy on a motorbike swung at the red brassiere, almost pinching it. The Muslim grocers in sandals, the Kosher felafellers, the Chinese and Vietnamese restaurateurs, the African marketers – all relinquished their posts to follow the red brassiere, each one with a massive erection, plainly visible, no matter the type of costume. Some were openly stroking themselves, with one hand or two, under and over their clothing. The men yelled women's names in a Babelous ruckus:

'Minou!'
'Bashira!'
'Habiba!'
'Wei!'
'Hong!'
'Falala!'
'Batool!'
'Odile!'
'Halima!'
'Shoshana!'
'Li Li!'
'Malika!'
'Ming!'
'Haboos!'
'Sultana!'
'Mei Xing!'
'Kalifa!'

'Hua!'

'Tzipporah!'

'Jing Yì!'

'Magali!'

Pascal reached for his mobile phone and tried to ring the police. He managed the 1 button twice but the gadget slipped to the ground and into a sewer grate before he could press the final 2. Pascal kept running, through the market stalls and along the shops on the margins, passing the sidewalk vendors and the crowds browsing their merchandise – sacks of dried lentils and peas, fruits and vegetables, bolts of African fabrics, plastic crates full of mini Eiffel Towers, flat displays holding cheap telephone cards. A man in front of the *Tout à 1 €* store stuck out a foot to trip him, withdrawing it in the last second.

The lanes of the Boulevard were filled with cars. There were few taxis and those present had solid orange roof lights indicating passengers. Pascal crossed the street, dodging the moving vehicles. He found a narrow alley, the width of one person. A man carrying two pillows on either side of himself approached from the opposite direction. Pascal managed to pass him but the pillows momentarily blocked the rush of the screaming pack on his heels. There was a *pop* and a million white and grey feathers filled the alley. The red brassiere ricocheted off the walls in a zig zag with the velocity of its forward propulsion. Pascal spotted a patch of grass beyond a decaying wooden fence matted with movie posters, away from the mêlée. He checked to see that the red brassiere was steadily behind him. It lurched over the barrier while Pascal scaled the structure and for a moment everything stood still.

The voices got louder, closer.

'Galia, I can smell you!' cried one man.

'Kumani, I know you're there!' screamed another.

'Mahmoode, I'm coming to get you!' bellowed a third in a caftan.

It was too late. The gang broke down the fence. The red brassiere gave off an odour of pure fear as its strap snagged on a café sign shaped like a top hat. One man scrambled onto the shoulders of another and dislodged the red brassiere, capturing it and yanking it down.

Droplets of nervous perspiration formed on the piece of lingerie. It crumpled and shuddered, then disappeared from Pascal's view obscured by the drapery of a sea of hands. One hundred erections pointed towards the red brassiere like hungry knives. The knot of men released an intense heat. There was the sound of cloth being ripped, and ripped and ripped again. When, finally, there was no more rending to be done the men retreated, man by man, each with a shard of red lace or silk as bounty. Three had hooks, three more eyes. One man held the small decorative bow from the front, still intact like a perfect unmolested rosebud. Short scarlet threads covered the ground, twitching like organisms under a microscope. Pascal sat forlornly, abandoned by the herd of men, holding the very last piece of the red brassiere, a tiny red sliver, off of which hung the tattered label – now a blank scrap without a name – soiled with shoe scuffs, a discarded grape skin. There was no smell.

In that moment, one by one, brassieres were seized from every corner of the city. Women strolling each rue, boulevard and avenue felt themselves coming undone – unravelled – the intimate harnesses drawn out through their sleeves. In thousands of boudoirs, from the 1er to the 20eme, drawers slid open, their contents unfolding and taking flight out windows and skylights. A parade of fantasy lingerie emerged from the department stores.

Street market brassieres fastened around headless mannequins unhooked and dashed away. In the Père Lachaise a half dozèn Wonderbras were pulled from the hands of young female tourists about to fling the apparel onto Jim Morrison's grave. The gigantic brassiere of Babar's cousin Celeste vacated Jean de Brunhoff's book illustrations and took to the air like a magic carpet.

Women all over Paris stood at their windows – topless and stunned – watching the silent ascension of silk, satin, lace and nylon in hues of white, yellow, orange, red, blue and green. One woman tried to loop a strap as it passed.

The brassieres formed tandem rows, filing through the streets and across the Seine – on and off bridges – the march of an invisible, scantily-clad army; bounding on cobblestones in a rainbow arc, going up stairs, turning corners in a calico jumble. People seated in cafés dropped their glasses at the sight of the promenading spectacle.

The brassieres headed skywards in Pascal's direction, single-file now, making dotted lines like trolley wires above the centres of streets, an airborne queue flanked by pitched rooftops. As they flew, other objects joined the mass in solidarity: a fleet of berets and handkerchiefs from Left Luggage at the Gare du Nord; bows from the hair of well-dressed children in the Parc Monceau and silk scarves from the necks of their nannies; one hundred paper airplanes set into motion by schoolboys in a hundred classrooms; pornographic passages ripped from paperbacks sold by the Seine bouquinistes; a stream of orphaned gloves from the Bureau des Objets Trouvés, forefingers all pointed towards Pascal. Rose petals fresh off the faces of women getting floral treatments at the hammam bundled with others plucked from the garland of florists and gardens woven through the city. Taxidermied birds left their gnarly branches at Deyrolle. Kites were whisked from small hands in the city parks. Braiding, embroidery, fans and parasols trailed from the two Musées de la Mode. The stockings of Madeline's Miss Clavel stepped up – in two straight lines, sails detached from toy boats on the pond in the Jardin du Luxembourg and peacocks lost their quills in the Bois de Boulogne. In the Père Lachaise Isadora Duncan's last scarf slid out her tomb like a long pink tongue while lipstick kisses unpeeled themselves from Oscar Wilde's headstone, hanging in midair for a moment like frightened spots off a cartoon leopard. Glittering in the evening's final light were sparklies from Josephine Baker's last revue, followed by feather boas from the Moulin Rouge, hose and garters once belonging to Kiki of Montparnasse, and, running to keep up, Edith Piaf's little black dress and tiny shoes.

The various objects filled the skies and soared towards Pascal, sitting long-faced in the grassy lot staring at the shattered red brassiere remains, both spirit and cock deflated. He welcomed the inventory, tethering everything together. Celeste's brassiere formed a hammock underneath him and he fell backwards into it as into a giant open hand. His cock immediately asserted itself, encouragingly resuscitated. Every item found its place as if part of a puzzle, creating a complex latticework. The craft rose with Pascal at the helm using scarves and straps as directional reins. The toy boat sails spined the ship like dinosaur's scales, acting as rudders. A poufed string of chef toques encircled the assemblage, jewelled with bits of cotton candy from the Bois de Vincennes.

The multilayered, multidimensional sling caught the wind and Pascal was pulled aloft by the cluster, a helix pulled high over the beige grey city. It began a large outward-moving spiral flight path mirroring the layout of the arrondissements below – a beignet, an escargot shell, a coiled snake.

Pascal veered away from Notre-Dame to avoid the low-voltage shocks intended for gargoyle-bound pigeons. Beneath him he saw the City of Light: the twinkling tiaras of the bridges spanning the Seine; the unbroken red and white meandering automobile beam stripe blurring the boulevards – a long slice of Tricoleur; the blinking green neon animation of pharmacy crosses.

From the Fontaine Stravinsky Jean Tinguely's shiny red puffed lips blew Pascal a kiss. In unison, the light-sensitive windows at L'Institut du Monde Arabe closed their shutters like camera apertures – 240 portals momentarily constricting in a conspiring wink – giving him the gazes of 1,001 Arabian nights from sheathed feminine eyes behind a thousand burqas. The Tour Eiffel grew another six inches – the full extension of its phallic architecture – and spouted fireworks from its tip in a lusty salute.

Birds spiralled around Pascal, now moving like a rapid current, intoxicated by the fragrant tufted cloud trapping him in a tempestuous tangled skein. Sharp gusts blew through the rigs of the vessel, stretched and knotted like harp strings, forging a primordial choir of women's voices – comprising every female utterance since the beginning of time: every moan, whisper and sigh – until that instant a lost bracelet of unheard sound adrift, swirling endlessly around the planet like Saturn's rings. Pascal felt the sonic vibration created by the choral hum. It entered his body as an electric ribbon, and surged through him, a vein of fire rising from his cock and balls up his torso and into each arm like unfurling tree branches of lightning. He stroked himself in sheer abandon as he inhaled the combined bouquets of the unseen women whose garments surrounded him, cradled him – the women who'd worn them and the women who might – women from past and future, known and not, spanning the centuries. Female names appeared on the hundreds of fluttering labels, writing and re-writing themselves in endless succession – like magic slates ad infinitum. Pascal laughed and sang while he alternately pulled at himself and guided the barrelling sphere. He rode the edge of light turning to darkness as night blanketed Paris. A golden swirl of shimmering Michelin stars, shot in a farewell booster from the restaurants below, formed a constellation around the flying contraption, raising it still further skywards, pulling Pascal up, upwards over the city – ascending far and away – his cock aimed towards the end of the sky.

About the Story

THE RED BRASSIERE WAS inspired by and is an homage to the late Albert Lamorisse's 34-minute 1956 film, *Le ballon rouge*, in my language known as *The Red Balloon*. My childhood memory of this film is that it was in black and white, a supreme error on my part, of course, given the work's title and premise. Yet, the post-War Paris *Le ballon rouge* portrays did impress me as being composed solely of grey tones. Perhaps this was because the rich colours, when they do appear, pop out in their Technicolor glory, making the city backdrop seem, well, greyer, by comparison. Also, my remembrance of *The Red Balloon* is conflated with my recollection of the accompanying book, an oversized hardcover predominantly illustrated with grainy black and white film stills, the red balloon and its coloured environs present only on eight pages.

Almost immediately upon learning of the *Sex in the City: Paris* project I knew I wanted to do a grown-up take on *The Red Balloon*, involving an object of desire more appropriate to an adult male whose favourite plaything is his penis. While a brassiere is not a direct correlative to a balloon in that it is generally not something found in the air, unless pegged to a clothesline, I thought it could work. And, although the little boy in the film is Monsieur Lamorisse's own son, Pascal, after whom my fictional hero is named in tribute, any resemblances to persons living or dead are purely coincidental.

Despite my beret collection and fondness for French surrealists, I have set foot in Paris on just a handful of occasions, each visit lasting a precious few days. As a result, my Paris remains an idealized one, and my vision of it comes more from the city as invented and interpreted in fiction – from Babar and Madeline to Henry Miller – movies, music and art, or documented by photographers like Brassaï, Henri Cartier-Bresson, Man Ray, Jacques Henri Lartigue and Andre Kertész, in all cases capturing a Paris either nonexistent outside the imagination or a city that has been lost for ever. The 20th arrondissement districts serving as the story's setting in *The Red Balloon*, for example, are mostly no longer extant, having been razed in the 1970s. I can now find bits and pieces of the Paris I seek while flying around Google Maps in "street view" mode, my mouse clicks whooshing me from rue to boulevard in search of crackled paint and architecture in need of rehabilitation. But, because of *The Red Balloon* I will always have Paris, preserved in time, primarily in black and white.

Author Biographies

M. Christian is an acknowledged master of erotica with more than 300 stories in such anthologies as *Best American Erotica*, *Best Gay Erotica*, *Best Lesbian Erotica*, *Best Bisexual Erotica*, *Best Fetish Erotica*, and many, many other anthologies, magazines, and Web sites. He is the editor of 20 anthologies including the *Best S/M Erotica* series, *The Burning Pen*, *Guilty Pleasures*, and others. He is the author of the collections *Dirty Words*, *Speaking Parts*, *The Bachelor Machine*, *Licks & Promises*, *Filthy*, *Love Without Gun Control*, and *Rude Mechanicals*; and the novels *Running Dry*, *The Very Bloody Marys*, *Me2*, and *Painted Doll*.

Carrie Williams is the author of three novels for Black Lace – *The Blue Guide*, *Chilli Heat*, and *The Apprentice*, as well as countless short stories in Black Lace anthologies, some of them under the pseudonym Candy Wong. Her erotic fiction has also graced the pages of *Scarlet* magazine and *The Mammoth Book of Best New Erotica*.

As an established travel journalist, Carrie visits and reviews some of the finest hotels, restaurants and shops around the world. Her adventures abroad inspire and inform her fiction, from street markets and temples in India to spas in the South of France, as do the many fascinating characters she meets on her travels.

Carrie began writing erotica after becoming immersed in the work of Sigmund Freud, Georges Bataille and the Surrealists while studying French literature at Oxford. She wrote her dissertation on the work of the female Surrealists, most notably the Argentine painter Léonor Fini, best known for her graphic illustrations for the *Story of O*.

Carrie is usually on the road but can often be found in London, Manchester or Paris. When not writing fiction, she enjoys gardening, the theatre and cinema, vintage clothes shopping and spending time with her Russian blues.

Alcamia Payne began writing short stories when she was a child and is a self-confessed book worm. Her favourite genres are erotica (she adores the writings of Anais Nin), crime, science fiction/fantasy and the classics.

She achieved degrees in Languages and English Literature before pursuing careers as both a linguist and teacher. Drawn inexorably to the written word though, she has gradually turned to what she loves doing best of all, putting her thoughts down on paper.

She says of writing. 'It's the hardest profession imaginable, requiring extraordinary dedication, but there's no feeling in the world like producing a satisfying story. I can't imagine not writing, not expressing myself, it's just a part of who I am. I love people, observing them, exploring what makes them tick, mentally, emotionally and spiritually and then building the fabric of a story around them. I particularly enjoy writing erotic and amatory dramas and creating atmospheric or unusual settings.

She writes several genres but has a passion for human

sexuality and erotica. Her stories have appeared widely and more recently in Scarlet magazine and under the Accent Press Xcite imprint. Her ambitions are to keep writing and improving and loving what she's doing. Alcamia Payne is currently working on a series of novelettes and a novel.

Debb & O'Neil De Noux: Debra Gray De Noux was the long-time associate publisher of Pulphouse Publishing in Eugene, Oregon. Her fiction has appeared in magazines and anthologies in the U.S., Great Britain and Germany. She is the editor of the anthology *Erotic New Orleans* (1999, Pontalba Press, New Orleans). Debra appeared in the short film *Waiting for Alaina* (2001) and has worked as a live nude model.

O'Neil De Noux has published five novels, six short story collections and over 200 short stories in multiple genres, which appeared in the U.S., U.K., Canada, Denmark, France, Germany, Greece, Italy, Japan, Portugal, Sweden and Ukraine.

De Noux's short story 'The Heart Has Reasons' won the Private Eye Writers of America's prestigious Shamus Award for Best Short Story 2007. The Shamus is given annually to recognize outstanding achievement in private eye fiction. His story 'Too Wise' won the 2009 Derringer Award for Best Novelette. The Derringer Award is given annually to recognize excellence in the mystery short form.

The Louisiana Division of the Arts awarded O'Neil De Noux its Artist Services Career Advancement Award for 2009-2010 for work on his forthcoming historical novel set during the Battle of New Orleans.

John Baxter was born in Australia but has lived in Paris for twenty years. As well as biographies of Robert DeNiro, Federico Fellini, Stanley Kubrick, Woody Allen, George Lucas and Luis Bunuel, he has written three books of memoirs, *A Pound of Paper; Confessions of a Book Addict*, *We'll Always Have Paris*: *Sex and Love in the City of Light*, and *Immoveable Feast: A Paris Christmas*. He also compiled *Carnal Knowledge: Baxter's Encyclopedia of Modern Sex*, and edits HarperCollins Perennial's *Naughty French Novels* series, for which he has translated *Gamiani*, *Journal d'une Femme de Chambre*, *Morphine* and *Fumée d'Opium*.

Kelly Jameson is the author of the indie thriller *Dead On*, film-optioned for two years with Gold Circle Films (producer of *My Big Fat Greek Wedding*; *White Noise*), and Runner-Up in the 2006 Do-It-Yourself (DIY) Los Angeles Book Festival. Her recently completed novella, *What Remained of Katrina*, placed in the top 3% of nearly 500 blinded submissions in the 2009 international Leapfrog Press fiction contest (entries received from 10 countries). Ken Bruen, author of *Once Were Cops* and *The Guards*, calls Jameson's second novel, *Shards of Summer*, "The Great Gatsby for the Beach Generation." Kelly's stories have been published in *The Summerset Review, The Mammoth Book of Best New Erotica* (volumes 8 and 9), *Dispatch Litareview*, *Amazon Shorts*, *Withersin Magazine*, *The Twisted Tongue*, *Barfing Frog Press*, *Big Stupid Review*, *Ruthie's Club*, *The American Drivel Review*, *sliptongue*, *ThugWorks*, and *Ramble Underground*. Kelly is at work on a screenplay, two new novels, and new short stories. She lives in the Philadelphia area with her family and doughnut-snatching dog.

Peter Baltensperger is a Canadian writer of Swiss origin and the author of ten books of fiction, poetry, and non-fiction. He began writing at an early age and has been writing ever since. He has also worked extensively as editor of various publications and anthologies and had his own literary press. He holds a B.Sc. from Switzerland as well as an honours B.A. in English Literature and a Specialist Teaching Certificate from Canadian universities. While teaching high school English, he received a Hilroy Fellowship Award for Innovative Teaching in Creative Writing. He now devotes his time to his retirement project of writing erotica. His short stories, poems, literary essays, photo features, periodical and newspaper articles have appeared in several hundred publications around the world. His erotic stories and essays have been published in *The International Journal of Erotica*, *The Mammoth Book of Erotic Confessions*, *In the Buff*, *Erotic Tales*, *Dark Gothic Magazine*, and *Sinister Tales*, and appear on-line in *Clean Sheets*, *Oysters and Chocolate*, *The Erotic Woman*, and *Black Heart Magazine*, among others. He makes his home in London, Canada, with his wife Viki and their two cats and a tortoise.

Toni Sands was born in the beautiful Vale of Glamorgan. At school she daydreamed about exotic places. In the real world, jobs in hotels and aviation claimed her, until love grounded her in Wiltshire. She and her husband converted a former Victorian school into a guesthouse but she found time to write short stories, which she broadcast on local radio. After becoming suddenly single, she began her first novel.

A move back to Wales and more time to write brought more published stories and articles. She enjoys mixing with other creative people who favour the quiet life but equally delights in the buzz of London when she can get away with it! Toni enjoys membership of a proactive group called Hookers' Pen – seven female writers who critique and support each other towards publication. As well as running her own creative writing workshops, she's constantly learning from other authors.

What sparked the interest in erotica? A friend detected a sensual quality within her prose. Toni relished the challenge and is convinced that editors in this genre are extra-supportive and passionate about quality of writing.

Her stories appear in two *Black Lace* (Virgin Books) collections and in a previous Accent Press anthology. For further details and to read an extract from her first published romantic comedy, please visit *www.tonisands.co.uk*

Michael Hemmingson wrote the independent film, *The Watermelon*, and has a few other movies in the works, including the film version of his 2002 novel, *The Dress,* which was also published in truncated form in Maxim Jakubowski's 1998 groundbreaking *The Mammoth Book of New Erotica.* Recent books include a collection, *Sexy Strumpets and Troublesome Trollops* (Wildside Press) and a crime noir, *The Trouble with Tramps* (Black Mask Books).

Savannah Lee's fiction has appeared in *Clean Sheets, The Mammoth Book of Best New Erotica 8, The Mammoth Book of Best New Erotica 9, Blue Earth Review* and *Neo-opsis.*

While in high school, she collaborated as one of the authors of *Mountain Sweet Talk*, a storytelling play which ran for several years at the Folk Art Center in Asheville,

North Carolina. She then took a lengthy writing hiatus to earn a PhD in art history. On the other side of the brush, she has exhibited paintings at Atticus Bookstore and Whole Foods Market, and was included in Spaightwood Galleries' *Womanshow 2000* exhibit. She currently works as a stay-at-home mom and freelance writer.

Savannah lives in the American Midwest, where she is taking teacher training in Alignment Yoga but despairs of ever achieving Chaturanga. Her essay 'The Other Side of the Story: Elia Kazan As Director of Female Pain' appears in the forthcoming anthology *Kazan Revisited*.

Maxim Jakubowski is a twice award-winning British writer, editor, critic, lecturer, ex-publisher and ex-bookshop owner. He shares his time between the wonderfully dubious shores of erotica and the perilous beaches of crime and mystery fiction. He is responsible for the *Mammoth Book of Erotica* series and the *Mammoth Book of Best British Crime* series, is editor of over 75 anthologies and counting, as well as being the author of two handfuls of novels and short story collections. He was crime reviewer for *Time Out London* and then the *Guardian* for nearly twenty years, and also makes regular appearances on radio and television. He also co-directs Crime Scene, London's annual crime and mystery film and literature festival, and runs the MaXcrime imprint. *I Was Waiting For You* is his latest novel.

Though based in London, he has been known to travel and frequent hotel rooms with depressing regularity, which no doubt inspired his *London Noir*, *Paris Noir* and *Rome Noir* collections, as well as the *Sex in the City* series. He has lived in, or regularly visited, every city featured in the *Sex in the City* titles published so far.

When not writing, he collects books, CDs and DVDs with alarming haste.

EllaRegina writes erotic fiction. Her short stories appear in the anthologies *Best Women's Erotica 2008*, edited by Violet Blue (Cleis Press); *The Mammoth Book of the Kama Sutra*, edited by Maxim Jakubowski (Constable and Robinson/Running Press); *Frenzy: 60 Stories of Sudden Sex*, edited by Alison Tyler (Cleis Press); *The Mammoth Book of Best New Erotica 8*, edited by Maxim Jakubowski (Constable and Robinson/Running Press); *Coming Together: Against the Odds*, edited by Alessia Brio (Phaze Books); *Sexy Little Numbers Volume 1 | Best Women's Erotica from Black Lace*, [two stories], edited by Lindsay Gordon (Virgin/Black Lace | Random House); and *The Mammoth Book of Best New Erotica 9*, edited by Maxim Jakubowski (Constable and Robinson/Running Press). Her work has also been featured online at Sliptongue, Cleansheets, the Erotica Readers & Writers Association and Literotica. EllaRegina's story, 'The Lonely Onanista,' was shortlisted for the 2007 Rauxa Prize for Erotic Writing. When not sniffing naughty words in the dictionary, the author can be found in her city or country online drawing rooms, making dirty pictures out of virtual lint, using a pair of tweezers: *ellaregina.blogspot.com* or *myspace.com/ellaregina* Contact: *hotelscribe@yahoo.com*. She will always have Paris.